Books by Irwin R. Blacker

FICTION

Westering
Taos
The Kilroy Gambit
Days of Gold
Chain of Command

NONFICTION

Irregulars, Partisans, Guerrillas
The Old West In Fact
The Old West In Fiction
The Golden Conquistadores
Conquest
Prescott's Histories
The Book of Books
Hakluyt's Voyages

JUVENILE

The Bold Conquistadores
Cortes and the Aztec Conquest

SEARCH AND DESTROY

SEARCH

RANDOM HOUSE

AND DESTROY

Irwin R. Blacker ●

New York

First Printing

© Copyright, 1966, by Irwin R. Blacker
All rights reserved under International and Pan-American Copyright Conventions. Published in New York by Random House, Inc. Distributed in Toronto, Canada, by Random House of Canada Limited and in London by Cassell & Company Ltd.

Library of Congress Catalog Card Number: 66-21492

Manufactured in the United States of America by
The Colonial Press Inc., Clinton, Mass.

Design by Victoria Dudley

For Dorothy Fuldheim, Jr.

EPITAPH ON AN ARMY OF MERCENARIES

These, in the day when heaven was falling,
  The hour when earth's foundations fled,
Followed their mercenary calling
  And took their wages and are dead.

Their shoulders held the sky suspended;
  They stood, and earth's foundations stay;
What God abandoned, these defended,
  And saved the sum of things for pay.

A. E. Housman

SEARCH AND DESTROY

●

NORTH VIETNAM •

THE WORK CREW looked like a swarm of bugs spread over the valley of the Song Koi and the mountains that rimmed it. Thousands of men with baskets on their backs walked in a seemingly endless line from the hillside, where thousands of others tore the loose red dirt from the open patch, digging deeper and deeper to fill the baskets which were then picked up and hauled away to be dumped into the great fill that dammed the river. Beyond and eastward another stream of thousands of men marched in route step down the poorly paved road and across the long bridge. It was a new bridge and they were in awe of what had been built by the able young engineers from Peking. The great span was broad with low fluted sides and supports that reached almost gingerly into the valley below. The bridge was shining white concrete, and when a burly soldier spat onto the bridge, a young officer in a drab, dust-colored uniform slapped the soldier's face and waited while he knelt down to wipe up the spittle. The officer was proud of the bridge. He believed the men should be proud to cross it.

And farther to the east was the tank farm: large, cylindrical metal tanks, painted black against the wear of rain and sun. Here the soldiers in the dust-colored uniforms marched back and forth protecting the thousands of gallons of oil and gasoline which had been hauled up the river in large boats and small ones. Nearby a rusty tanker from Iraq pumped petroleum like blood from its bowels into the newly constructed tanks.

Not far as a plane flies, or even as a man can ride in an ox cart, the airfield lay spread out over the flat land between the mountains. The edge of the runways had recently been lengthened, topped with concrete and then covered again with brush and the limbs of trees. The airplanes, which were no longer new but which were polished and treated with extraordinary tenderness, stood under the trees and the spread nets woven with leaves and painted green. The planes had seen battle in Korea, had flown over the coastal islands and had been used to train a thousand pilots. They were slow by some standards, but they were the best the small pilots with the dark faces had available to them. And they were guarded with care against fire and sabotage by rigid-backed sentries who walked their posts in regular order—twenty paces in one direction until they met a second sentry and twenty paces in the other until they met a third. The pilots were proud of their planes, and the sentries were proud of them both. They had no others.

Every so often a sentry or a pilot would look up and listen to the sound of a train that chugged down the mountainside past the airfield and disappeared into the tunnel that led through the mountain beyond. Sometimes a sentry would stand to watch the troops riding the box cars or count the cars filled with ammunition and explosives or observe the small artillery which would later be unloaded and hauled south into the jungles by the sweat of oxen and men.

The whole valley between the mountains crawled with activity. For almost a thousand years it had been quiet, although men had marched across it into battle and had come back or had not come back. Caravans carrying trade goods north to Yangnin passed in one direction or another; but then they had moved slowly, had gone their way and left the valley undisturbed. The men who came now intended to leave their mark on the land; their holes punched through the mountains, their concrete aprons spilled white on the valley floor, their dam would hold back the river and their bridge, they knew, would last a thousand years so that future generations would know these men had paused here on their southward drive. They did not care about the valley or the people who lived there—they had no reason to care about them. The valley was only a point of departure into a greater world, a rich world that could feed a half billion people, a world of rice and jungle and opportunity for those who were willing to grab that opportunity. The people in the valley lived as their parents and grandparents had lived; they were not important except as they could haul dirt for the dam or trees for camouflage or lead the ox carts that carried large drums of fuel to feed the strange-looking tank farm that spread near the airfield. The only thing that was important to the men who had so recently moved into the valley was that their secret be kept and that they be ready to move on when the orders were flashed to them over the radios in the shacks they had built to house their officers and equipment.

Above the valley the sky was bright blue with a few scattered clouds, and high beyond the sight of the men on the valley floor —or even those posted on the mountaintops—the black plane with the blunt-edged wings sailed the currents of thin air. Inside, the pilot checked his instruments and flicked the lever which started his camera motors turning synchronously. He had a long way to travel before dark; and he had already been over South China and the China coast. No one could bother him, even though a radar screen might reveal his presence as a faint blip. When he completed his flight, he would land his plane at the military airfield outside Saigon, turn over his films and look up the small Annamese girl who was so playful under the covers.

He could not see the valley below and could not have cared less what images his cameras captured. They were not his problems. He was paid almost two thousand dollars a month to fly this plane, and that was more than both of his brothers together made working in the coal fields of West Virginia. He had a job to do. He was doing it.

Below in the valley that lay between the mountains, the swarms of men and women continued hauling their sacks of dirt or marching southward over the white concrete bridge. They, too, had a job to do.

SAIGON •

A HALF HOUR after the U-2 plane landed at the airfield near Saigon, the pilot was on his way to meet the Annamese girl and the films were already out of his cameras. Without even waiting to develop the films, the colonel commanding the base slipped them into a pouch which he handed to an Air Force major. The two stood beside the large C-135, waiting for the plane to be checked out and the jet engines warmed. They talked about a dancer they had been with the night before—a Javanese girl who could twist her pelvis with greater ease than an eel. The major envied the colonel his opportunity to see the Javanese girl again, and the colonel envied the major his flight back to the States. The sergeant in charge of the ground crew called that the plane was ready for take-off and the two officers shook hands while making an obscene comment about the Javanese dancer. Five minutes later the major was airborne.

WASHINGTON, D.C. ●

THE C-135 landed at Andrews Air Force Base two hours before dawn. Stepping into a waiting sedan, the major sped directly to the Photo Interpretation Lab in downtown Washington, where he turned his pouch over to a waiting lieutenant general from the Defense Intelligence Agency.

An hour later, with a complete interpretation carefully typed on a cover sheet, one set of the air photos was on its way to the Georgetown home of the Under-Secretary of Defense and another to the home of the Director of Central Intelligence in Northwest Washington.

Sitting up in bed, the Under-Secretary of Defense listened to the quick briefing given him by the Deputy Director of Defense Intelligence, Lieutenant General Hyde MacWolfe. The light on the night table was inadequate to show the fine points of the films which MacWolfe was discussing, so the Under-Secretary asked his wife, who had already poured coffee, to turn on the overhead light. He was still staring at the prints when the phone rang. The Director of Central Intelligence wanted to know the Under-Secretary's reaction. Putting one hand on the mouthpiece of the phone, the Under-Secretary grinned at General MacWolfe. "CIA wants to know our reaction, Hyde. Do you want to throw them into a tizzy?"

MacWolfe, a stocky, tough-minded sometime tank commander, considered the implications of the prints that were spread on the bed before the Under-Secretary and the further implications of any action he might request. "Let's label it a flap," he suggested. "And then let's see if we can carry the ball on it."

The Under-Secretary looked at him a long time before he shook his head. Talking once more into the phone, he said, "The Old Gray Wolf thinks we have a flap on our hands. I'm inclined to agree." There was silence for a moment, and then he argued, "I'm sorry, but I don't think this is your bailiwick. You brought in the information, and I'll tell the President that I think bringing it in was wonderful, but any action plan should be decided by GENOPS," indicating the General Operations Agency, headed by Major General Richard LeGrande.

MacWolfe looked at the Under-Secretary and half nodded in agreement. "I'll have MacWolfe get on this with General Le-Grande and we'll see what General Operations can come up with. Meanwhile, we'd both better get over to the White House." The Under-Secretary looked at his watch. "I'll try to set a meeting for eight o'clock breakfast." After a pause he was saying "goodbye" with a grin.

The General, dressed in full uniform, felt uncomfortable in the Under-Secretary's bedroom, with the Under-Secretary's wife, dressed in a robe, sitting and watching as the two of them gathered the aerial photos into a stack.

"LeGrande's agency will have to handle this if the President agrees," the Under-Secretary was explaining. "If I'd asked for Defense Intelligence to handle it, CIA would have screamed like a stuck pig. If I'd let CIA handle it, as he was suggesting, then I'd have had to scream. If the decision is made to do anything about it overtly, then it's up to the Joint Chiefs to come up with a plan. If the decision is made to get into the bag of dirty tricks, then it's LeGrande's."

MacWolfe nodded. He understood the politics of the situation, even if he did not agree with them. The small agency known as General Operations had been assigned by Congress the responsibility for covert operations which involved action—"irregular operations" as its director General Richard LeGrande always called them. To MacWolfe that phrase would never mean anything except guerrilla warfare. To LeGrande irregular warfare meant anything in the way of sabotage, guerrilla operations, assassination, or action in support of such operations.

The Under-Secretary was out of bed now and handed the photos to MacWolfe. "Stay with LeGrande on this. Offer him what help he needs." After a moment's thought as he slipped on his robe, he added, "I'll clear that with the Chairman of the Joint Chiefs." MacWolfe was excusing himself and was about to leave the room when the Under-Secretary asked, "You'll get right to Le Grande with this and be in touch with me as soon as he has any suggestion regarding how he wants to act?"

"Yes, sir." Then MacWolfe asked, "Where shall I find you?"

The Under-Secretary looked at the alarm clock on the table and thought a moment. "Make it ten o'clock at the White House. We'll be at a National Security Council meeting. This will probably top the agenda."

When MacWolfe had left, the Under-Secretary smiled at his wife. "I'm told they've called him the Old Gray Wolf ever since he graduated from the Academy. I wonder if that's because he snaps like one or because of the way he thinks about women?"

She considered this for a moment and then smiled. "He's probably good-looking, if you're the kind who likes bulldogs."

But the Under-Secretary was already thinking of what he was going to recommend to the President.

General MacWolfe's driver sped through the empty streets of the Capital in the early morning, crossed the Potomac at the bridge south of the Tidal Basin and drove on past a still sleeping

Alexandria southward to the tall apartment building near Hunting Creek, which once marked the northern edge of George Washington's plantation. Without waiting for the drowsy doorman to help him, the General stepped out of the car and mounted several steps into the carpeted lobby of Potomac Towers. Looking about quickly, he asked the doorman to call General LeGrande's suite and announce that General MacWolfe was coming up to see him.

In the elevator MacWolfe opened the envelope which held the aerial photographs. He shook his head in disgust. At the ninth floor he hurried out, crossed the empty corridor and rang the bell of the General's suite. A moment later Janet Garner opened the door and let him in. She was wearing a silk robe, and he could tell from the hairbrush still in her hand that he had caught her before she was ready for company.

"It's that important?" she asked him as she stepped aside and let him pass her into the living room.

For a moment the two of them stood alone in the large room with white carpets and dark floors. MacWolfe had known Janet ever since she had become LeGrande's mistress more than six years earlier. He had met her before that, but until she and his old friend and classmate had established the apartment together, he had not paid much attention to her. In the years since, she had become a friend to both MacWolfe and his wife. And after six years, Janet remained a puzzle to MacWolfe. A man of simple and direct methods, he could not understand a woman executive, could not really imagine working with one the way Richard LeGrande did with his Director of Personnel, the post which Janet held at GENOPS.

As she took MacWolfe's hat, Janet waved to a chair. "He'll be out in a moment," she said, aware that the stocky Pentagon officer had not answered her question.

MacWolfe waited until Janet sat down on the sofa and then settled himself in a large easy chair. "It isn't six o'clock yet, and you're the third woman I've seen in a silk robe." He thought a moment, and then added, "That's a record for me."

Janet nodded. "There was Lil, but who was the other one?"

"The Secretary's wife," MacWolfe said, knowing that somehow the luster had gone off his boast.

And as he spoke, Janet realized that he had come directly from the Secretary's house and that whatever he wanted to talk to Richard about had to do with the envelope that he still had in his hand. Before she could make any comment, General Le-Grande came in from the bedroom. In white shirt sleeves and with a tie thrown over his shoulder, he stood looking down at MacWolfe. "Isn't this a hell of a time to come calling, Hyde?"

MacWolfe nodded. In the thirty years since they had first met, he had become accustomed to LeGrande, and only on rare occasions did he take umbrage. "You've got a busy morning ahead of you," MacWolfe warned, as Janet rose and excused herself to get dressed.

The tall, almost square-faced general with the steel-gray hair stood looking at MacWolfe. Then with a gesture toward the rows of ribbons on the uniform, he said, "Any more medals on that manly bosom, Hyde, and you can open your own hock shop."

"Maybe it's going to be your turn to earn one," MacWolfe countered, as he handed the envelope to LeGrande. The morning sun had already lighted part of the room, but to assure himself better light, LeGrande took the photographs from the envelope, tossed it on the coffee table and then strode out the French doors to the balcony beyond. There he stood alone for several minutes reading the photographs and the cover sheet which identified the locations and the times the photographs were taken. When he was done, he looked up and saw MacWolfe beside him.

"Where have they been?" he asked as he turned the photos over and looked at the time stamp on the back which indicated when they had been printed.

"I sent a set to the Director of CIA and took one to the Under-Secretary of Defense."

LeGrande nodded. The sun was clear in the eastern sky and he knew it would be a warm day. Glancing down, he saw a small sailboat leave the pier of the apartment harbor. He was trying to avoid thinking about the prints in his hand. Finally, he held them up and scanned them once more. "I make out an airfield, a bridge, a dam, a tunnel and a tank farm," he said.

"That's what I see," MacWolfe agreed.

Shuffling the prints, LeGrande studied an older set. "They weren't all there last month."

"You're getting warm, Dick," MacWolfe said.

For a long time neither of them said anything. LeGrande heard Janet preparing breakfast in the kitchen. He saw a 707 pass over the river toward the Dulles National Airport.

"You have any bright ideas about it?" MacWolfe was asking.

After a pause LeGrande shook his head. "Confirms things that have come in from other sources. Spells them out, in fact." Then he fell silent for a moment. "Your being here, I gather, means that this is my problem?"

Smiling, MacWolfe said, "We'd love to handle it, but there's always . . ."

"CIA," LeGrande finished the sentence for him. The Director of GENOPS was beginning to think clearly, though he would have been the first to admit it was much too early in the morning. "When does the Security Council meet?"

"At ten."

Reaching out, LeGrande turned MacWolfe's wrist so that he could read the time. "I presume that I have the Deputy Director of Defense Intelligence just panting to assist me unofficially on this?"

"That's about it, Dick." Then MacWolfe shrugged. "Every time I have to chase to the Secretary's house and then either here or to the Chief's or the Old Man's I feel like a messenger boy."

"They aren't usually dressed so pretty," LeGrande consoled him as he walked back into the living room. "Has the Old Man been briefed yet?" he asked, wanting the assurance that the Chairman of the Joint Chiefs knew what was going on.

"The Secretary said he would talk to him."

Standing in the small entrance foyer, LeGrande knotted his tie as he called to Janet.

She appeared from the breakfast room, already dressed; both officers appreciated what they saw, for Janet, in her late thirties, was still a very good-looking woman.

"I've got a flap," LeGrande explained. "I'm going to take the Old Gray Wolf's car and get to the office. Will you call Harry and ask him to get in as quickly as he can?"

"Do you want me to come in with you?"

LeGrande shook his head. "When the sergeant comes, he'll bring you in." He thought a moment, "As soon as you get there, see what you can do to find me an Annamese who speaks English. Male. Able to take care of himself."

Seeing Janet's head cock to one side as she weighed the problem, he added, "I'll explain when you've found him." He was already taking his suit jacket out of the foyer closet and slipping into it.

As the two men started to leave, MacWolfe crossed to the coffee table and picked up the envelope marked TOP SECRET. Assuring himself that it was empty, he handed it to Janet. "Better get rid of that."

"You're learning this intelligence business, Hyde. You know, of course, that's the best way not to get another star."

For a moment he was not certain how he was supposed to take the remark. Then he looked at the open front door and gestured with his hand. "I didn't tell Dick to get himself off the merry-go-round," he said, knowing that she referred to the fact that LeGrande had not been promoted since the Korean War because he had become a specialist outside the Army chain of command.

When he heard LeGrande calling him from the hallway, he shrugged. "Not only have I seen three women in silk robes this morning, but I missed coffee with all three of them." Then he was gone and Janet was alone in the apartment. She looked at the brown envelope in her hand and, without realizing that she was doing it, very carefully shredded the paper. In two hours the maid would be in and she herself would be sitting at her desk in GENOPS headquarters. She was not sure she would not have preferred to stay home and clean up the apartment herself. As she walked into the kitchen and poured herself a cup of coffee, she wondered if Mary LeGrande, the General's estranged wife, had ever cleaned house for him. She did not think of Mrs. LeGrande very often. They had never met, and the General himself had seen her only once since the Second World War, when they had agreed to separate without the divorce which she felt would hurt her socially. Janet wondered about a woman who was so concerned about her social status and so little concerned about the man she had married. Looking out of the kitchen window at the river below, she knew that this was a fruitless line of thought. She never resented Mary LeGrande. In fact, ever since that lonely weekend in Quebec six years before when she and the General had found themselves together without the pressures and formalities of the agency, she had somehow pitied her. Before that she had pitied herself: married at seventeen, separated at nineteen and widowed before she was twenty. Then the long years alone in Washington, shifting from one agency to another until GENOPS and the General. And now she was thinking of Mary LeGrande, and she wondered why. Then she recalled MacWolfe's comment about the women he had already seen in silk robes. Her coffee drunk, she set the cup on the sink. MacWolfe. He was like a child much of the time, but Richard always said that given a tank command he could fight like a bear, crushing everything about him with a giant paw. These two generals whom she knew best were very different animals. Hers was no bear, but more a panther—hard, flashing, swift. As she stood at the sink, rinsing out the cup, she smiled. What in the world did Dick plan to do with an Annamese male who spoke English?

By eight o'clock General LeGrande had worked out the basic outline of his proposal to the National Security Council. In the spacious conference room of GENOPS he had discussed the outline with Harry Fuller, his deputy, and with MacWolfe. They agreed that the plan he was going to present was possible, but both of them concurred that it would not only be difficult, but would perhaps cost lives. LeGrande sat back in his chair and stared at the other two as if they were strangers. Then, after a moment, he rose and walked over to the large globe which filled a corner of the room. With effort he rotated the globe so that Southeast Asia was before him. Looking down from the South China border he could see the entire sweep of what was known a century before as Little China and now went under the many names of the Vietnams, Laos, Cambodia and Thailand. It was a world in itself and was almost cruelly soldered onto that of the larger China which was trying to thrust itself aggressively into the twentieth century.

The conference room was plain in its decorations—map boards were carefully covered from curious eyes, and several field tables with files were scattered along the walls of the room. In the center was a large oval conference table with a single telephone and interoffice communications speaker set beside the chair which LeGrande had just vacated.

Swinging back to look at Harry Fuller and MacWolfe, LeGrande shook his head. "Those pictures we've seen. You can't make them pull all of that back without taking a risk of lives."

MacWolfe nodded and looked to Fuller for comment. Harry Fuller was as difficult for MacWolfe to understand as Janet. Harry, a short, wiry, nervous man, was a civilian operations specialist, who could plan an assassination or move guerrilla supplies into enemy territory. What he could not do was realize the importance of MacWolfe or any other military man. By nature a civilian, Harry knew only one soldier he respected, and that was his superior, and LeGrande did not wear a uniform. "You'd be mounting this thing," MacWolfe commented to Harry. "Haven't you any ideas?"

Harry did not know if this was intended to be a criticism of his reluctance to talk in front of an outsider, or if MacWolfe really did not understand his function. Before he could answer, LeGrande interrupted. "Harry's ideas will come when we have a policy. That's what we haven't got now."

At that moment the intercom buzzed and an angry LeGrande crossed the room and flicked it on as he looked at the other two men. "Can't get that wench to understand when I say no calls . . ." Then into the intercom, "What is it?"

"There is a call for General MacWolfe from the Chairman of the Joint Chiefs of Staff on line 404."

The Pentagon officer reached over and picked up the phone as he shrugged to indicate he did not know why he was being called. After three "yes sirs" he hung up. "The Old Man wants to see me before the meeting of the Security Council."

LeGrande nodded and waited; there had been three "yes sirs."

"And he wanted to know if you had a proposal. Told him you had."

LeGrande waited as MacWolfe pulled down the front of his uniform blouse. "We're going to need an alternative, in case your plan fails," MacWolfe finally said.

This made sense to both LeGrande and Fuller, but it was Fuller who pointed out, "The only alternative could be war."

Then with that tough-mindedness and lack of subtlety which set MacWolfe apart from most men, the Deputy Director of DIA shook his head with complete disdain for the civilian; "They aren't building up a base of departure to play pattycake." Turning to LeGrande, "I'll try to get to the Security Council meeting. If not, I'll talk to you later in the day." Reaching over, he picked up the set of air photos and strode out of the room.

When he was alone with LeGrande, Fuller laughed. "The way he took those pics, I think he doesn't want to play marbles with us, Boss Man."

LeGrande shook his head. "The Old Gray Wolf is suddenly in Intelligence and has an overdeveloped sense of security right now."

Harry laughed again. "What you mean is that he doesn't trust *me* with those pics."

"That's right. You're a civilian. You have to be patient with the Gray Wolf—he's never known many civilians. His father was Army. His grandfather was Army. And his sons will be Army, or

God help them." The General leaned over and switched on the intercom. "Mrs. Garner, please. General LeGrande." He smiled at Harry, who had learned a long time ago that the smile on the General's face was never in any way related to how he felt at the particular moment. "Janet, have you found my Annamese?" A soft curse under his breath. "No, I don't want any favors from CIA. Find our own." He clicked off the intercom. "That's just what they'd like. Someone to tell them how I function."

He stood for a moment with one foot on the chair as he considered the plan he had formulated. "Try to break that damned idea down now," he told Harry. "If we get a go-ahead, I think that time will be everything."

Harry nodded in agreement, handed the General the file of the morning's Intelligence and left him standing beside the conference table. Finding himself alone, LeGrande glanced at his watch—an hour and a half to the Security Council meeting. Then he started to read the Intelligence reports.

The meeting with the Security Council went very much as LeGrande expected it would. He arrived fifteen minutes early and waited for almost an hour to be ushered inside the Cabinet Room of the White House. He knew everyone there, even if only slightly. It took him half an hour to present his plan, and then he was told that he would be contacted in the event it was accepted. And so it was almost noon when he returned to GENOPS. Going directly to his own office, he tried, without much success, to assess the Security Council meeting. There had been the questions he had anticipated. From the maps and papers spread out on the table, he knew that before he had presented his proposal the Chairman of the Joint Chiefs had offered an alternate plan of action should the Defense Department be called upon.

Sitting in his own office at GENOPS so many blocks from the Pentagon, LeGrande wondered how his plan had been received. The President had not smiled, but then he rarely did at

Security Council meetings. The Council was not called to ponder pleasant problems. It was not a place for politicking or kind words. From these meetings came the life and death decisions for a nation, and no one present had the time to be more than courteous. LeGrande wondered if they would actually call upon GENOPS to meet the present threat. If the President decided that an immediate air strike could stop the build-up in the valley of the Song Koi, then he could order it and hope that it would not trigger a war. LeGrande believed that it would. Obviously, the Council did too, even though its members had already made their decision that the immediate bombing of certain targets in the Hanoi area would not months before when they had taken the risk and had authorized the bombing of petroleum installations. They could take the risk again and blow one or more of the targets revealed in the air photos. However, at this moment anything might trigger a war. A dam, a bridge, a railroad tunnel—these were all signs of natural progress of the kind the United States was telling the world it wanted in the Far East. To take them out with bombers would belie all of the promises to help Asians build a better Asia. The airfield and the tank farm were gratuitous. They could be treated as part of the same package, and with less danger than the other three targets. LeGrande knew he was thinking in circles as was almost everyone else who was forced to deal with the problem of Vietnam. Trying to put first things first, he admitted to himself that the chance of starting the larger war was the most important factor. And placing second things second, he admitted that the Security Council had to avoid anything that would force the Russians to make a final choice between the Chinese or neutrality. And the one thing the Council hoped for at this moment was Russian neutrality at minimum, Russian alliance at best. But a bombing that wiped out the villages of the Song Koi could not be tolerated by Moscow, if only because Russia would lose any chance it still had at the leadership of the Communist world; at the same time the United States would lose any hope it had of keeping the continued neutrality of the so-called non-aligned nations. The more he thought about the area involved, the more LeGrande respected the Chinese selection. It met all of their needs and was protected by the United States' clear decision not to overtly escalate the war further. LeGrande knew that he was only thinking about the excuse for war and not the reason. If the Security Council did accept his plan, he knew he had to make certain that nothing could be laid to the door of the United States, that nothing could be proven in any way. He shrugged. The Chinese did not need an excuse to intervene, but at the same time he could not afford to give them one. Putting his elbows on his desk, he flicked on the intercom and asked his secretary, "Did we get the National Estimate today from CIA?"

A moment of confusion, and she said, "I think so, General. Do you want me to bring it in?"

Very patiently, he said that he did and turned off the intercom. When the young woman brought him the small document in the blue cover with TOP SECRET printed on it, he thanked her and settled back to read it. The twelve men at CIA who were supposed to tell the President what would happen in the event of any particular emergency hedged as always. If this happens, then this will happen, but if this does not happen, then this might happen, unless this happens, etc. But at the end of the report LeGrande found what he was looking for—the basic notion without the equivocation. It read simply that if we overtly attack these new installations, they will counter with added force. Tossing the document on the desk, he believed the President and the Security Council had to come to the same conclusion. That left them three alternatives, as far as he could see: provoke the war by bombing out the line of departure from which an invasion would begin through Little China; wait for the enemy to be fully prepared and give him time to build up both his total strength and his propaganda to pitch and let him start the war; or accept the risks involved in the GENOPS plan.

Satisfied that he knew which way the President had to decide, LeGrande walked out of his office into the reception room, where he told his secretary, "There are classified documents in there. Call for a guard," and then by way of explanation, "I'll be with Mrs. Garner."

The secretary watched the tall, dignified figure of the General stride out of the office and wondered what Mrs. Garner had that shot down a handsome two-star. The relationship between the Director of the agency and his Personnel Director was no secret. The newspapers had hinted at it broadly enough several years before when LeGrande had come under Senate investigation. There were those who maintained the agency would be larger and richer if the General did not get his meat and potatoes where he worked. And there were those who thought that the Personnel Director had too much influence in the agency. But those who knew the two of them brushed off such comments as being irrelevant. One of the reasons GENOPS existed at all was because the combined strength of Richard LeGrande and Janet Garner was such that they had taken on all of the people who wanted to sink the agency by turning its budget over to the CIA and its functions back to the Pentagon. Although many who worked for the agency did not understand this blunt fact of life, many in the Washington Establishment did. And understanding it, they were reluctant to clash with the pair. LeGrande's reputation was that of a killer and Janet's that of an operator; both knew how to reach the sources of power and when to use them.

Walking into the reception room of the Personnel Office, where a number of men and women were filling out application forms or waiting to be interviewed by Janet's staff, LeGrande looked about hoping to see an Annamese male who knew how to take care of himself. If Janet had found him, he was not to be seen.

"I'll tell Mrs. Garner you're here, General," her secretary was offering, and LeGrande nodded.

"Anyone with her?"

"No, General. She's on the phone. Been trying to locate someone—an Annamese male—all morning."

Seeing all the heads about the office come up with puzzled expressions, LeGrande wondered if there could be such a thing as security in Washington. "Thanks," he said, as the secretary alerted Janet on the intercom.

Inside her office, he waited while she finished the call she was making. "Any luck?"

"I think so, but I'll know more in a couple of hours." She lit a cigarette, and then she brushed her hair aside and clipped her earring back in place. "What about you?"

He shrugged. "They'll let me know if I made sense in their context." He sat down in the chair across from her and swung his feet up onto her desk.

"When do you think you might hear?" she asked.

"Late today. Maybe tonight. They know they'll have to squirm before they okay what I proposed. They'll want to clear it with people in SEATO."

Janet shook her head as she watched him rub his chin with the back of his hand. "There goes your security."

"I don't know. If I move as fast as I have to, maybe not." Then with a completely irrelevant grin, "I'd like to play some bridge tonight. The Old Gray Wolf and Lil."

Puzzled, Janet asked, "It's important?"

He nodded. "Very. I don't care what else they're doing. Tell Lil it's my birthday or something, but be sure she comes."

"Am I supposed to become jealous about you and Lil? Or," and she laughed, "do I just play the madam with your best friend's wife?"

"Just play the madam."

Janet nodded as she picked up the phone. "You want to talk to her alone?"

To her surprise, he nodded. "That's right."

Dialing, she asked, "And what's Lil got that I haven't got?"

"Hyde," he said. "Hyde and a fascinating past." And he left her looking after him as someone answered the phone she was holding.

•   •   •

Through the afternoon LeGrande worked on the details of the plan he had presented to the Security Council. And while he worked, he waited for a phone call. Finally, at six o'clock, he told Harry Fuller to alert the duty officer that he would be at home for the evening and asked Harry to be available in case he had to call on him. Satisfied there was nothing more he could do at the office, LeGrande met Janet at the entrance of the building where the sedan was waiting for them. On the way home, the General explained in as much detail as he could the plan which he and Harry had been working on. When he was done, Janet nodded her agreement. The President would have to call on GENOPS if he wanted to increase the odds against war.

"I made them no promises," LeGrande told her. "We may blow the whole thing, but they understood that."

"I wonder what kind of a money-back guarantee you could have offered," Janet commented.

He stared at her, the setting sun through the car window fuzzing the edge of her soft silhouette. After a time he reached out and, putting his arm about her waist, drew her to him. She leaned back and his lips brushed against her hair. She was staring out the window now, watching the river muddy south beside them. "You aren't going to do this yourself, Dick?" she asked. His arm tightened about her waist. For a long time he did not answer her, and she moved away so that she could look up at him. "Dick?"

"I was leaving the Cabinet Room when the Old Man stopped me. Asked me the same thing, and when I said I was thinking about it, he made the comment that it was time I grew up." He drew her back to him, and after a rigid moment she yielded with the remark, "You haven't answered my question."

Again he was silent, and then he said, "I haven't made up my mind yet." As he felt her start to draw away, he held firmly to her waist. "Relax. I think I might have someone who can do it better."

She waited for him to explain, but instead, he asked, "That man I asked you to find?"

"I found one," she said. "He's coming in from France."

LeGrande considered this. "None here?"

Janet nodded. "I ruled out a lot of them. Came here for one reason or another and I didn't think you would have taken them."

"The one reason or another?" he was pressing now.

"Fled the French or fought the French with the Vietcong. Now that their nations are independent, they have no part of either side."

He was puzzled now. "I don't get it. I don't give a damn about the French in the area."

Janet agreed. "Nor do I, but there are people who liked them, and they wouldn't want you to send someone back who had fought them. There were those who did not like them or the Vietcong."

Finally, LeGrande understood. "You were looking for someone neutral?"

"Less controversial anyway."

The car drove up the circular drive in front of the apartment and the two stepped out. LeGrande waited until his sergeant closed the door behind them before he told him, "Return to your barracks and stand by. I'll call you if I need you." The sergeant stepped back, saluted, and was about to return to the car when LeGrande reminded him, "Stand by. No excuses will be accepted."

Then he and Janet were walking into the building. As they went up to the ninth floor in the elevator, LeGrande returned to the subject of the Annamese. "If this one coming from France doesn't work out?"

"There are two here," she advised him. "Second choices, but they might serve in a pinch."

Accepting the limitations of her recommendations, he asked, "And the one who's coming?"

"He was offered an interview with an engineering company. They're paying his way to fly right in."

The cover story satisfied the General. He could always turn the man down and send him back none the wiser. A construction job in Vietnam would need a man who knew the languages.

Inside, Janet put the dinner which the maid had prepared into the oven and joined the General on the balcony, where he was waiting with an extra drink in his hand. Taking the martini, she reached up and kissed his cheek as his arm went around her. "The Old Gray Wolf should be here about eight," she said. "I'll get him into the kitchen to tell me how you should not take this assignment on yourself while you talk to Lil."

LeGrande winked. "Be careful alone there in the kitchen with Hyde. He's hell on women."

Three hours later, while they were playing bridge with the MacWolfes, the phone rang. Janet and MacWolfe both set their cards down and watched as LeGrande crossed the living room and picked up the phone. He acknowledged who he was and then he listened. Finally he said, "Yes, sir. At once." Then he cradled the phone and returned to the card table. Picking up his hand, he asked, "Whose bid is it?"

MacWolfe left his cards where they were as he shoved his chair back and looked at his friend. "Aren't we playing it cool tonight, Dick."

"Did you get the go-ahead?" Janet asked.

Uncertain about what was going on, Lil MacWolfe looked from one to the other. A woman in her early forties, there was still something chic about Mrs. MacWolfe. She was a large woman, almost as tall as her husband, and though she was dressed for the evening, she retained the look of someone who had spent the day horseback riding. "Is this a game of button-button?" she asked.

LeGrande shook his head. "It was only this morning that your noble husband, that fearless commander, said I was the eager beaver around here." He was smiling, but Janet saw that he had put his cards down again and was fumbling for his pipe. She assumed that he had the orders he had been waiting for.

Looking around the table, he suggested, "Let's call an end to the bridge. I had a lousy hand anyway, and if you," looking at

MacWolfe, "had had a good one, you would have loused it up. So we're even."

While the MacWolfes were trying to understand what was happening, Janet rose from the table and said, "I'll put on some coffee if Hyde will open the can for me." As she walked into the kitchen, both LeGrande and Lil MacWolfe watched a puzzled Hyde rise and follow her.

"A drink, Lil?" LeGrande offered.

She shook her head. Then rising from her chair, she stepped out of the living room onto the balcony beyond. The General followed her and closed the French doors behind him so that they were alone; only the light shed through the draperies cast their shadows on the dark stone railing.

"You wanted to ask me something?" she said, as LeGrande stood beside her, his elbows on the rail. Both of them were looking at the lights on the river below them.

It took LeGrande a long time before he could bring himself to the subject.

"Barney," he said, and he was aware that she stiffened. "Can Barney be trusted to get a job done?"

Lil MacWolfe stared at the moving lights, but she could not see them now. She could only see the image of Barney Fannin. A bear of a man, one who might seem clumsy but who actually moved with grace. An angry man. A man who had hurt her and whom she had hurt.

"I was there when you married him," LeGrande said, to give her time to think. "The first man in our class and the first to get married. Hyde and I held swords that day. I don't think anyone else knows Barney Fannin as well as you do."

She turned her head slowly and looked at the tall man beside her. She had known him as long as she had known Barney Fannin, longer than she had known Hyde MacWolfe. All three men were Army. And so was Lil MacWolfe. Her father had been a general in two wars. Her grandfather, until he was killed, had held a cavalry command under Longstreet. "Are you asking me to pass judgment on him, Dick?"

LeGrande shook his head. "No. You sort of did that when you left him. What I want to know is if I can trust him to get a job done."

Lil considered the question. "He could not hold the job you do. Hyde's would leave him confused. Unlike the rest of you, he really is suited only for the battlefield. He might have been remembered if he had been killed on one. He certainly would have been happier." Then, recalling the few years she had lived with him after the war, she added, "And I don't mean to be cruel when I say I would have been, too."

LeGrande nodded. "There are men who cannot come to terms with peace. Robert Rogers was one. George Rogers Clark another—even Lawrence of Arabia. They only came to life when they were fighting."

"Well," Lil agreed, "that's Barney Fannin. If you have a regiment you want led into hell, he could take it." She thought a moment and added, "I would never trust him with a division, because he couldn't think of all the things that had to be done with it."

"But a regiment to hell?" LeGrande asked again to make certain he had understood her.

For a long time she looked away into the darkness and then nodded. "Barney's been there and could lead the way." Then she turned and stared at LeGrande. "You're not going to involve him in some bag of dirty tricks and get him killed?"

He reached out and put one hand on her arm as if to calm her. "You'd care?"

After a moment she said, "He's the father of two of my children."

The General's hand squeezed her arm affectionately, "I'll try to bring him back," he promised. Then he stepped away, opened the French doors and followed her into the living room. "Your car's downstairs?" he asked a surprised MacWolfe.

"Yes. Want it?"

Looking at the tray of coffee and sweet rolls set on the table, LeGrande apologized to Janet, "I'm sorry. Will you call Harry and tell him I'll meet him at the office. Then call my sergeant and tell him the MacWolfes will need him tonight." With a grin, he added, "It isn't every day I sport a Pentagon sedan with three stars." He was already in the foyer closet taking out his jacket when MacWolfe started to slip into his own.

"If you have your orders, I'm coming with you."

LeGrande looked back at the two women. Both of them nodded. "Damn," he exclaimed. "It doesn't mean as much with a three star in the sedan." He apologized to Lil MacWolfe for leaving her and walked to the elevator door with Janet. "Get those calls made. Suggest to Lil she stay over tonight. We won't be home." He tipped her face up and kissed her. The elevator came and he stepped aside for MacWolfe to enter. As the door closed, he winked at Janet. "I knew I wouldn't be able to lose him, but the surprise is going to be his."

When both generals were seated in the long black sedan, MacWolfe told his driver to take them to the GENOPS headquarters building. Then he leaned back in his seat and pulled out a cigar. "You aren't going in on this one yourself, Dick." It was not a question.

The headlamps of a passing car lighted the interior of the sedan for a moment and LeGrande could see that his friend was looking at him and waiting for an answer.

"I'm not going in if I can get the man I want."

MacWolfe remained silent as he lighted the cigar.

"That offer of help the Pentagon keeps pushing on me all the time; how good is it?" LeGrande asked.

Puffing deeply for a moment, MacWolfe considered what he was letting himself and the Pentagon in for. Then he shrugged. "I guess you get a blank check." The car sped through Alexandria and on toward the lights of the city beyond. "What do you want?"

"Barney Fannin." He could hear the man beside him stir. The sedan passed the National Airport and Gravely Point. The only light was the faint glow of MacWolfe's cigar.

"Do I get him, Hyde?"

"I don't think that's the only point involved." The Pentagon officer was trying to be objective, and both of them knew this was difficult. But LeGrande had to know MacWolfe's reaction, because he and Fannin had been together during the war.

"What else is involved?" LeGrande wanted to get the matter aired as quickly as possible.

"You know I'm the wrong person to be talking about him." Silence for a moment. "He gave Lil a hard time. He's not one of my favorite persons."

"You're probably not one of his, but then I'm not organizing a country club."

Then MacWolfe said bluntly, "Barney never grew up. He plays at being a soldier."

"Is that all of it?"

"All of it? I don't know. Something went wrong with Barney. I won't guess when. Maybe Lil could tell you." Then with a snort, "But I'm sure that's what the two of you talked about while Janet and I held hands."

LeGrande shrugged off the discussion with Lil for the moment. "I want to know what you think the rest of it is."

"The day we graduated, Barney was the top man in our class. That doesn't always mean the man who'll go the farthest. Just means at that moment he was good. He had something. Then the war, and he couldn't handle his job. Time after time, someone said, 'Give Barney Fannin a chance,' and he got his chances, Dick. He flubbed every one of them."

"Be honest, Hyde. Did he flub every chance?"

MacWolfe was silent for a long time, as if he was thinking of something else. Finally, he shook his leonine head. "No. He was a good man in combat. Would have been a fine company commander." Then, almost regretting the waste, "But he couldn't do anything else."

LeGrande nodded. "Lil thought he could have handled a regiment. You cut him down to a company." And his hand went up to cut off any protest. "It's really the same thing. All you're both telling me is that Barney Fannin is a soldier and not a commander."

The cigar came out of MacWolfe's mouth and he held it for a moment as he grudgingly conceded. "A hell of a soldier, Dick." "Isn't that what I need right now?"

The sedan drew up in front of the GENOPS building. Stepping out, the driver opened the door and the interior light went on. LeGrande sat studying MacWolfe, who nodded. "That's what you want, Dick." He remained where he was, staring straight ahead, and added, "However, if I were you, I would not use Barney Fannin. I think he's broken. Done. Finished." Before LeGrande could comment, he said, "But if you use him, I hope he doesn't come back."

"Do you really mean that?"

Again, MacWolfe nodded. "For what the son of a bitch did to Lil, I mean it."

It was a long moment before either one of them stepped out of the car.

The Night Duty Officer approved their credentials; and after they signed in, they went directly to LeGrande's office. Neither of them spoke until they were inside and the door was closed behind them. LeGrande waved MacWolfe to a chair across from the desk and pushed a telephone toward him. "Will you call the Night Duty Officer at G-1 and get Barney on a special plane? Orders to follow."

MacWolfe picked up the phone and held it for a moment. "You're sure this is what you want?"

LeGrande nodded. "I've been thinking about it ever since I left the Security Council this morning."

A longer hesitation. "I'm going to call the Old Man first."

Annoyed, LeGrande agreed, "If you think you have to."

"I do. He's had opinions about Barney for some time now."

Rising from behind the desk, LeGrande leaned across it. "And what are they?"

"Retirement. Barney's not going anywhere. You know it, and so do I. Give the Old Man credit for seeing the same thing."

LeGrande considered this. It was the duty of the Chief of Staff of the Army to know his senior officers, though at the rank of colonel, Barney Fannin could not be considered a senior officer. And though he was no longer Chief of Staff of the Army, the Chairman would remember Barney Fannin. He was not an easy man to forget.

While LeGrande was thinking about the call, MacWolfe dialed. A moment later he was discussing the matter with the Chairman. Then he listened to the reaction and held out the phone to LeGrande. "He wants to talk to you."

Holding the phone away from his ear for a moment, LeGrande weighed his original decision in relationship to a disagreement with the Chairman. Once, long ago, he had been the Chairman's protégé. And once, during the war, the Chairman had referred to him as *Das Wunderkind*. The name had been picked up by the newspapers, and for a time LeGrande had been a public hero. His career had been built in part on the mutual respect he and the Chairman had for each other. Sighing, he said, "LeGrande, sir." Then he listened to the question he had expected. "Yes, sir. I think he can do it." A moment of listening, and he said, "No, sir. There is no sentiment involved here. If Colonel Fannin is not available to me, then I shall undertake the assignment myself." He knew that this was his prerogative as the head of his own agency and the person responsible to the Security Council for the mission which it had approved. He waited for the Chairman to respond, and the wait was longer than he expected. Finally, he said, "Yes, sir. Good night, sir." He cradled the phone and pushed it back to MacWolfe. "Will you call G-1 now?"

MacWolfe stared at him for a long time before he took the phone again and dialed G-1. Once he had given the orders for Fannin's immediate transfer to Washington, he waited until the Night Duty Officer located Fannin. "He's in Georgia," MacWolfe said as he hung up the phone. "They'll try to get him on a plane tonight."

LeGrande nodded. "Thanks."

"Don't thank me. You have just lost another chance at that star you want so damned much." He saw that LeGrande was trying to ignore his remark, and he added, "Don't threaten the Old Man. He doesn't like it."

"Agreed," LeGrande said. He was standing by the window now, looking down into the street, where he saw a car stop at the entrance of the building. He assumed it was Harry, and without turning he asked MacWolfe, "Hyde, will you do me a favor?"

"What am I supposed to say?"

Both of them were smiling now as LeGrande turned to look at him. "Hold down your own office at the Pentagon. I'm going to be wheeling and dealing tonight and will want you where you can press the right buttons for me. Transportation. Men. PR. Supplies. Equipment. Everything that will have to be moved into place for this. As Harry and I lay out what and where, I'll call you and let you handle the logistics from there."

MacWolfe considered this. "You want me out of the way so you can do something foolish?"

LeGrande laughed. "Sometimes I think you don't trust me." Then he was serious. "No. I want help, and as fast as I can get it."

Nodding, MacWolfe came to his feet. "Call me at this number," he said as he quickly jotted down the private number to his office. He was about to leave when LeGrande said, "Lean on them to find Barney and get him moving."

FORT BENNING, GEORGIA ●

THE DUTY OFFICER at the Post Headquarters building at Fort Benning started to look for Colonel Fannin at the Bachelor Officers' Quarters, but the Colonel's room was empty. Because of the urgency of the Pentagon call, the duty officer, a young captain from Missouri who could not understand why anyone would want Colonel Fannin in the middle of the night, started knocking on other doors of the BOQ. Finally, a middle-aged National Guard major on a training cycle thought he remembered Colonel Fannin saying that he would be in Panama City, Florida. The Captain nodded. Fannin would stay at a motel there, and Panama City had at least fifty motels. Two rooms farther on, and after listening to the curses of two superior officers, the Captain located a lieutenant colonel who had gone to Panama City with Colonel Fannin two nights before. The Hayseed Motel. "But," the Light Colonel warned, "be it on your head to disturb him."

Back at the headquarters, the duty officer weighed the perils of ignoring the Pentagon against disturbing Colonel Fannin. Although the Colonel was a formidable figure, the Pentagon was a looming, vague dragon that consumed captains and spat them out disemboweled. Gathering all of the courage he could muster and remembering the varied slogans around Fort Benning, where the infantry trained its leadership, the Captain dialed information and, learning the number of the Hayseed Motel, placed his call.

PANAMA CITY, FLORIDA •

FIVE MINUTES after the duty officer at Fort Benning placed his call, the motel clerk at the Hayseed answered the phone. He admitted he had a Colonel Fannin registered. Plugging in the switchboard, he took great delight in ringing the Colonel's cabin.

Inside the seedy cabin, the phone rang twice before a buff-naked Barney Fannin reached over to pick up the receiver. The girl beside him turned over and asked if he had to answer. Fannin shrugged and started to reach for one exposed breast when the phone rang again. The girl moved closer, and he was holding both of her breasts and kissing her neck when the phone rang a fourth time. Annoyed, Fannin rolled over onto his back, pulling the girl on top of him as he did so, and reached for the phone. "What the hell do you want?"

He listened a moment to the excuse that the clerk did not want anything, but that someone at Fort Benning did. Swearing beautiful oaths, Fannin said, "Plug the idiot in." Then he listened to the apologies of the duty officer before he interrupted. "Get to the point, sonny." His hand ran down the bare spine of the girl, making her squirm as she giggled. Fannin listened for a long time. His hand came away from the girl and he brushed her off him. Ignoring her pout, he asked, "Who called from Washington?" He thought about the answer he had received and shook his head. "It's pretty damned late for the G-1 himself to be calling for one lousy colonel. You sure you have this right?" Again he listened to the recitation and finally he nodded, ignoring the fact that the Captain obviously could not see him. "They said any means of military transportation is authorized so long as it gets me there tonight?" Again the long confirmation.

Suddenly, as if just awakening, Barney Fannin sat up in bed, letting the sheet slip down to his waist. "Call Tyndall Air Force Base. Pass those instructions on. If there is any confirmation needed, tell the duty officer to check out with G-1 Pentagon." He reached for his watch on the night table. "I'll be there as soon as I can. They had better have a jet waiting to haul my butt north as fast as they can blow it out their engines." He paused a moment. "Do you understand your orders, Captain?"

The confirmation received, he hung up as the girl beside him rolled over, offering an arched back. Rising, he jerked the sheet off the bed and looked at her in the faint light cast by the motel's sign outside the cabin. She had a good figure, though not as nice as others he had seen. Her ankles were thick. Her shoulders were larger than those of most women. But he approved of the rest of her. Leaning over, he swatted her exposed buttocks so hard that she yelped and sat up staring at him.

"Papa Fannin's going bye-bye," he informed her.

"Not tonight," she protested. When he nodded, she cursed him so creatively that he smiled as he pulled on his shorts. "I could have found someone else," she objected.

"Well you might have," he agreed. "But you lost the target for tonight."

A few minutes later he was fully dressed. It was going to be cold in Washington, and he wished he had brought a bag and civies, but he had left the post too late to change or pack, and so he would live with what he had. Leaning over the bed, he took the young woman in his arms and kissed her solidly. One hand wandered over her breasts and down the length of her flat stomach to pause at her thigh. She tried to hold him but he broke away. "Duty calls," he said cynically.

"That transfer you offered me to the Post Exchange?" she asked as he started for the door.

Fannin looked back at her. "You just keep plugging in that switchboard till I get back," he suggested. Then, taking a ten-dollar bill out of his wallet, he tossed it on the night table. "You pay the motel and take a bus back to Benning."

The girl nodded as Fannin stood for a moment looking at her mussed hair down about her shoulders and then at the shabby motel room. The bare floor was partly covered with sand and the furniture had been battered by too many drunken infantrymen relaxing from the strain of jump school or infantry training.

Then he was outside. Five minutes later he turned onto Route 98. Thirteen miles farther on he pulled up to the sentry post at the gate of the Air Defense Command field designated Tyndall. A military policeman stepped forward and asked if he could be of help. Rummaging through the pockets of his uniform, Fannin located his ID card and waited until the MP verified the picture with the face. "Now," he asked, "where the hell do I find the duty officer?"

The MP pointed to a building some distance away.

Snorting his thanks, Fannin drove slowly through the small

air base to the indicated building. As he stepped out of his car, an Air Force major approached him. "Colonel Fannin?"

Wondering if the MP had phoned ahead, Barney grunted. "That's right."

"The orders from Washington were to have your plane ready for departure, sir. If you'll leave your car here, we'll drive over to the plane by jeep."

Impressed with whatever orders were shifting him about with such dispatch, Fannin looked at his own car for a moment, flipped the keys to the major and decided to see just how far he could press this VIP treatment. "Will you see that that"—gesturing to the convertible—"gets driven to Benning. Have it placed in my parking slot beside the BOQ."

The major said, "Yes, sir," hopped into the jeep and drove directly onto the runway. At the far end was a T-39 jet, its engines whining loudly. Speeding down the concrete path, the major wondered who Colonel Barney Fannin was that made him so important. "We had to have that jet flown in from Eglin," he explained.

"You made good time," Fannin said, not terribly impressed, because he had no reason to concern himself with Air Force logistics.

Five minutes later he was settled in the small cabin as the pilot gunned the motor, hurling the plane down the runway and jolting it into the air. Fannin looked about him. The furnishings included a desk, two seats facing each other with a large bolster set between so a man could stretch out to sleep. Some brass hat would scream when he learned his plane had been commandeered. Glancing at his watch, Fannin figured that he would be in Washington a couple of hours after midnight. Slipping off his tunic, he laid it across the seat beside him. It would never do to arrive in Washington in a wrinkled uniform. He thought of taking off his trousers and decided against it.

As he stretched out on the seat, he was thinking of the girl with the sad look in her eyes he had left at the Hayseed Motel in Pan-

ama City, and of his existence at Infantry Training School. He
was in his late forties, weary of being shuttled from army post to
army post. He had written up so many training schedules that he
felt he had prepared several armies for battle.

The whine of the jet as it streaked over Florida and Georgia
was the only sound in the night. The sky beyond the small port-
hole was black mixed with very few stars. His hands went behind
his head, and he wondered if this was what death would be like,
a vast darkness with a few stars. The subject had rarely crossed
his mind in recent years, but the hour and the place brought him
to it. There had been times since he had returned from Europe
at the end of the Second World War when he had thought of
death often. Those last few years he had lived with Lil and the
boys, when there had been nothing for him to do. He had run
an ordnance depot in Iowa, a small training camp in North
Dakota, been an ROTC instructor in northern California, been
assigned as a National Guard liaison officer in Ohio. Then he had
thought of death, because as far as he was concerned, he was already dead. It had not made any difference to him that he had
lost one assignment because he had been drunk, another because
of a poor efficiency report, a third because he had told a stupid
superior that he was, indeed, stupid.

Finally, Lil had had enough and he was alone. The years between had been little more than marking time. He had spent six
months in Korea before he had been shipped home with another
medal and then six months to collect himself, which meant that
he had lost his temper again and one more superior officer had
had his fill of Barney Fannin. Benning was only another training interlude since Korea. The Hayseed Motel was only one more
quick dive into a soft bed with an available woman. Now the
Pentagon. He wondered what he had done this time that was so
very wrong they had sent a special plane for him in the middle
of the night. Lil could be ill, but he knew that Hyde MacWolfe
would not be calling Barney Fannin. The boys could be ill or
injured, but the last time one of them was sick he heard about it
three months afterwards, when he had called while drunk from a

filling station in the Texas Panhandle. Hyde had answered the phone and called Lil. She had brought him up to date on the boys. His oldest was posted in Saigon. And when he hung up, he realized that she had not even bothered to ask how he was or what he was doing.

Barney Fannin wished he could close his eyes and fall asleep, but he could not. He wished he had a drink, but he doubted if the Air Force had left any bottles around the plane. Now, if he had traveled National or Pan Am . . . Smiling to himself, he made up his mind that the next time the Pentagon sent for him, he would demand a plane that served a drink. The next time the Pentagon sent for him . . . He had every reason to believe it never would again. He was at the age where the Army had to fish or cut bait—pin a star on him or kick him out—and he could not think of any reason why they would pin a star on Colonel Barney Fannin. Not now. Not with Lil's father a four-star and Hyde MacWolfe a three-star. In fact, he could not think of a single reason why he was going to Washington. No one needed a soldier there, an over-ranked dogface. He remembered the comment that Vinegar Joe Stillwell had been the highest-ranking battalion commander in history. Maybe he would go into the lists as the highest-ranking platoon leader, because no one would trust him with much more.

The T-39 passed over Georgia. South Carolina lay in darkness below.

WASHINGTON, D.C. •

IT WAS ALMOST one-thirty in the morning when LeGrande and Harry Fuller made their last phone call to MacWolfe at the Pentagon. They had ordered the supplies they wanted, the plane to carry them, the free hand to select personnel as quickly as possible and to shift them about the world as they wished. The afternoon's planning had come to fruition at this point, and now as the two men sat with the maps and plans laid out before them on the conference table in the GENOPS planning room, they were satisfied that they had done the best they could. Both men were in shirt sleeves. The Night Security Officer had twice sent for coffee, and the paper cups were lined along the window sill.

The General rubbed his chin with the back of his hand and smiled at Harry. "We're going to get you out from under the paperwork on this one. I haven't decided how just yet, but this operation is going to take a full-time boss, and you're it."

Harry Fuller, a man in his early forties who had spent most of his professional career in dubious operations, nodded. He had heard this promise from the General many times, but when the time actually came to shepherd an operation through to the end, it was LeGrande who worried out the final details which made for success or failure. Harry had reconciled himself to sharpening pencils on the special operations and handling the routine ones which seemed at times to bore LeGrande. They had worked together for over five years, ever since Janet Garner had heard about Harry from some friends in the State Department and had tracked him down.

Now, as he relaxed and waited for the jet flying north, Harry thought about that first meeting with Janet. Any first meeting in intelligence work must, by its very nature, be a kind of minuet, small steps hesitantly made because no one knows just how far he can move safely. And as a man with a fully developed sense of security, Harry moved more slowly than most operators. After the meeting with Janet had come the meeting with Le-Grande. And only then did Harry know the agency for which he was being screened. He had always considered it a kind of handicap that GENOPS had for its director a man who had been a national hero—the face of General LeGrande was too well known for his work to be kept as secret as it might otherwise have been. But Harry, for all of his distrust and dislike for Washington intrigue, was also prepared to admit that LeGrand's stature helped them more than it hindered. Most men in Washington thought twice before they said no to the tall General who rarely appeared in uniform and almost never in public. Harry had heard a senator one night speak of the LeGrande mystique, admitting that it was an awesome thing even when one was close to the General. When he had mentioned this to Janet and the General, both of them had laughed. The mystique might have awed some, but it rarely seemed to frighten either the Pentagon or Central Intelligence, both groups always being ready to move in on Le-Grande's minute domain.

"Tired, Harry?" the General was asking.

Fuller shook his head. "Tomorrow, maybe. But right now, I'm just worried."

LeGrande sucked in his cheek as he considered this statement.

He tried to remember when Harry Fuller had not been worried and then decided that he had better worry the moment Harry stopped. "The team?" he asked.

"That's right, Boss Man. I'm taking for granted that the man you've picked is as good as you must think he is, though he sure hasn't been in the papers or latrine talk. But those who are going with him"—he shook his head—"they worry me."

"You said you could move enough of our own staff into position to go with Fannin."

"That's right. But will they be able to work with a stranger without even an introduction?" The dark lines under Harry's eyes appeared even darker as he leaned over and doodled on the pad before him.

LeGrande weighed the team problem for the hundredth time since he had made his presentation to the Security Council and knew that he would have to go with what he had. When Mac-Wolf had asked about the team, he had brushed the question under the table with the comment that he would work out the problem with Barney. MacWolfe had remained skeptical. Now Harry was dubious. But as far as LeGrande was concerned, there was nothing he could do about it until he and Barney had a chance to talk together. He looked at his watch.

"It's almost two, Boss Man." Harry was also aware of the time.

The silver T-39 moved into the landing pattern at Andrews Air Force Base, and after a moment the wheels descended and the pilot cut his jets, touching down as gently as he could. The co-pilot walked quickly through the plane, passing the large, rough-hewn Colonel who was buttoning his tunic. The door of the plane swung open and the co-pilot stood beside it.

Barney Fannin nodded and stepped into the darkness. Beyond he could see the lights of Washington. Above he made out the scattered stars. A young army major approached and saluted, "Colonel Fannin?"

Fannin nodded.

"They are waiting for you, sir," and he started to lead the way toward a chopper which stood nearby, its blades slowly turning.

All the comforts of home, Fannin thought, as he strode over, hauled himself inside the helicopter and nodded to the major. He would have liked to ask who the hell was waiting for him. He thought it would be nice to know, but then there was always the chance that he might be spoiling someone's fun. Never a person to dampen a surprise party, Barney Fannin decided he would take this ride as far as it went.

They were off the ground now; leaning toward the city, the chopper moved over the broken countryside, the lights of streets below. Then Fannin saw the Capitol dome, washed with spotlights and looking like a bad five-cent tourist photo. Once it would have thrilled him. Now it only meant that he was in Washington again; back in the hubbub of the universe, a place where he did not belong. In the years since the Second World War, Barney Fannin had learned what many men never did—what he himself was. And though he could not change the fact that he was Barney Fannin, he had found with difficulty a way to live with that fact. He lost the way only when intruded upon by superiors or problems he knew were not the kind he could cope with. He had tried to explain his self-discovery to Lil one night just before she left him, but she had been too unimaginative to see that a man was cast in a mold and that what he was was irrevocable.

The lighted dome brought thoughts of Lil and the boys back to Fannin and he looked the other way. More lights, and he knew they were coming in at the National Airport. A puzzled look at the major brought no response. Fannin had expected to come in at the Pentagon, but he was along for the ride and did not argue.

The chopper settled down with a bump, and then the two officers were walking across the concrete toward a waiting sedan. The major held the door open for Fannin, and then, to Fannin's surprise, closed it and stepped into the front seat beside the sergeant, who was driving. Without waiting for anything more than a nod, the driver sped out of the National Airport and north toward the city. A few minutes later they crossed the bridge near the Lincoln Memorial and came to a stop behind a large temporary building. The major stepped out, opened the door and said, "We're here, sir."

Nodding, Fannin emerged from the car.

The high gate in the cyclone fence opened and a guard waited for Fannin to enter. He looked back toward the major, who saluted him and remained where he was. Shrugging, Fannin followed the guard, who locked the gate behind him and led the way into the building past a second guard who moved out to the gate. The efficiency of the movement made Fannin smile. Almost as neat as a general's desk.

"This way, sir," the guard said as he led Fannin through a darkened corridor, turned right and down another corridor until he came to a flight of stairs. "Up there, sir," he pointed. "The first door to your left at the head of the stairs."

Grunting, Fannin mounted the steps in the semi-darkness. He had gotten into someone's private preserve, and somehow, from the smell of it, he knew it was not Army. The walls lacked the usual dull pep-up signs, the GI furnishings, the overscrubbed look. At the top of the steps and in front of the first door to his left, Fannin found another guard waiting. He approached and started to enter when the guard stepped in front of him.

"Your identification, sir."

For a moment, Fannin was ready to laugh. He had not asked to go in, was not even certain he would like what he found inside. Shrugging, he pulled out his ID card and waited while the guard turned his flashlight on it and on Fannin's face as if the corridor light was not bright enough. Disgusted with the seeming excess of security, Fannin reached out, pulled his ID card out of the man's hand and started to walk away when the door opened.

"Come on in, Barney."

He turned back to see Richard LeGrande in his shirt sleeves standing in the doorway. "I'll vouch for the Colonel," LeGrande assured the guard as he stepped aside. Nodding, Fannin entered the room and heard the door close behind him.

Inside, he found that LeGrande was not alone. In full uniform, Lieutenant General Hyde MacWolfe stood with his back to the window on the far side of the room. An Air Force major general stood beside a large conference table, while a man who was obviously a civilian sat at the end of the table.

"You know Hyde," LeGrande was saying. A nod of recognition passed between the two, and LeGrande presented Major General Elliot Canby of the Air Force. Canby's hand went out and Fannin shook it as LeGrande introduced the civilian as his deputy, Harry Fuller. Fuller rose and shook hands with Fannin, and from the way he stared at him, Barney was not sure he had not done something wrong.

Looking at MacWolfe, Fannin half-smiled as he said, "May I be the last to congratulate you on your third star, Hyde. It gives me that onward-and-upward feeling, because I've been under the illusion that they only sold shirts with eagles on them these days." Looking at LeGrande and Canby, he smiled. "I see I'm wrong." A sardonic chuckle. "But then I'm sure you didn't get me out of that warm motel bed to talk about stars at this time of the night."

MacWolfe looked at LeGrande. It was the director of GENOPS' mission, and if he wanted to back away from Barney Fannin, no one would hold it against him. The Air Force officer remained silent, too, because he had only been asked in as an advisor.

LeGrande walked over to the table and Fannin followed him. Picking up a set of aerial photos, the General handed them to Fannin. "What do you make of those, Barney?"

A quick and trained eye scanned the top photo. "A rail tunnel punched through a mountain." A fast shuffle and he identified the next laconically, "A dam." A pause as he looked at it a moment longer. "Jerry-built." And to the next photo, "Petroleum tank farm." The next: "A bridge," and then, "A jet landing field—twenty, twenty-five—forty medium bombers." With that he tossed the photos on the table and waited.

LeGrande had known from the moment he had decided to ask for Barney Fannin that the Colonel would not be easy to deal with. That was, strangely enough, part of the reason for making the decision. There was a basic toughness about Barney Fannin which the mission needed. But he knew, too, that he had to give the orders or he would lose control. Very quietly, he said, "Take the chip off your shoulder, take off your coat and sit down."

Fannin's head came up with a snap as if he were about to dispute the point, but he did as he was told. LeGrande motioned for the others to take their places at the table. When everyone was settled, LeGrande started to brief both the Air Force general and Fannin.

"Those installations you identified were photographed here," and he pointed to the valley of the Song Koi in North Vietnam. Four weeks ago our air recon revealed none of them."

Fannin shook his head in near disbelief. "Built in four weeks?"

"That's right, Barney. This is a build-up. It could move in any of several directions once it starts."

"Several directions?"

"They don't have to move down the coast. They could peel off and move southwest into Laos, Cambodia, Thailand, or head for Burma."

The others in the room nodded.

"One question," Barney was asking.

"Go ahead."

"What's this got to do with me?"

The others waited for LeGrande to explain what they already knew. Slowly and deliberately, as if he were emphasizing every word, LeGrande said: "Those installations will not be there ten days from now, or they will be used in fifteen." Then he gave his orders. "You will seek out and destroy them."

Anyone looking for a reaction from Barney Fannin would have

been disappointed. The leathery features of the Colonel did not indicate that he had even heard what had been said.

"Why the airfield? It can be replaced in hours."

LeGrande nodded. Whatever had happened to Barney in the years since he had seen him, Barney had not lost his senses. "You're right. But if we knock it out, they'll know we know what they are up to. It's gratuitous. A target of opportunity rather than necessity."

Fannin shoved back his chair and reached for the map of the area on which the installations had been outlined with red marking pencil. Without looking up he said, "What do I get to work with?"

The others let LeGrande answer. He thought for a moment. "I can give you everything but time, Barney."

The map was tossed onto the table and Fannin picked up the photos again. "What are the alternatives?"

LeGrande nodded to Canby, who answered. "We can bomb them out. It would take two flights to insure it. Three squadrons from two carriers. Sixty-four planes."

Then LeGrande nodded at MacWolfe. "The Strike Force could go in—a division coming down on top of that valley and moving through it."

Fannin looked from MacWolfe to Canby and then, shaking his head, he turned to LeGrande. " 'The effect of discussions, making a show of talent, and calling councils of war will be what the effect of these things has been in every age; they will end in the adoption of the most pusillanimous or—if the expression is preferred—the most prudent measures, which in war are almost uniformly the worst that can be adopted.' Napoleon."

The Director of GENOPS had difficulty not smiling as he watched the other two generals react to what they no longer remembered. He knew now if he had not known before why Barney Fannin thought shirts came with eagles on them. Barney was deliberately trying to embarrass all of them.

" 'Appear at points which the enemy must hasten to defend;

march swiftly to places where you are not expected.' Sun Tzu," LeGrande said with a smile.

The other two officers at the table wondered if they were listening to a game of one-upmanship or a showdown between the two.

Fannin accepted LeGrande's rejoinder. "You want to get me off my butt, Dick?"

The General nodded. He thought he was beginning to understand Fannin better.

"You're offering me a chance to volunteer?" Fannin asked.

"No one's ordering you to go on this, Barney. No one's promising you a return ticket."

"One thing more, Barney," MacWolfe interjected. The others turned to the stocky Lieutenant General. "If you agree, you can't let Dick down on this. His neck is stuck all the way out." MacWolfe's distaste for Fannin was obvious.

To the surprise of Fuller and Canby, Fannin chuckled and answered wryly, "I'm so sorry that he will be sticking his neck out."

Then LeGrande laughed. "Hyde, the decision has to be Barney's." He grinned. "And without untoward influence from his friends."

Everyone was silent now as Fannin looked once more at the photos and the map. "How free a hand do I have, Dick?"

"You will have to clear details with me."

" 'He will win who is not interfered with by the sovereign.' Sun Tzu."

" 'Only skill and discipline will insure victory.' Vegetius."

Again the others at the table were confused by the exchange. LeGrande and Fannin were completely serious about what seemed to be a joke.

Fannin nodded. "How large a team did you envision, Dick?"

LeGrande knew he had his man. "You and three others. Someone to take over in case you get killed. A radio man. A good man with explosives."

"That's the way I see it." Then Fannin rose from the chair and stood looking at LeGrande, "One restriction, Dick."

LeGrande weighed whether he should allow any and decided to listen. "What is it?"

"I pick the team. It's my back that will need covering."

LeGrande also pushed back his chair and stood up. He walked over to the window where the paper cups were strewn and stood staring out. What Fannin was asking made sense from one point of view because, as Barney had said, it was his back. But Le-Grande was not certain he could trust Barney's judgment. The old sharpness had shown itself, but the attempt to be the Barney Fannin who had once been so brilliant had been paraded like a schoolboy. The General doubted that Barney would have spoken that way to impress anyone other than a classmate; yet it had been a childish exchange, and because of that he was concerned about the men Barney would select. Finally, he decided that he had to have faith in the man or forget him. He was tempted to reject Barney Fannin because the mission was important and he wanted to assume the responsibility himself. Then he recalled the Chairman's comment about the need to grow up.

Turning back, he said, "Harry Fuller will clear the men you need. Security. Mission cover. We'll arrange to get them here even if Elliot has to fly each one in." He was aware as he spoke that Fannin relaxed for the first time since he had entered the room. LeGrande knew it was because someone was taking the Colonel seriously and allowing him to make a decision. LeGrande wondered how long it had been since anyone had trusted Barney; and as he wondered, he felt sad about the waste of talent. Lil had thought Barney could handle a regiment. Hyde had brought it down to a company, and Barney was pleased because the man who was trying to be his friend had trusted him with a squad of three men. And what made LeGrande feel more guilty was the fact that he was not actually trusting Barney, because he was going to add one more man to that squad himself.

It was three-thirty in the morning when the conference broke up. Generals MacWolfe and Canby left the two GENOPS directors and Colonel Fannin alone in the large conference room. Barney settled back in his chair to decide the names of the men he wanted to take with him, while LeGrande told Harry that he had better find a safe-house in which the team could assemble, one that would meet all of their needs—a place to be briefed and equipped, to eat and sleep.

Leaving the General alone with Fannin, Harry walked down the dark corridor to his own office and, opening the safe, took out the list of houses GENOPS already owned or rented.

Finally, Barney, now in his shirt sleeves, his collar open, shoved a piece of paper across the table to LeGrande. "These three will get it, Dick."

The General picked up the list. None of the names meant anything to him, and he knew that there was no reason why they should. He was willing to accept the fact that over the years every man meets those persons to whom he would be willing to trust his life, and no two men's lists would be the same. "Which is the demolitions man?" he asked.

"Zing Miller. Was in my regiment in Korea."

LeGrande considered this. "And the radio man?"

"Joe Brodsky—a kid I ran through training a couple of years ago." Fannin thought about Brodsky for a moment and then added, "You get a feeling about kids when you watch them train. Some have it, and some never will."

The General wondered if Barney could remember that there had been a time when everyone thought Barney had it. He knew that he was not being fair to Barney. The young man who had graduated the Point and the Barney Fannin who sat now with his feet on the chair were no longer the same person, any more than General Richard LeGrande was the same person he had been. Handing the slip back, he asked, "Put down the place you last knew these men to be. Harry will chase them down."

Nodding, Barney picked up a pencil and jotted down the most recent information he had on each of them. "About Brodsky, the Army will have a record of him. Zing"—he paused—"a drifter, it may take a bit longer." Then he smiled. "Carl Sprague will be right where I saw him last. Upright citizen. Pillar-of-the-community type."

The General considered this information. "How many of them have wives and kids?"

For a long time Barney was silent, and then he said simply, "Sprague has three kids and a wife. But then, Barney Fannin has two."

LeGrande accepted this, wondering if it was some kind of implied criticism of himself for having asked the question. But before he could say anything, Barney asked, "The boys—they're all right?"

"You could have asked Hyde."

Barney shook his head. "Come on, Dick. You know that I wanted to, but I wasn't about to give that bastard the satisfaction."

"As far as I know, they're fine." Then, realizing that Barney would want to know, he added, "And so's Lil. Just fine."

Fannin nodded. "I guess a man likes to think his wife is still pining for him, wasting away with regret at having walked out on him." He was trying to treat the matter lightly, but he was having difficulty.

Standing up and walking over to the window, Barney looked out into the darkness for a moment. His head tilted back and he stared at the few stars visible beyond the reflection of the city lights. LeGrande watched him, the slip of paper still in his hand. After a few minutes, Barney turned back and looked about the conference room. "You spend much time here?"

LeGrande nodded.

"It would choke me," Barney said without any emotion. "Choke me."

Both of them were silent again and LeGrande considered the Old Gray Wolf's comment made hours before, "Something went wrong." The General suspected that MacWolfe was right, and that even Fannin knew it.

"If Harry can get these people," he said, holding up the slip, "here in the next forty-eight hours, then you can leave. That will give you twenty-four hours to get there and five days in action."

Fannin nodded. "Nights, Dick. I'm not going to be able to get much done during the day."

Pleased that Fannin understood the problem, LeGrande agreed. "Nights. But until these men get here and agree to go with you, you might as well get all the rest you can." He did not want to say that Fannin looked as if he had been on a four-day binge.

Picking up his tunic from the chair beside him, Barney started to put it on. "BOQ at Meyers or a hotel?" he asked.

Reaching into his pocket, LeGrande took out a set of keys and, removing one, tossed it to Fannin. "I'll call about this." Puzzled, Barney waited with the key in his hand as LeGrande picked up the phone beside him and asked the night operator to dial his apartment. A moment passed and Le Grande could envision Janet waking up in the darkness and fumbling for the receiver. "Dick," he finally identified himself. Then, with a laugh, "All right, so I'm a bastard. You've company with you?" He sighed with relief. "I'm sending Barney Fannin out. Will you put him up in the guest room. I'll be here a few hours yet, and then I'll come home for breakfast and a shave." Listening, he could imagine her shaking her head at the thought of making up the extra bedroom at this hour. He wished he were there with her, warm and ready to fall back to sleep with one arm about her. "Thanks, dear," he said softly and then, cradling the phone, he looked up at Barney. "My place. Janet will have the spare room, which I call a study, made up for you." He jotted down an address and shoved it toward Fannin. "The Pentagon car that brought you should be waiting at the rear gate."

Fannin picked up the slip of paper. Then he stood looking down at LeGrande. "Why, Dick?"

"Why what?" LeGrande did not want to explain his motives now, not to Fannin.

"The assignment? The house key?"

The first part LeGrande faced honestly. "The assignment because I need you for it. If it's not you, it's me, and the Chairman told me it shouldn't be me."

"And the key?"

"It's only to an extra bedroom." He smiled. "You may have forgotten—but I haven't—that we're friends, that I slept on your couch a dozen times after you were married. So, I've got a bedroom instead of a couch."

Fannin nodded. This much he believed could be true, and this much LeGrande knew was only half true, because what he really wanted was Janet's evaluation of Barney Fannin. She was the Personnel Director of the agency because she knew people, and at this moment he needed that understanding of hers more than ever. As Hyde MacWolfe had put it, with all of his usual insensitivity, LeGrande's neck was, indeed, stuck out. So was the agency's, the country's and most of all Barney Fannin's, though this was, sadly, the least important.

"I'll see you at breakfast," he said, and Barney nodded.

Two hours later Harry Fuller had cleared the three names with the FBI and Central Intelligence files. As far as he could determine, the three were clean. And so, before six o'clock in the morning, the search began. Once it was under way, LeGrande left the details to Harry and drove to his own apartment. It was almost six-thirty when he arrived, and as he stepped out of the elevator, he recalled he had given Barney his key. He hesitated before the door debating whether to have the doorman open it for him or to wake Janet. A glance at his watch: six-thirty, and there were things he wanted to discuss with her. Pressing the buzzer, he waited. A moment later the door opened and Janet in a silk robe stood shaking her head at him.

He stepped inside, kissed her lightly and then asked, "Our guest?"

Janet shrugged. "Came in, picked up a bottle from the sideboard and retreated to the bedroom without even a good night."

LeGrande's arm still about her waist, they walked into their bedroom. He settled down on the edge of the bed, and she watched him for a minute.

"The drinking bother you?" she asked.

"I don't know. He has all kinds of reputations, but that has never been a large part of it."

She took off her robe and tossed it across the foot of the bed. "What is it, then?"

"Somehow, I thought he would try to ask you a lot of questions."

Janet hesitated a moment before taking off her nightgown. "What kind?"

"GENOPS. Us." Seeing that this did not explain what she was after, he added, "He's very . . . well, bright's an odd word to use when you're talking about a man in his late forties. Let's just say that he knows or finds out what's going on."

She was pulling her nightgown off over her head, and for an instant some of it clung to her. Holding it before her, she said simply, "What makes you think he cares about either GENOPS or us?"

She tossed the gown at him, and when he reached out for her, she turned and disappeared into the bathroom. He thought about her question, aware that the very fact that Barney Fannin had not cared was what was disturbing him. Then he heard the shower running. With a smile he picked up her nightgown and threw it across her dresser. He was unbuttoning his shirt when the phone rang. The clock beside it read six forty-five. Annoyed, he picked up the phone. "LeGrande speaking. Go ahead, Harry. In the stockade at Ord?" He laughed, "That's par for the course. What for? Off limits and striking an MP? That all?" He listened to Harry's confusion for a moment and then said, "In the parlance of the gang, Harry, 'spring him.'"

Laughing, he hung up to see Janet standing in the doorway of the bathroom, drying herself with a large white towel.

"Spring whom?" she asked.

"One of Barney's buddies."

Janet stood very still for a moment. "One of the team?"

LeGrande nodded.

"Harry's bringing them in?"

"That's right. And I want you to meet each one of them. Talk to them. Evaluate them." His shirt was off now and he was watching her as she dried her back.

"Just like that," she said.

"It would be nice if you could run them through that battery of tests you and your headshrinkers have devised, but we haven't time."

He was walking across the room toward her as he spoke, and without blinking, she tossed the large white towel in his face and disappeared once more into the bathroom. He settled down on the edge of the bed to wait for her to get dressed.

Through the door he heard her ask, "Can you bring any of them back, Dick?"

He had been thinking about the same thing all the way home, and even now as he waited for her. "I don't know," he said. "Take that into account when you talk to them."

"Meaning?" and he could tell from the noise beyond that she was brushing her teeth.

"I don't give a damn if they liked their mothers or not. I only want to know if they can hold up for five days."

The door opened and she walked over to her closet. "Five days. Who knows who can hold up for five days?"

Reaching out, he put his hands on her bare hips and started to draw her to him. A quick slap on his hands and he released her. Without getting up, he watched as she slipped on her bra and then stepped into her girdle. The movements always fascinated him, and because she knew it, she wrinkled her nose in disapproval. She was reaching for her dress when he walked into the bathroom. He stood in the doorway a moment and, looking back at her, asked, "Talk to Barney. Take him to lunch if you have to."

"Just to lunch?" she asked.

"Just to lunch." He stared at her a moment and then said, "You are a bitch this morning, my dear."

"I didn't wake you at three-something to put up an old class-mate, and I didn't ring your doorbell at six-thirty." She was settling the dress about her hips now, and he approved with a smile.

FORT ORD, CALIFORNIA •

THE DUTY OFFICER at the Military Police Barracks looked at the TWX handed him and shook his head. It was four in the morning and it made very little sense. He knew it would not have made any more sense at noon. Crossing the orderly room, he opened the file containing the reports of upcoming court martials and pulled out the one labeled "Brodsky, Joe." Flipping it open, he scanned the contents. It looked like a good six months for Brodsky, and the date for the hearing was only a week away. He glanced again at the TWX and shouted for his sergeant.

"Take these," he ordered, handing the sergeant the file and the TWX. "Get Private Brodsky and take him over to the chopper area."

The sergeant saluted and walked out to the stockade. Calling one of the guards, he told him to bring Private Joe Brodsky out at once. The guard wondered what had bitten the sergeant so early in the morning, and, walking down to the small barracks where the prisoners were housed, he opened the door and shouted for Brodsky. Inside, on his bunk, a sleepy young GI in fatigues rolled over and asked, "What the hell do you want?"

"Up and at 'em, Killer. You're wanted by the sergeant."

Brodsky, a lean-faced young man in his early twenties, rubbed his hand over his barely stubbled cheek. "Sure you got the right man? I'm not due to be heard for a week."

The guard snorted, "If your name's Brodsky, I've got the right man."

Wondering what he had done wrong now, Brodsky swung his feet over the edge of the bunk and sat up.

"Now!" the guard ordered. Having only recently tangled with the MPs, Brodsky pulled himself slowly to his feet.

At the gate of the stockade, the sergeant asked, "What've you been pulling, Brodsky?"

The morning light hurt his eyes, and the young soldier shook his head in complete confusion. "I don't know what the hell you're talking about."

The sergeant remained dubious. "I've been in this man's army for twenty-five years, and this is the first time I've ever seen the Pentagon send for a dogfaced P-V-T by name."

Twenty minutes later, the sergeant drove Prisoner Brodsky over to the chopper, saw that he was aboard and handed the TWX along with the file to the pilot.

The captain who had met the chopper at Edwards Air Force Base deposited the prisoner on a jet bound for Washington, D.C. He passed along the TWX and the file and told the flight sergeant on the jet, "He'll be met at Andrews. Give the officer who meets him these papers. He is a prisoner and should be watched."

Brodsky nodded his complete approval of the captain's handling of the matter and said, "I'll tell the President that you did a fine job, Captain."

Then, on the orders of the flight sergeant, Brodsky took his seat in the plane. He was both confused and somewhat frightened because he had no idea why he was being sent to Washington. Only after the plane was airborne did he think of asking if the

MP he had slugged was dead. But by the time he thought of it, there was no one to ask. Washington. He whistled. Whatever he had loused up this time, it must have been something important.

WASHINGTON, D.C. •

JANET AND THE GENERAL were about to sit down to breakfast when Barney Fannin joined them. Janet rose to set an extra place with the apology, "I thought you might want to sleep."

Barney shook his head. "No soldier sleeps late." He thought about what he had said and explained, "It's against regulations or something. And I think I've been getting up ever since this"— gesturing toward LeGrande—"husband of yours and I first arrived at what we so laughingly called the Point."

Janet looked at LeGrande to make the explanations as she went into the kitchen to get the coffee.

"Sit down, Barney," the General began. "And so you won't be embarrassed, Mrs. Janet Garner and I are not married."

Fannin looked from LeGrande to the kitchen and back again. He realized now that the Janet who had introduced herself when he had arrived at the apartment in the early morning was the woman the papers had written up when LeGrande was under Senate investigation a few years earlier.

"Whatever anyone ever tells you about Barney Fannin," he said, "remember one thing, Dick. He at least has the biggest mouth in the Army." Then, politely, "I'm sorry."

"Don't be," LeGrande reassured him.

And both of them half rose as Janet brought in the coffee.

When they were all settled, LeGrande asked, "You bring any civies, Barney?"

The Colonel shook his head. "Left Benning in a rush and didn't have time to change. I was away from the post when your call came last night."

LeGrande thought a minute. "Janet's office will issue you a check. You'd better get a couple of suits and whatever else you'll need for the next ten days."

Fannin looked at Janet. "Your office?"

"Director of Personnel at GENOPS," she explained.

Trying to understand, Barney merely nodded.

"And after that," LeGrande was saying, "you and Janet had better go over what you can tell her about your team. As much detail as you can remember. She likes to keep her records straight.

"I've got a day at the White House and back at the Pentagon." He thought for a moment and then suggested, "We can drive in together." Looking at Janet, "You'll have to meet your friend coming in from France." She nodded. LeGrande looked at his watch. Not eight yet. Too early to contact the other two men of Fannin's team without alarming their families. Although Harry would know how to use discretion, LeGrande regretted not having started Janet on this instead. He chalked it up as his first error in the mission and hoped that nothing would go wrong because of it. Smiling at the other two, he started to tell Barney about the Washington Underground as he lived in it and as Janet was teaching him to fight it. The field soldier listened, partly bored and partly disgusted at the waste of a man of LeGrande's talents playing footsie with politicians when he should be commanding an army in the field.

And as she watched the two of them, Janet realized that neither one really could hear what the other was saying. And in her own way, she felt as sad as the two officers.

As he had suggested, LeGrande left Barney and Janet at GENOPS and took another sedan to the Executive Office Building to report on the plans they had discussed and modified the night before so that the Executive Secretary of the National Security Council would be abreast of the situation.

At the GENOPS office Fannin sat down with Janet and Harry in the conference room while Harry detailed what he had done during the night. Brodsky would be met at Andrews Air Force Base and taken directly to a private home in Virginia where he would be kept incommunicado until Fannin and the others had an opportunity to meet with him. The first contact would be made with Sprague as soon as he arrived at his office. So far, no one had been able to locate the demolitions man, Miller. Harry had the FBI working on that. The orders were specific—locate but do not contact until ordered.

Sitting in the conference room, where the maps were covered by wall boards and the oversized globe of the world filled the nearest corner, Fannin listened to Harry Fuller's report. He had been in a thousand briefing sessions in his life, but the intricacies of dubious operations were new to him. He was impressed with the ability and power of both Janet and Harry to wheel and deal as they saw fit. At the same time, he was surprised that LeGrande delegated so much authority to two civilians. He knew that he never would have.

When Harry was done, Janet lighted a cigarette and looked at the notes she had taken as well as the papers Harry had handed her. She had the address of the safe-house and the name of the agent who was stationed there. She had been to the house once a year before and thought it would be excellent for their present needs. It was located in a residential neighborhood on a quiet street two blocks from an elementary school. A large lawn and trees would hide what took place behind the circular drive. She wondered whom Harry had put in the house in the past year. It was his custom to sublet these houses for a year at a time, leaving one or two open for a month or so between sublets so that he would always have a "decontaminated" one available for use.

The agent assigned to meet with and handle the team was Cliff Carter, returned from several years in West Berlin and a man both Janet and the General respected. He was using the name of Charles Clifford. Satisfied that Harry had done as well as anyone could have, she suggested he go home. "The General wants you rested. There's going to be a lot of work in the next few days, and I'll take over at this stage."

Fannin looked from Fuller to Janet and saw the Deputy Director of the agency nod. "If you think so," he agreed. Then he added, "You know where to reach me?"

Janet smiled. "Unless you've moved since I called last night."

"There's always the possibility that my wife moved out on me. She thinks this job takes too much of my time." He was not complaining, just stating a fact of life. "Thinks that someplace there should be a PR job for a man who knows the world. What she doesn't realize is that I only know the dark side of it, and no one does much selling to the people we deal with."

"Go on home, Harry," Janet said with a smile, and he nodded.

"I'm stalling," he said, "because I won't feel comfortable until this team's gone."

When Harry finally left, Fannin asked, "Is he always that way?"

Puzzled, Janet nodded. "If you mean he talks in *non sequiturs*, yes. If you mean is he confused, the answer is very negative. Harry's the best operations specialist in this city."

Taking the file in hand, Janet looked at the information the FBI had been able to TWX from Columbus, Ohio, about Carl Sprague. Insurance executive. Small company. Employed there for three years. Before that Harvard Business School for two years. Before that five years as an insurance actuary. Korea in the 32nd Infantry. Married and two children, boy nine and girl seven. Wife a graduate of Ohio University, 1956. Born, as was Carl Sprague, in Columbus, Ohio.

Looking up from the file, Janet saw that Barney Fannin was standing by the window. She watched him for a few minutes. His hands opened and closed and she could see that he was uncomfortable. At first she thought it too soon for the man to be upset by his proximity to the Washington milieu. Then she realized that there was more than Washington involved here. "Were you with the 32nd Infantry?" she asked him, skirting the problem for the moment. Fannin nodded without looking at her. "Sprague was in your command there?" He nodded again and turned to face her.

"Company commander. Bright and hard as nails when he had to be."

This seemed to satisfy Janet. Picking up the intercom, she asked her secretary to have a check prepared for Colonel Barney Fannin. Five hundred dollars. She thought a moment and told the secretary, "Have that drawn on the Imperial Western Pipeline Company." She was looking at Fannin when she said, "The Colonel will pick it up in ten minutes." Switching off the intercom, she reminded him, "That shopping trip the General wanted."

Fannin nodded. "The Imperial . . . what?"

"A cover account of the agency's," she explained. "Wouldn't do for you to start flashing a GENOPS check. In fact, we don't have such things."

Revealing his curiosity for the first time, Fannin asked, "Then how do you get paid?"

"Some people get paid through State. Some through Defense. Most through companies we set up and use for a month or so and then fold up; no complete set of records could be put together from any one company that would reveal who or how many work for Genops."

Fannin weighed the complexity of this. "You have your own finance office?"

"It comes under Personnel," she said and, seeing the question on his face, added, "It helps confuse anyone prying."

"What about something like a charge account, a credit card, a service like a telephone? What do you people do?"

Janet was almost happy with the General's choice for the first time, because until this moment all she had seen was a dull soldier who tried to be a boor. "We get companies to say our people work for them. Just a few agents to a number of companies with only the personnel director and the president of the company ready to admit these people are on their payroll. And even the executives have to be cleared. We usually take people who have already been cleared for classified work in missiles or atomic energy or the like."

"Nothing's easy," Barney said, and then as if he had no interest whatever in their discussion, he seemed to back away from it. "I'll get that check."

"My office is down the hall. Third door to the left." She waited until he reached the door and then said, "I'd appreciate it if you came back here when you were done shopping."

Barney looked at her, uncertain if he was being given an order or a suggestion.

Aware of his uncertainty, Janet added to it. "Park that uniform someplace. I don't think it should be taken out to the safehouse."

"Yeah," Barney grunted and walked out without looking back.

She remembered the General's comment that something had happened to Barney Fannin somewhere, sometime after he left the Academy. This man was not as obvious as he tried to appear. She glanced at her watch. It was time to get in touch with Carl Sprague, Columbus, Ohio. She looked at the TWX from the FBI and decided to make the call from an outside phone. She flicked on the intercom and informed her secretary that she could pick up a file from the security guard and that she herself was going out. Looking at the phone number once again to be sure she had memorized it correctly, Janet left the conference room, handed the file to the guard at the door and walked down the stairs and out of the building, where, ignoring the General's driver, she flagged a cab and asked to be taken to a real estate office in a small building several blocks away. Once there, she went inside. The receptionist said there were no calls for Mrs. Williams. Nodding, Janet agreed that business was slow and went into an office beyond the railing. From here she dialed the Pentagon to backstop her story and then placed her call to Columbus, Ohio.

COLUMBUS, OHIO •

THE SMALL OFFICE of Carl Sprague was busy at nine in the morning. Two stenographers were typing up report forms when the telephone rang. "It's long distance for you, Mr. Sprague."

Sprague excused himself and picked up the phone. "Carl Sprague speaking."

At the other end of the line he heard the operator tell someone that she had Mr. Sprague and then he heard a woman's voice asking if he was the same Carl Sprague who had been in the 32nd Infantry in Korea. Puzzled and wondering what was happening, he said that he was, but before she could say anything else Sprague informed the woman that he was no longer in service.

She said that she knew that, but that someone who had been in the service with him was very seriously ill and wanted to see him. A certain Colonel Barney Fannin.

Sprague, a man in his early forties with graying hair and a slight paunch, leaned forward, putting his elbows on his desk. "I know him, but you sure it's me he means?"

The woman said it was the same one—a company commander under Fannin's command in Korea. Then, before Sprague could think of an excuse why he could not go to visit his old commander whom he had never really known very well, the woman was saying, "The Air Force has a jet waiting for you at Lockbourne Air Force Base. If you drove over there now, you could be in Washington this morning and back home for dinner this evening."

Sprague thought about Old Barney Fannin, as the men had called him; he had been as rough as a cob on a cold winter's night, but he had been decent as far as Captain Sprague was concerned.

"You sure I can be back by tonight?" he found himself asking, surprised that he was even considering the trip. But the woman was already assuring him, "On the same plane, Mr. Sprague. It will bring you into Andrews Air Force Base and be waiting to take you home." Then, to add to the necessity for his coming, she said, "If you can't make it today, well, Colonel Fannin won't be seeing anyone tomorrow."

Sprague wanted to know what was wrong with the Colonel, but somehow asking at this moment seemed to be quibbling. "All I want to be certain about is that you are sure I'm the one he wants to see."

Reassured for the third time, he started to think about the flight when the woman said, "Then you will drive straight to the Base and identify yourself. They are waiting for you."

Before he knew exactly what he was saying, he said, "Yes." He hung up the phone and looked at it for a long time before he turned to the salesman. "A crazy kind of thing. My old colonel's dying and wants to see me in Washington."

The salesman shook his head. "It's a lot of bills flying there and back to say goodbye to an army buddy."

Sprague shook his head. "Won't cost anything, but we weren't really that close."

The salesman, a former sergeant who believed he knew all there was to know about both the army and what he termed the military mind, shook his head. "Sad, these guys in uniform never really knowing anyone."

Sprague nodded. Then he told his secretary that if his wife called to tell her he would be back in time for dinner and would explain where he had gone then. Puzzled, he admitted to himself that a round trip to Washington was certainly an exhilarating idea to be sprung on him so early on a Monday morning.

He walked out to a small lot where his Ford Galaxie was parked and wondered if he should take anything with him. Back by dinner, the woman had said, and now as he thought about the call, he wished he had asked her name. It took him almost an hour to reach the air base, but when he arived at the gate the MP said the plane was waiting for him and pointed to the place where he could park his car. Fifteen minutes later Carl Sprague was airborne for Washington.

WASHINGTON, D.C. ●

AFTER she had completed her call to Columbus, Janet left the real estate office and returned to GENOPS, where she made arrangements for the Air Force to contact her as soon as the Sprague plane had an estimated time of arrival.

It was already ten o'clock and she had a meeting with a certain Annamese engineer at the Mayflower Hotel. Her assistant had called the hotel and affirmed that the man had checked in at five-thirty in the morning. She looked in the files to be sure she had the right name—Hac Quan. Leaving a message that she would like to see Colonel Fannin for lunch in the President's Room at the Mayflower, she called her assistant once more to see if anyone had been able to locate Fannin's demolition man. When she heard the answer was negative, she called LeGrande's secretary and asked her to tell the General to consider someone else if they had not located Zing Miller by three in the afternoon. Then she went to her meeting at the Mayflower.

● ● ●

While the General's driver was taking Janet to the Mayflower, the jet bringing Joe Brodsky landed at Andrews Air Force Base. The flight sergeant was surprised to find that he was asked to turn the prisoner's papers over to a civilian, and for a moment he hesitated until the base security officer assumed the responsibility. Joe Brodsky himself was impressed by the attention he was receiving, even though he could not understand what he had done to cause it.

Once the civilian, who identified himself as Charles Clifford, was seated in his small two-door with Brodsky beside him, he said, "Relax, soldier. This is going to be painless."

Not quite sure how he should take this, Brodsky nodded. "I only slugged an MP," he said. "I never thought anyone took them that seriously."

Charles Clifford, a neatly dressed man in his late thirties, smiled to himself as he joked with a straight face. "The MPs take themselves seriously, son. Never forget that."

Then both of them were silent. They paused in Alexandria only long enough for Clifford to buy a quiet Brodsky some civilian clothes. Then they drove directly to the safe-house. When the car pulled into the circular drive and came to a stop, Brodsky whistled. He was impressed.

"This is where you will stay while you're in Washington," Clifford informed him. "There will be no going out without permission from me or others you will meet. Break that rule and you will be a very unhappy soldier."

Then Clifford led the way into the house. It was large—eight rooms, and all well decorated. "Make yourself at home," he suggested. "Get rid of the tie and the jacket if you want to. Put your feet on a chair or raid the icebox. This is your place."

Still confused, Brodsky sat down in an overstuffed chair and waited for something to happen. Clifford watched him for a moment and then grinned. "Knock it off, soldier. In the kitchen you'll find a bottle of Scotch. Pour us each a drink and put some soda in mine."

Brodsky nodded and disappeared into the rear of the house to look for the kitchen.

Cliff Carter, the man assigned by GENOPS to shepherd this team, looked at his watch and then, picking up the phone, dialed an unlisted number at the Pentagon. He waited a moment and then was informed that the plane carrying Carl Sprague from Columbus would arrive at one-thirty. Deciding he might as well relax with the kid, he went looking for Brodsky and found him gaping at a well-stocked liquor cabinet. The young man shook his head in awe.

"That comes to one hell of a binge," he exclaimed. Carter laughed.

The short, stocky Annamese sitting across from Janet was not what she had expected. As they sat together in the small bar off the lobby of the Mayflower Hotel, Janet watched the dour expression on Hac Quan's face as he tried to understand why he was being interviewed by a woman about a job as an engineer, a woman who obviously did not know engineering. For twenty minutes they had talked about everything but the job he had been flown across the ocean to discuss. She had been surprised that he spoke English as well as he did, and the fact that he had spent three years working on the water system of Hong Kong did not seem to satisfy her curiosity about this subject. She was also surprised when he said he had no relatives left alive in North Vietnam, as if she did not know that there had been a war there for over twenty years. There was an ingenuousness about her questions which baffled him and made him regret having come so far to discuss employment. The job the French had offered him in Africa was good, but anyone knew that American salaries were higher than French, and so he had made the flight. When she suggested a second drink, he shook his head.

"Mrs. Williams," he said, "I do not know what you expected or just what you want."

Janet had been skirting the central reason for her meeting with Hac Quan; it was an old dance she had played many times in the past, trying to get hold of something she could evaluate before she exposed herself or her agency to a stranger. In this case she had already come to a conclusion. Hac Quan was much tougher than he was letting on. He had fought in the war against France on one side or the other; she could tell a soldier when she met one. The thing she could not establish was whether this man had been Vietcong or not. This was something she had to know. What she had learned about him was that he was calm, controlled, intelligent, assured, though impatient with her handling of the interview. If he could be trusted, she believed he might meet the General's needs. However, only the General could decide that. In the meantime, she had made the decision that if Hac Quan was unacceptable he would have to be kept incommunicado until the mission was completed one way or the other.

"Would you excuse me a moment?" she asked. "I'll call and see if the head of our company can meet with you this afternoon."

Hac Quan looked at this American woman and nodded. She was not what he had expected, and as she walked away, he knew that she was not what she pretended to be. But he could not decide what she actually was. His story about Hong Kong had been the truth. He had, indeed, worked there. The other jobs he had held and the rest of his past were his own business, and he intended to keep it that way.

Janet looked around for a phone booth and, seeing one all the way down the long lobby that extended for almost a block, paused. There was always the chance that Hac Quan might not wait for her. She tried to evaluate what he might have learned and decided that if he would not want to wait, she might as well know it now. Walking down the length of the lobby, she stepped inside the booth, turned so that she could watch the entrance to the bar and placed her call. When it was completed, she walked into the lobby and seated herself some distance from the bar.

Fifteen minutes later she saw three men enter the crowded bar, and soon after they emerged with Hac Quan between them.

His arrest by the police had been swift and efficient, alerting no one. Satisfied that she would be able to locate him when she wished, she called the police back and said that she would be in later in the day to prefer charges against the man who had stolen her money. The desk sergeant on the phone said he was satisfied so long as his men did find her stolen purse in the foreigner's pocket. Knowing that they would, Janet hung up the phone and walked down the lobby to the President's Room, where Colonel Barney Fannin in a new gray sharkskin suit was waiting for her. She smiled at him and at the head waiter who led them to their table.

General LeGrande caught Janet's message about the demolitions member of the team when he returned from the Pentagon. It was already one o'clock in the afternoon. Half an hour later he heard from Janet that the Annamese male was in the Washington police station. She thought he was worth talking to. Setting the phone down, LeGrande evaluated the problem of the demolitions specialist. This man was basic to the structure of the team, and the General wished he could place one of his own men into the slot. He considered telling Fannin that his selection could not be located and that they had no more time to search. But he recalled his decision made in the early morning to let Fannin pick his own team.

He was preparing to leave for the police station when a call came through from the FBI informing him that they had found a carnival barker in Keene, New Hampshire, who seemed to be the man he was looking for. The description matched, and from what they could learn by poking around him, he had been in the Second World War with a Colonel Fannin. LeGrande took the number where the man could be reached and then hung up the phone. If he was going to get Miller to Washington, he could not waste time now. He pushed his chair back from the desk and strode into his secretary's office. Handing her the number, he told her to have Mrs. Garner paged at the President's Room at the Mayflower and to give her the number on the slip. Then he said he would be gone for an hour. Down the corridor into Harry Fuller's reception room, past the secretary and into Harry's office.

Harry, shaven now and with several hours sleep behind him, was going over the reports he had been able to collect on Brodsky and Sprague. He had reservations about both men, but this was not the time to discuss them with the General, who appeared to be standing on one foot.

"Who is meeting Sprague and how?" the General asked.

Satisfied that Janet, the General and he were on top of all the moving situations, Harry said, "I've got him, Boss Man. I read Janet's report of her call to him. I'll waltz him around for a time and then, if I feel comfortable, I'll take him to the safe-house."

From Harry's office LeGrande went to the Washington police station, where he asked to see the captain. Alone in the captain's office, they talked for ten minutes. The elderly police officer, who was waiting for retirement, knew the General and had cooperated with him in the past. They had been able to keep this cooperation secret from the others on the force, and LeGrande had every reason to expect the help he needed.

"But," the captain protested, "Mrs. Garner will have to use something other than that purse gag next time. One of my men is apt to catch on."

LeGrande laughed. "I'll bet it wasn't Mrs. Garner who had him arrested."

The captain looked at the note on his desk. "Mrs. Williams."

"Now, isn't that better?" LeGrande asked.

Shaking his head in disapproval of what he did not fully understand, the captain picked up the phone and told the desk sergeant to bring the prisoner Hac Quan to his office and to see that they were not disturbed.

When Hac Quan, bewildered and angry, was ushered into the office, the captain stepped outside and took his place in a chair just before his office door. He did not know what the General wanted with this foreigner, and he did not want to find out.

LeGrande greeted the short Annamese engineer with a smile

and a handshake. "I'm Major General LeGrande," he said, introducing himself. "And you are Hac Quan, Hanoi-born and French-educated?"

The engineer shook the hand dubiously. He did not know this American who introduced himself as a general and yet was not in a uniform. Nor did he know why he had been arrested by the police and charged with the theft of a purse. For an hour he had been trying to convince the police that he had not taken that purse and that he did not know how it had come into his pocket. However, the police had only smiled and nodded. He was leery and wished that he was back in France, preparing to fly to Africa where someone wanted a bridge built over a river he had never heard of in a place impossibly called Mali.

"Better sit down," the American was saying, and Hac Quan took the hard chair pointed out to him. The General perched himself on the edge of the police captain's desk, one leg swinging loosely as he stared at the Annamese.

"I'll wager we've confused you," the General said with a smile.

Hac Quan agreed. "I am confused."

A pause, and he could see that the General was trying to make a decision; but LeGrande felt he had no choice. He would have to trust Hac Quan to a point, and if this did not work out, he would hold him until the operation was completed and then release him, denying any contact had ever been made.

"I need someone to go into North Vietnam for me. A man with some guts who knows the country around Hanoi and the Song Koi valley."

Startled, Hac Quan tried to understand what he had just heard. "North Vietnam?"

The General nodded.

"Why?"

"Details will have to wait," LeGrande said, backing away from too great a commitment at this juncture.

The Annamese rose from his chair and walked about the police captain's office, looking at the plaques on the wall. An award for bravery in the capture of an escaped convict. A plaque for helping the Police Benevolent Fund. After a time, he looked at the tall American whose leg swung back and forth. "And why should I do this?"

"To stop a war."

Hac Quan nodded. "And we would be able to do this?"

A smile came to LeGrande's face. "Possibly. Only possibly. But it is the kind of thing a man has to try."

The Annamese nodded his agreement. "There is no job for me as the lady said?"

"Just this one. And I don't usually pay for this kind of work because I don't know how much a man's life is worth or how much stopping a war is worth. You could say everything, but no one can afford to pay everything."

Hac Quan smiled. "At least you are honest about that, General."

LeGrande's head came up. "Was there something I was not honest about?"

The Annamese's hands went wide. "Arrest. A position as an engineer."

LeGrande nodded. "But would we have met if I had told you I wanted to risk your life to stop a war?"

The smaller man shook his head. "Probably not." Both of them were silent now.

It was Hac Quan who spoke first. "And if I say that I will help you, will I learn more?" Then, as if he had to explain, "I want to know what I am supposed to be doing."

The General agreed. "That's fair enough. However," he added, "you will have to accept a polygraph test."

They were silent for a time as the engineer considered the request. He knew enough about the lie-detector to know he did not have to worry. Many men had said that the Annamese were by nature liars. He did not know if this had been proven on the machine with the wriggling needles, but he was willing to pit himself against it. Hac Quan nodded. "Where do I take this test?"

Picking up a telephone, LeGrande dialed nine and then a number. "This is General LeGrande. Will you ask General MacWolfe to send a polygraph team to the Central Police Station to check out a security for me?" He waited a moment and then said, "Now, of course." Then he cradled the phone and walked to the door. He paused a moment and looked back at Hac Quan. "I hope that we can work together." Opening the door, he asked the police captain to hold the prisoner in his cell until the Pentagon team completed a security check. Then he closed the door and said softly, "If they say he does not check out, please hold him for ten days. If he does, send him by car to the Mayflower and tell him to wait until we contact him."

The police captain agreed. "Maybe some day, General, you'll let me get some police work done in there."

LeGrande laughed. "Not just yet." He was about to walk away when he turned to the captain again, "Don't let him loose unless they say so."

When the T-39 put down at Andrews Air Force Base, Carl Sprague stepped out and looked around the field. He had assumed he would be met, since he had no idea where he was to go. For several minutes Harry Fuller sat in his sedan and watched Sprague. He recognized the type. An ex-officer who had never really been military. Somewhat gone to seed behind a desk. He did not know why he had pictured a shorter man. Sprague was over six feet tall, and though he had a slight paunch, he appeared to be in good physical condition. Harry knew that if he had a couple of months to get him ready for the mission he would have no trouble. But as he had said only a short time before—the mission had to be on its way within twenty-four hours. Only Sprague would know if he could hold up for five days in the field.

Stepping out of the car, Harry approached him and introduced himself. "I'm Phil Harmon, and I guess you're Carl Sprague."

Sprague accepted the hand which was extended and said, "I'm supposed to see Colonel Fannin. I understand he's ill."

Harry nodded. A plane came down the runway and jolted upward with a loud whine, drowning anything Harry might have been saying. "Let's get out of here," he shouted and led the way to his car. A moment later they were on the road leading toward the city.

"I really don't know Colonel Fannin very well," Sprague said, assuming that Harry knew why he had been called to Washington.

"You fought under him in Korea."

Sprague nodded as they sped past a truck on the highway.

"Did you do anything in particular that would have impressed him?" Harry was curious because the Korean War had been fought by the Carl Spragues—retreads from the Second World War.

The insurance agent thought about this for a moment and then said, "There was a battle near the reservoir. He had told me to hold my ground." Then with almost a shy feeling of saying too much, "I did, until only two of us could walk out."

Satisfied that he knew now what he had been looking for, Harry said, "Colonel Fannin is perfectly well."

The first shock of this information passed quickly and Sprague became indignant, which was the reaction Harry had expected. "Then what the hell am I doing here?"

Harry glanced into the rear-view mirror and, seeing that the road behind him was clear, pulled over to the shoulder. Cutting off the motor, he turned so he could see Sprague better. "I was told to level with you. The Boss Man put your credentials simply —'He's an American. He's Colonel Fannin's choice. He came when called.'"

Carl Sprague glanced at his watch. He should have let his wife know that he was going to Washington instead of waiting to tell her when he returned. Now there seemed to be no excuse for having taken the trip. Harry saw the impatience and knew that hearts, flowers, mother and country might not be enough.

"Who's the Boss Man and why am I here?" Sprague asked.

Harry nodded, accepting the questions as reasonable. "The Boss Man you'll meet. Now as to why you're here . . ." He thought a moment and then set it out as neatly as he could. "Colonel Fannin has been asked to take on a mission which could mean war or peace. It could mean your kids and mine being incinerated or not. It could mean that we are a country two weeks from now or that we aren't."

Sprague started to laugh. "You're joking."

"If I'm joking why did the Air Force send a plane to bring you to Washington? We don't run tourist flights in T-39s."

Sprague's laughter ceased in the face of the evidence. "But where do I come in?" He touched his paunch and put one nervous hand to his hair.

"The Colonel said he wanted to pick his own men to help him, and he put your name on the list."

"Me?" The incredibility of the whole notion seemed to astound Carl Sprague, and Harry tried to see it from the other man's point of view.

"You."

There was a long silence and then Sprague asked simply, "And if I say yes, what am I expected to do?"

Harry thought a minute. "Jump out of a plane and blow up five targets to upset an invasion timetable."

A longer silence this time as Sprague tried to comprehend the meaning of this in relationship to his home and business, to his wife and children.

"Why me?"

Harry did not smile when he asked, "Why not you? Why should someone else get killed saving your wife and kids?"

Sprague was not taken aback this time. "What about my family?"

Harry could see that they were now beginning to talk details, and he respected Sprague. "If you meet with the Boss Man and the Colonel tonight, tomorrow your family will be notified that the plane in which you were returning to Columbus crashed. You will have taken out $200,000 in flight insurance which will be paid to them over a period of years. In the event you return from the mission, well"—and he grinned—"you were in a hospital and could not be in touch with them. A mistake will have been made and all kinds of apologies expressed by one of the airlines."

There was a low whistle from Sprague. "Just like that?"

Harry nodded. "I could arrange a fancy funeral, if that's what you would want, but it gets complicated, and we don't have much time."

The silence was longer now, and when Sprague spoke, he asked, "Can I have some time to think about this?"

Harry shook his head. "The other night the Boss Man told Colonel Fannin he could give him everything but time. We've got about two hours. I know a place where you can take a long walk and think."

Both of them were smiling when Carl Sprague said, "Thanks."

Harry started the car once more and took the road to Rock Creek Park. "I have your promise not to make a phone call?"

Sprague thought about this and then nodded.

The nod came too fast to suit Harry, who made his mind up that there would be no opportunity to make that phone call even if he had to walk with Sprague, but he did not tell this to Sprague until they reached the park.

KEENE, NEW HAMPSHIRE

ZING MILLER sat on the edge of his bed in the shabby boarding house and stared at the phone he had just set down. Colonel Fannin wanted to see him in Washington. The matter could not be explained on the telephone. Zing had been honest. He was broke. He did not even have money for a car or bus trip to Washington. The Williams woman on the other end of the line had told him to take a cab to the Air Force Base just across the Vermont line and the base security officer would pay the cab fare. From there a plane would bring him directly to Washington. Zing had agreed, partly because he was curious as to what the hell his old Colonel would want with a broken-down carnie who couldn't find a sideshow to bark in, and partly because he could not think of a single reason why the hell he should not go to Washington. His time was not so valuable. He rose from the bed and started to pack his clothes. Both pairs of pants and the other pair of shoes. He had three shirts in the local laundry, but he did not have the sixty cents to get them out. Maybe sometime, if he was unfortunate enough to find himself in Keene again, he would have the change.

Looking about the room, he realized that he had only one problem now—the landlady. She would be waiting in the living room, where she always seemed to be when he went in or out. He looked at the window and thought of doing the dishonorable thing—tossing out his bag and then walking around the house and picking it up after telling her that he was going for cigarettes. Then he looked at the bag in his hand and started to laugh. Why the hell did he need two extra pairs of slacks and a pair of shoes that had a hole in the bottom? He tossed the bag on the bed and walked out.

A block from the house he flagged a taxi. It took almost two hours to reach the Air Base and the pilot of the T-39 was waiting on the field. As soon as Zing Miller identified himself, even before he had a chance to sit down, the pilot hurled the plane down the runway and jerked it into the air.

WASHINGTON, D.C. •

It was almost five in the afternoon when General LeGrande assembled his staff in the GENOPS planning room. He had been in touch with Janet and Harry through most of the day, but until this moment he had seen neither of them. Before him on the table lay the files of each of the members of Colonel Fannin's team as well as the file on Hac Quan. He could tell from the expression on Janet's face that she was tired. Lines which he normally would not have noticed could be seen about her eyes. The inevitable cigarette was between her fingertips, but she was not really smoking it. He looked at Harry, who had had so little sleep the previous night, and he could see that Harry was as weary as he himself felt. Twenty-four more hours, give or take a few, and then there would be little he could do except worry.

There was no agenda for this meeting, so LeGrande just picked up the first file before him. "The soldier Brodsky?" he asked of neither of the other two in particular.

Harry shrugged. "Cliff Carter met him, took him to the safe-house. A boy who may always be a boy. Tough and fairly bright, according to Cliff's first reactions. Confused, but, hell, Boss Man, who wouldn't be?"

"Did he check out the boy's knowledge of radio?"

"I did," Janet offered. "His 201 was complete when Cliff sent it in." She pointed to the file before the General. "Went to school at Monmouth and came off high in his class. Might even have been sent on to an officers training program, but he was just too argumentative."

The General grinned. "That's a good word for a loudmouthed dogface." He was silent a moment. "Have we any negatives?"

Janet laughed. "He wasn't exactly up for a good conduct medal when we 'sprung' him this morning."

"Do we give a damn?" Harry asked.

Janet was the first to agree that she could not care less. "But it doesn't exactly make one feel he is the most responsible person we could send in."

The General was shaking his head. "I've known too many of them. Can't spend years making up bunks and policing cigarette butts at a post, but can be a first-rate soldier in every other way."

Harry and Janet glanced at each other. LeGrande did not seem to be aware that he was giving them part of his own autobiography and all of Fannin's.

Closing the file with the comment, "You'll talk to him tonight, Janet," the General moved on to the next. "Sprague, Carl. Our possible Number Two Man."

Harry answered. "Wife and kids. Intelligent enough. Wanted to think about the the thing and walked through Rock Creek Park just thinking as I walked behind him. Finally, he turned to me and said something I think indicates his personality. 'One more fling before I go fat.'"

The other two weighed the comment with the word *fling* the only thing that bothered them. "Then he'll go?" LeGrande asked.

Harry nodded. "Once he made up his mind, there was no reason not to accept him. That was when I called you and we agreed to take him to the safe-house."

LeGrande looked at the others. "Any second thoughts?"

"The family?" Janet asked.

"Will be informed of his tragic death tomorrow," Harry said. "Airline crash. Non-sched. Insured."

"No second thoughts." Janet closed the subject.

LeGrande agreed. "Talk to him tonight."

Then he opened the file marked Miller. "This third one, the carnival man. You met him, Harry."

The Deputy Director laughed. "He's been seeing too many movies. The glib tough guy. Humphrey Bogart on the late show. I put it to him straight. 'You could get killed doing this.' He nodded and said, 'I'm supposed to owe someone a death,' and then he shrugged. We talked explosives for an hour and he knows them as well as anyone I've ever met."

This evaluation satisfied LeGrande. But Janet had a reservation. "If he's foolhardy, he could get someone killed."

"I'll grant you that," LeGrande conceded. "But I'm not worrying out how many we bring back."

"Will you explain that, Richard?" Janet challenged him.

For a long time the General looked at her and then he rose from the table and walked over to the wall map which he had unlocked before the meeting had begun. Southeast Asia lay spread before him. "What do you think the chances are of getting a man back after he has blown five targets?" Then, without waiting for an answer, he went on. "Damned slight. I'll concern myself with it after the team has gone. But I think this time we must be prepared to pay the cost. This team has less chance than any I have ever sent out, than any either of you has ever assembled. Don't think I haven't thought of the cost. A plane where the survivors can be met. A sub in the Tonkin Gulf. These and a date I can give them. But I'm not going to think of the chances for survival. They are just too damned slim."

Le Grande was back at the table now, closing the file with the comment, "And you'll talk to this man called Zing?"

Janet nodded, wondering when she would be able to meet with each member of the team.

"Now that leaves us Hac Quan. He checked out on a polygraph.

There are some fuzzy edges. But he isn't Vietcong and he isn't in favor of Ho Chi Minh. What didn't emerge, and what I think we'll have to live without knowing, is the real reason why he is willing to go back. From what the Pentagon inquiry brought out, he's wanted there." The General shoved the Pentagon report toward the center of the table in case the others wanted to look at it.

"Do we know why he's wanted?" Harry was asking.

LeGrande shook his head, "And I'm not so sure that it really matters. If we had weeks to mount this, I'd check further. But as it stands, I'll live with what we have." A pause, and then he added, "Unless you two think we shouldn't."

Janet shook her head and Harry shook his.

LeGrande nodded and turned to Janet. "What, my dear, did you think of our Colonel Barney Fannin?"

"I don't understand Barney Fannin," Janet admitted. "He baffles me."

LeGrande waited for her to continue, but Janet shook her head. "I don't want to commit myself to an opinion now."

Both Harry and the General were surprised. It was Janet's job to commit herself on personnel. After a moment, LeGrande accepted the fact that she meant what she had said. "Where is he now?" he asked.

"At our apartment. The three American members of the team are at the safe-house and Hac Quan is at the Mayflower."

Harry considered this for a moment and then said, "Let's leave it that way tonight, Boss Man. The Americans can get used to each other with Cliff there. The Colonel knows them already."

The General had already arrived at the same conclusion. "And Hac Quan can be brought in too late for Fannin to turn him down and find someone else. Remember, they've got to be free to come and go. Better they quit now than later."

"I'll go to the safe-house for an hour or so," Harry offered. "I'll meet with them and try to make them comfortable. Tomorrow I'll have to equip them, but that seems to be pretty much in hand, and the plane is actually standing by." What he was really worrying about, and all of them knew it, was the possibility of a breach of security if any of them defected now.

Janet considered the implications of the plane being ready. "I wouldn't move them before tomorrow. Let's get to know them better and not take a chance of anything happening that could bring attention to them."

LeGrande nodded. "And you'll talk to them tonight?"

"I'll go out to the safe-house after dinner," she said. "You might as well count on going home when I get there."

The arrangement appeared to suit LeGrande, who nodded absent-mindedly as Harry left the planning room. Alone with Janet, the General asked, "What happened between you and Barney?"

There was an instant's hesitation, and she said simply, "He propositioned me."

Startled, the General stared at her. "Am I supposed to laugh or get angry?"

But Janet was shaking her head. "I think you should worry."

"You sound like Harry."

"There's something wrong with a man who would propose that I jump into bed with him just because I am a woman and he is a man and there is a hotel bed handy."

Considering this for a moment, LeGrande asked, "Do you think he's a Don Juan?"

She shook her head. "He's not sick that way. I'm not shrinking his head, but I don't believe he had to have a woman."

"Then what is it?" LeGrande had accepted her advice: he was worrying.

"He has to louse up whatever situation he is in. There's all that talk about people who are winners and people who are losers."

"And you think Barney Fannin's a loser?"

Janet was shaking her head. "It's not that simple. I think he may have what it takes to be a winner, but he wants to be a loser. This town is filled with women, has the reputation of being an

oversized whorehouse on an official basis with government buildings provided. But Barney Fannin asked *me*. The mistress of the
man who for some reason or other is trying to help him."

LeGrande was following her with some difficulty. "You think
he wants me to drop him?"

Again she shook her head. "I don't believe your Barney Fannin
was thinking at all. I don't believe he has actually thought for a
long time. I believe he is reacting in every possible way to what he
sees as a world he never made. He's the man on a white horse
without a white horse. He's the hero with nothing to be heroic
about. He's the best damned platoon leader in the world, but has
no place to lead it."

LeGrande was grinning at the way in which she was piling up
her arguments as if someone was arguing with her. "Lil said last
night that Barney Fannin has been to hell and can lead the way
back again."

Janet laughed softly. "Now there's your melodrama. The Ulys-
ses looking for his lost love down below." Then she was not laughing. "If you really want to oversimplify things, Dick, I would say
that the problem with Barney Fannin is that he knows no one
wants him any longer because he has embarrassed them by being
a failure. And so now, like a little child, he doesn't want anyone."

"And he thought I'd give him up if he went after you?"

Janet nodded.

But LeGrande shook his head, "That's too simple." Both of
them were silent as he put one hand out and placed it on hers.
Then he said, "We'll have to keep the record open on Barney
Fannin." He drew her out of her chair and to him. Janet did not
resist as he took her face in his hands and tilted it so that he could
kiss her. Her arms came to rest on his shoulders, and one of his
hands came away from her face and passed gently over her
breasts. They remained as they were for a moment before she
stepped back. When she did, he could remember the softness of
her.

"Let's get the hell out of here and go home. Then we'll drive
over to that house later."

She accepted the suggestion and began to gather up the files. "I'll meet you at the car in five minutes."

He nodded and paused to watch her touch her hair with one hand to assure herself that he had not disarranged it.

"I'll make a mess out of you when we get home," he threatened, and she wrinkled her nose at the idea.

"You have company at home," she reminded him.

A puzzled look on LeGrande's face, and then he recalled, "Barney." And he added with a sigh, "The sacrifices I make for my country."

It was almost midnight when Barney Fannin was met by Janet at the gate of GENOPS headquarters. She had called him after the General decided that Barney should hear the tapes she had recorded with the team members. The interviews had been as casual and informal as Janet could arrange for them to be. The liquor had flowed readily at the safe-house, with Cliff Carter acting as host and the General sitting and talking to the three men who had been brought together for the first time. During the evening, Janet had managed to get off alone with each of the three to talk about any problems they might have. She had not put it that way, but when the polish was washed from her remarks, a perceptive team member could have seen what she was trying to do. What none of them had known was that they were being taped and that even their ability to understand the situation was being evaluated.

Passing the Night Security Guard, Janet led Barney Fannin directly to LeGrande's office. The General already had his suit jacket off, his tie open and a bottle of John Dent on the desk with three glasses poured. Waving Barney to a seat, he asked, "Long evening?"

Fannin shrugged. "Still don't know what the hell you're holding me back for?"

"Strategy, Barney. Strategy. Let them worry about you and the mission until we're ready for them to meet you, and then for the damnedest reason—your being there—they'll be relaxed when they leave."

The Colonel could see that LeGrande was in good humor, though as far as Barney knew, he had spent a dull evening in the sitting room of the LeGrande apartment watching a bad war movie on TV.

Janet ignored them as she set a tape into the Wollensak and pressed the button. Every so often she would pause to listen to something that seemed to be nothing more than a series of *non sequiturs*. Then when she was down to that part of the tape in which she was particularly interested, she pulled up a chair with the comment, "This is the young one—Brodsky." She picked up the drink which had been poured for her. "I think that Cliff started him drinking early this afternoon for lack of anything better to do with him." She thought a moment and then smiled. "Cliff did say they swapped lies for a couple of hours, and the boy can hold his own with any of you." She enjoyed the reaction on Barney Fannin's face, and she could see that the General was smiling at that reaction.

Then she pressed down the button on the machine and the three could hear her voice and Joe Brodsky's.

Sure, Colonel Fannin is a nice guy for an officer, but I can't see what he wanted with me.

Don't you think you can do the job he will expect of you?

A laugh. Nobody told me what the job was, lady. They just brought me here and bought me these. A silence. This is the first honest-to-god suit I ever owned that wasn't worn by one of my brothers first.

Do you expect me to believe that?

A silence. Why not. Not everyone is rich and lives in a house like this. I didn't, that was all. I didn't. My pa worked as a puddler in a steel mill, and when that closed we moved out to a farm. Me and my brothers worked the farm while my old man kept telling us how hard he had worked in the steel mill. Then the local draft board got cute and picked

*me to fill a call they received. That's the only kind of fill
they ever take. Guys whose fathers can't make waves and
black boys from the swamp country nobody cares about.*

*Then you don't think you should be here? Maybe the
Colonel should find someone else to go with him?*

A silence. *That's not what I meant. I'm here and there's
this job Mr. Clifford keeps telling me has to be done and
that it may be dangerous.* A silence. *Hell, lady, I don't know
no one's got less to lose than Joe Brodsky, and so as I'm
telling this Clifford—why not?* A silence. *Maybe I'll come
out of it a hero. Me, Joe Brodsky.*

Is that what you think, Joe? A silence. *Do you think you'll
be a hero?*

*No. I'm just blowing my mouth off. I imagine like everyone
else I'll get sick and puke and maybe I'll live and maybe
I won't.* Another silence. *But as I said, no one I know's got
less to lose than Joe Brodsky, and that, lady, I mean.*

Janet reached over and switched off the tape recorder. For a
moment she sat where she was with the drink in her hand.

"Funny," Barney was saying, "I thought he was a happy kind
of kid. Bounced all over the obstacle course. Bumped right up to
the top of his radio class."

The General nodded. "I haven't heard anything that makes me
say he isn't your man."

"Yeah," Barney agreed almost reluctantly.

LeGrande nodded to Janet, who removed the spool of tape
from the machine and threaded up a second spool. Again, she
ran it down to what she thought was the crux of the interview.
Before she turned it up for the others to hear, she looked at Barney. "This one's the demolitions man. Harry says he knows his
business."

Having already vouched for that fact, Barney said nothing as
he looked at LeGrande. "Did you have to pump these guys?
They did come of their own accord and they did agree to go."

The General looked at the Scotch in his hand and smiled.

"You thought Brodsky was a happy kid. I want to know as much as I can about these men and you'd better too. It's that split second when knowing or not knowing about one of them may make a difference." He reached over and picked up the stack of files he had taken out of the safe. "When we're done, you can read these. The reports we've gathered on these men."

Smiling, Fannin shook his head. "For years people have been saying, 'That nice sweet boy, Dick LeGrande, has gone bad.' Now I know what they mean."

Sucking in his cheek, the General considered the awesome innocence of Barney Fannin and all of the men like him who thought a uniform was to wear when you charged, gun in hand and gung ho, at the enemy. He nodded to Janet, who turned on the Wollensak.

I'd like to get something out of it. If I'm going to be sticking my neck out, maybe something ought to come back to me.

You mean you want to be paid? A silence. You're thinking of money? A silence.

I'm not so sure that's what I'm talking about.

You want medals, Zing? Your name in headlines?

Laughter. *Everyone wants that. A silence. No. I'm talking about that . . . A silence. That thing, that . . . oh, hell, Mrs. Williams, I'm the glib boy. The one who can-do with a capital can. But when it comes down to talking like this to a lady about something other than a toss in the hay . . . I guess I'm not much good at words. A silence. Colonel Fannin. He can be sometimes. I've heard him when we were liquored up. Just the two of us and him telling me what it was like to be in a uniform and be trained at West Point and be that special kind of soldier who makes his living by getting killed. A silence. Colonel Fannin's good with words, but not when he's with other officers or generals. I've watched him. He's sort of uncomfortable then. Laughter. Like I am now, talking with a lady and not about that toss*

*in the hay. Alone, he's some guy, that Colonel. You know
him well?*

We've met. A silence. *But you were telling me about that
thing—to use your word—that you think you should get
because you're sticking your neck out.*

*Yeah. That thing. It's like a stake. Dough. Moola. Cash.
That which the eagle used to crap out on pay day.* A silence.
*But it isn't that. It's maybe just nothing more than a break.
Maybe I want my own carnie stand. Maybe I don't want to
be a shill. Maybe I want a white collar and a tie that wasn't
tied in the factory. Maybe what I'm talking about is just a
chance to not go broke pushing a goddamned pea under
walnut shells, if you know what I mean.*

*You think because you are going to risk your life that
somehow when you get back the risk should be taken out of
things. Is that what you're trying to say, Zing?*

A silence. *Almost. But what I mean is, maybe if I do this,
there should be some kind of a job a slob who knows how
to shill and handle explosives can do so he can maybe get
married and go home nights and at the end of the month find
him a paycheck.*

Wouldn't you think that kind of square, Zing?

A silence and then a nervous laugh. *Maybe it's time a guy
becomes square.*

Janet turned off the machine and, rising, poured herself a second Scotch.

"Maybe it's time a guy becomes a square?" Barney Fannin repeated what he had just heard. Then he looked up at Janet, who
stood before him. "Looks like both of them feel they've missed
something and think they'll find it when we go."

She nodded. "It bothers me, because they're not going to find
anything." She paused and shrugged. "But by the time they learn
that, it'll all be over."

"Is that all you make of it, Janet?" The General was asking.

"No, Dick. These men are both have-nots."

LeGrande smiled his agreement. "You're thinking of that guerrilla account Julian Amery wrote some years ago. The best guerrillas are the have-nots. As Brodsky so neatly stated it, 'I know no one with less to lose.' "

Janet finished her drink, watching Fannin over the top of the glass as he considered what he had just heard. She had put him in the same category shortly after they had sat down to breakfast that morning. She wondered if he had now so categorized himself.

The General looked at his watch. "We've got a long day tomorrow. Let's hear that last one."

"Yeah," Colonel Fannin agreed.

Still watching him, Janet switched the tapes on the machine. She could see that Fannin was troubled. Maybe this whole idea was not as good a one as she had first thought. Maybe she was shaking Barney Fannin, who at this moment shouldn't be shaken. But then she thought of Lil MacWolfe, who had been married to Fannin for over ten years and had not been able to shake him. Janet was not so vain as to think she would be the one finally to get to this man.

Pressing the button on the recording machine, she stood on the far side of it so that she could watch Fannin as he listened.

I don't know. Maybe I didn't have the right to say I'd go. I've been thinking about it, and maybe I should be back in Columbus.

Do you want out now?

Well, not really. A silence. *What does a man say? This sounds like kids' stuff. There's that boy Joe in the living room with the new suit he's so proud of, and the other one who acts as if he was uncomfortable out of a whorehouse. Maybe this is for them.*

But you said you didn't want out.

A long silence. I've got a wife. She's almost my age. A nervous laugh. *I'm no kid, you know. Forty-three. Then there is the boy and the girl.* A silence. *I've got to think of them.*

I don't understand.

Well, let's say I'd be thinking of them if I said I wanted out. I could go home and forget I ever came here. Or I could say I was thinking of them and go on this mission because if it's all Mr. Harmon said it is, then it's important, and the Colonel thinks I can help him.

You feel caught in between? Is that what you're trying to say?

Something like that. When the Second World War was over, I thought I'd had it. Done my bit and all that hogwash. Then I was retreaded for Korea. It meant breaking up the house and knowing that if I lived I would have to start all over again.

You think that's what this means?

I don't know. You've been asking me the questions. I guess that's what you're supposed to do. Will you let me ask one?

A silence. *I can't promise to answer it.*

That's fair enough. But if this thing comes off and I come back, how long will it have taken?

A silence. *You come through this and you'll be back in your office in Columbus in three weeks at the outside.*

Then this really isn't the same as Korea.

Did anyone tell you it was?

A silence. *No. I just thought . . .* A long silence, and both the General and Barney started to say something, but Janet shook her head. *My boy, he's smart the way a man wants his son to be. Kind of the all-American type you see in ads. I've even thought of using him in some of the ads we get out for the company. You know—he's why you take out insurance.* A silence. *That's all kind of cornball, but maybe being a father is. Tell me, Mrs. Williams, how does a boy grow up without a father?* A silence. *Maybe I shouldn't have asked the question. Not that one, anyway. Maybe I should ask why should a boy grow up without a father when he doesn't have to. Or a girl. Why should Marge grow old without me?*

It isn't what we planned. A silence. *We didn't plan it that way.*

Do you want to forget the whole thing?

No, I said I'd do it.

Don't feel as if you're bound by your word. I am sure Colonel Fannin would understand. He has two boys himself.

I didn't know that. One never thinks of him as being very human. He was a kind of machine out there. All polished and ready for someone to pull the trigger.

Do you want out?

A silence, and Janet explained to Fannin and the General, "He shook his head."

Do you want that fling you mentioned? The one before you get fat?

You and Harmon discussed that? But then, I guess that's your job. Fling? It's a way of feeling that everything isn't over—the dreams of being more than an insurance man, though don't think I'm not proud of being one. I am. Worked myself to save the money for Harvard Business School, and for a man with a dime-store background, that took some work. But the fling you were talking about. That sort of makes the whole thing cheap and unimportant, and if this isn't important there's no sense in my being here and her growing old without me. A long silence. *It is important, isn't it?*

The President thinks so.

He knows about this mission?

Yes. He said it should be tried.

A long silence. *And so a kid in a store-bought suit, a carnie shill, a Colonel who couldn't quite make the grade and one frightened insurance salesman are being written off. No, I'm not asking out. I'm just trying to look at it. Trying to be honest. It isn't always easy.*

Janet let the tape run on, though there was nothing more to be heard. When it came to the end and started to slap loosely on the spool, she turned off the machine. "That's your second in command," was all she said.

"A have," Fannin said, evaluating what he had just heard. He was looking to LeGrande for comment.

"Let's give him the best of it—an honest one. He's without any illusions, and so he won't be let down."

The craggy face of the Colonel set. "You can't have it both ways, Dick. For the others the mission is too brief for them to lose their illusions, and for this one he won't be let down."

Pleased that Fannin had caught him playing word games, LeGrande smiled. "He did not want out, and Janet gave him every chance to get out."

"You think that's important?"

"It's your team, Barney. If you don't want him, say so."

Janet rewound the tape and stood with the three spools in her hand as she waited for Fannin to make up his mind.

"I'm taking him. Just because he knows what he has to lose doesn't make him a coward."

LeGrande nodded. And Janet knew he was hoping the same thing that she was, that the moment would never come when Carl Sprague, suddenly faced with the reality of losing what he had, would try to seek the way out she had offered him when there no longer was a way.

"I'll put these tapes in the safe in my office," she said, knowing that the two men would want to speak for a few minutes without her.

After Janet had left the two alone, Barney Fannin smiled. "Did she take a tape on me at lunch?"

The General shook his head.

"But she told you what I said?"

"You wanted it to get back to me, Barney."

The Colonel picked up the bottle of John Dent and looked at it a moment before pouring himself another drink. "She's quite a woman." The comment was gratuitous, and the General did not think an answer was expected of him. "You're in love with her?"

"Have been for six years."

Fannin nodded. "I was in love once. Lil. I don't know what happened to us." He held the bottle out and laughed. "The answer isn't in that or in any bed with someone else."

"Now you're feeling sorry for yourself, Barney." LeGrande knew that this was expected of him.

"Yeah." Then with a grin, "Zing said it. I don't know what to say to you or Hyde or the others."

LeGrande pushed his chair back. "Want to glance through those files?"

Fannin shook his head. "Anything there I don't know?"

After a moment's thought, "Not really. You've got them pretty well summed up. The Brodsky boy's father runs a grocery. Always did. The background he gave himself is all his own invention."

"Is that bad?"

And LeGrande could see that Fannin did not really know how to judge it. He shrugged. "People run away down different paths. Take Sprague. He wants to run away from that office, but he keeps telling himself that he's doing it for wife and kiddies. He is, but only in part, and that's what's dishonest."

There was a wry smile on the Colonel's face when he asked, "And what are you running away from, General? *Das Wunderkind* bit?" Then almost ingenuously, "I was counting on you getting up to the top before Hyde. You've let me down."

Janet wondered why both of them were laughing when she walked back into the room. "The Night Security Officer handed me this," she said, holding out a manila envelope to the General.

He turned it over, noted the TOP SECRET stamped on the flap, and, tearing off the end, slipped out the contents. Photographs. One after another, he looked at them and passed them to Barney, who read them and handed them to Janet. When the last one was in Janet's hands, the General shook his head.

"We aren't giving ourselves any too much time."

Barney agreed. "I didn't think they'd move that fast. The runway is all finished. The dam's in use, but maybe that already was. I didn't notice the lake backing up behind it in the earlier pic."

LeGrande shook his head. "That's not it. I took for granted they were all pretty much functional in the other pictures. It's the traffic on them that I didn't expect."

He could see that Janet looked puzzled, and he explained, "It's heavy equipment. They've got a hell of a lot of motor transport." He thought about this a moment. "They aren't planning an oxcart invasion."

He looked at his watch as Janet crossed over to the safe and put the aerial photographs away with the files which had been lying on his desk. She looked around for anything else that should not be unsecured, and with a shake of her head picked up the bottle of John Dent and set it into the back of the safe. Barney and LeGrande watched as she closed the safe and looked at her watch. Then, holding out her hand, she waited for LeGrande to pass her a pen which she used to initial the report form on top of the safe and put down the time she had closed it.

The General had already slipped on his suit jacket, and they were walking out of the building when he asked her, "The final pawn been moved?"

"About half an hour ago," she said, knowing that he was asking about Hac Quan.

Fannin looked from one to the other but said nothing. After the three had signed out of the building and stood for a moment in the darkness of the street, Fannin stared up at the sky. A few scattered stars and the rest was darkness.

"I'll meet the team in the morning?" he asked.

"First thing," the General said. "And by tomorrow night you're going to be on your way."

The sedan driven by the General's sergeant pulled up and Janet stepped in, followed by the General. Then, to the surprise of both of them, Fannin closed the door, remaining on the sidewalk. He leaned down to the window level. "That key you gave me, Dick. I'll use it when I come in later."

For a moment Janet expected LeGrande to say something, but instead he waved his hand. "Night, Barney." Then to the driver, "Home, Sergeant," and the large Imperial pulled away from the curb, leaving Barney Fannin looking after it. Janet, glancing back over her shoulder, could see him staring up at the sky. When she turned to the General, he shook his head. "I'm not Barney Fannin's keeper."

"Somebody should be," was all she said as he put his arm about her waist and drew her to him.

It was almost two in the morning when Barney Fannin banged on the door of the small apartment off Massachusetts Avenue. He waited a moment and was about to bang again when the door was opened by a young woman in a nightgown.

"You said you were coming an hour ago," she reproached him.

"Yeah," he agreed, and pushing the door wide, walked into the living room and slammed the door behind him.

"Take it easy, Barney," she warned. "I've got to live here after you go."

He swung back and scooped her up in his arms. Before she could protest, he kissed her firmly on the mouth and then the neck. Her head fell back. Her arms came about his shoulders and he carried her through the small living room into the bedroom beyond, where he dumped her on the bed.

"Always said when I got back to Washington, you and I would have another go-round," he explained as she watched him take off his suit jacket and drop it unceremoniously on a chair. Her legs came up under her chin as he started to jerk his tie open.

"Howd'ja find me, Barney?" Her voice was soft. She was wearing no makeup and the light from the living room cast shadows over her cheeks.

Barney paused to look at her while he unbuttoned his shirt. "Just called the Pentagon and threw some weight around, and sure enough, the duty officer at Ordnance told me you still worked there."

Sitting on the edge of the bed, Barney crossed his legs and started to remove a shoe with one hand while he put his other on her cheek where the shadows lay. She nuzzled closer to him and his hand went from her cheek to the neckline of her nightgown and then inside it. She smiled and pointed out that he had one shoe off and the other on. His hand came away and he jerked his second shoe off. A minute later he was pushing her down on the bed as he whispered, "I came all of the way to Washington for this." And though both of them knew he was lying, for this moment both of them wanted to believe.

Richard LeGrande had finished shaving and was standing before the mirror in the bathroom, bared to the waist, staring at the gray hair that covered his temples. Once he would have thought it distinguished, but as he smiled at himself now, he knew it was merely that he was growing older.

"There are plenty of homes for old soldiers," Janet said, and he swung around to see her, already dressed in a blue skirt and white blouse, watching him from the doorway. She knew what he had been thinking, and he was annoyed, because, as he always told her, "there are some things a man wants to keep to himself."

Taking the towel off his shoulder, he tossed it on the edge of the basin and reached for his shirt, hung on the back of the door. Janet looked from him to the towel and back again. "Next time one of you Academy boys starts telling me about the tough restrictions you faced, how damned neat you had to be . . ." She did not finish the sentence, but picked the towel up and hung it on the rack.

"I didn't say I was done with it," LeGrande protested in self-defense.

She looked at him and shook her head sadly, "That would make fascinating conversation, 'I am done with this towel.' "

Buttoning his shirt, he asked, "And what would make fascinating conversation at six-thirty in the morning?"

"Well, for starters, we could talk about your Colonel Fannin, who isn't here yet." She reached up and touched a dab of shaving soap which remained behind his ear. Almost angrily, he reached for the towel again and wiped the soap away. She knew he was thinking of Barney Fannin and worrying about his absence.

"I told you last night," he snapped, "that I'm not Barney Fannin's keeper."

Janet looked at him tolerantly as she patted his cheek as though he were a child. "Maybe you should be."

He started to reach for her, but she ducked under his arm and into the bedroom. He followed her as she stood in front of the full-length mirror hung on the closet door.

"What would you have me do?" he asked.

"Do? About what?" She was pulling her skirt so that it hung more evenly.

"Barney. Do you think I should have held his hand all night or hired a keeper to sit with him?" He was selecting his tie now. Janet stood before the mirror, and when she did not answer, he added, "Now we both approve of what you're looking at."

With a wry smile, she turned to him. "The nicest thing you've said this morning." Then shifting the subject to what she knew was troubling both of them, "Barney doesn't need a keeper. He needs a baby-sitter."

LeGrande started to knot his tie as she sat down on the edge of the bed, watching him. "How do you know that wasn't what he went looking for last night?"

Janet was about to answer when the doorbell rang. Both shrugged.

"It couldn't be Barney," the General assued. "He said he had a key."

She nodded in agreement and remained where she was.

He slipped the tie knot into place and shook his head as he started out of the bedroom. "It's got to be someone."

Janet smiled as she nodded in full agreement, and he only realized the inanity of his statement when he reached the foyer. He opened the door to find Hyde MacWolfe.

The two Generals stood looking at each other. "I know," Le-Grande said, "you want coffee."

MacWolfe nodded and walked past him into the living room. "Perceptive, Dick," and he handed the manila envelope he was carrying to LeGrande. The Director of GENOPS looked at the classification and was about to open it when he asked, "The recon photos of the valley?"

"You are bright this morning."

Handing the packet back, LeGrande explained, "I saw them last night." He thought a moment. "And if I had to take a guess, you knew that, because they were sent from your office to GENOPS, and if you didn't know I was at GENOPS, you would have had them sent here."

"Brighter and brighter."

Janet joined them in the living room and she smiled as she always did when she saw the Old Gray Wolf in full uniform with all the rows of spangled confetti on his broad chest.

LeGrande looked at her and shook his head. "Ever since he's been appointed to Intelligence, he keeps thinking that there is some direct relationship between his job and his title."

Looking from one to the other, Janet opened her palms wide to show that there was nothing she could say. "I'll get the coffee." Then, to MacWolfe, "How's Lil?"

There was a moment's pause, and he looked at both of his friends. "I wish Dick had not brought up Barney's name to her. She thinks Dick is getting Barney in over his head, even though she doesn't know what it's all about."

Janet started to say something and then, changing her mind, she left the two men alone.

Throwing open the French doors that led to the balcony, Le-Grande stood in the doorway a moment thinking about the implications of Lil's emotional involvement with Barney Fannin and what it could mean to a man like Hyde MacWolfe, who was now her husband. To his surprise, it was MacWolfe who changed the subject. "I'm glad your team's all ready."

LeGrande swung about on his heel and stared at the Deputy

Director of the Defense Intelligence Agency. "If there's anything I won't stand for, it's people running operations to check up on mine."

Realizing that LeGrande was serious, MacWolfe backed away from the subject. "We're involved here, too."

"You know where the safe-house is?"

MacWolfe nodded. "Our plane came in. One of your boys met it and drove straight there."

There was a long silence as LeGrande evaluated this breach in his security. He knew there were too many breaches in security at all times, but he was still angry. "Don't play games with me, Hyde. I'm not the reason you use your counter-espionage. The only justification for that is to protect your own men. And a warning: operations inside the territorial limits belong to the FBI."

MacWolfe smiled ingenuously. "I'll catch on to how all of this works some day. Where's Barney?"

"Are you concerned?"

The smile became a grin as MacWolfe said, "No, but I thought you might be." Reaching into his pocket, he pulled out a slip of paper.

LeGrande took it and, reading the name and address, asked, "You sure?"

"He called up the ordnance duty officer last night after about four other tries." Then to show how much he did know, "Do you want the names of the ones he tried and didn't find home?"

LeGrande shook his head angrily before he glanced at the paper, "All right, you've been through the Ordnance Personnel files already this morning. What's a Betsy Lou Hogan?"

"Brunette. 5'2''. 110 pounds. La Jolla, California. Thirty-two. Twice divorced and from a simple deduction—available."

LeGrande considered the implications and did not believe there were any. "Security clearance?"

"Sweet and clean as a scented whore."

Convinced that MacWolfe was only showing the power of the Pentagon to function and at the same time using that power to learn what he could about Barney Fannin, LeGrande changed the subject. "Let's have some coffee." He was angry at another agency checking up on his own operation, and for reasons he could not quite explain to himself, he was angry because of some vague injustice being committed against Barney Fannin. Thinking about Barney, he sat down with his coffee before him and saw the clock on the breakfast-room wall. In two hours he had to be at the safe-house with Barney. Even if it meant pulling Barney Fannin out of the bed of . . . and he looked at the note again . . . Betsy Lou Hogan.

LeGrande quickly left the table and went into his bedroom to place a phone call.

The taxi in which Barney Fannin was sitting had circled the block three times, and the driver wondered how long this glum-faced man would sit, shoulders hunched up, staring straight ahead of him. The driver was wondering, too, if he would be stopped by the MPs for just circling the block in Fort Meyers. Unable to tell from the identification his passenger had shown just what his connection with the Fort was, the driver felt uncomfortable. Finally, as the cab started around for the fourth time, the tall man in the back seat straightened up. "Stop here," he ordered, and he reached over and dropped a five-dollar bill on the front seat.

The cab came to the curb and the passenger stepped out, slammed the door and, bending down, told the driver, "There's another five in it if you wait for me."

Calculating his possible morning take, the driver asked, "How long?"

A shrug. "Fifteen minutes. Maybe more. Maybe less." Then, without waiting for an answer, Barney Fannin strode up the walk to the two-story red brick home. Meyers, an old fort that has served Washington for more than a century, housed the men with enough rank to bump out the others in the chain of command. Stopping in front of the oak-paneled door, Barney realized that Hyde MacWolfe's three stars gave him certain prerogatives. He was about to ring the bell when the door opened. Lil stood there in jodhpurs and boots, a riding crop in her hand. "The boys aren't home," she said, before Barney could ask her anything.

Barney nodded. Lil looked older than when he had last seen her. There was more gray in her hair now, but her figure was as full and young as he liked to remember it from before the war. But the way she had changed the most was a quiet look about her face that had not been there the night she had told him she was leaving him. It had not been there in any of the years that he could recall after the war.

"Bill is away for the summer. My father's place on the Cape."

Again Barney nodded. He remembered the place on the Cape. He remembered, also, the General who had told his son-in-law that he did not have what it took to go anywhere, that he was personally going to tie a can to Barney's career. But Barney remembered, also, the hours he had spent on the beach at the Cape with Lil beside him as the two of them had stared at the stars.

"And Bob?"

She hesitated a moment. "He made first lieutenant when they shipped him to Saigon last month." Lil was trying to be polite, but she was afraid of Barney Fannin, and though she tried to recall when she had ever had this feeling before, she could not. It was something which had grown on her in recollection. "Was there anything else you wanted, Barney?"

Very slowly, as if it were a difficult task, he shook his head.

"I'd ask you in for coffee," she was explaining "but you know Army posts."

"The major flattens the captain's wife, and the captain flattens the colonel's, while the colonel's flattening the major's." He spoke as if by rote. Then he shook his head. "You've got it all wrong, Lil. It isn't played that way any more. Those days are done. And besides, your reputation's safe because it's common knowledge that everyone's afraid to sleep with the General's Lady."

Both of them were silent for a time and Lil MacWolfe became increasingly nervous.

"I just came to say hello, Lil." Then with a cynical smile, "Maybe I also wanted to see how you looked."

"And how do I look, Barney?"

"Like someone who caught the tail of a star."

"You mean a comet." She did not know if she was supposed to be pleased or not.

But Barney removed any doubt when he shook his head. "I meant a star, Lil."

Before she could say anything else, he turned and walked back to the taxi that was still at the curb. Just before it drove away, he looked back at her. He wondered how she would have felt if he had told her that he had spent himself the night before so that when he saw her she would not know how much he wanted her.

It was almost eight when Betsy Lou Hogan stepped out of her apartment and started to walk toward Massachusetts to look for the cab that would take her to the Pentagon. Usually, she waited for the bus on the corner, but she felt richer this morning by a hundred dollars and she was happily weary. Her hair blew in the faint breeze and her face turned up toward the sun so that she could feel the warmth. She did not see the long sedan that drove slowly behind her until it moved ahead and two men stepped out of it to block her path. They were middle-aged men, neatly dressed, and both of them, she noticed, wore hats, which since the arrival of John Kennedy in the White House had become less common. She became frightened and started to turn.

"Don't, Miss Hogan," one of the men said softly.

She felt herself freezing where she was, even though she wanted to scream or run. Then the man was showing her his identification in a plastic case. Criminal Investigation Division, Department of the Army. "It's all very formal and official," the man was saying. "Actually, you are in no danger, and we merely want to make sure that nothing happens to you. If you want to go back to your apartment and pack your bag, you can take what you want with you."

But she could not seem to understand what he was saying, even after she asked, "Where am I going?"

"We have orders to take you to Fort Huachuka, Arizona. Business. You will be there about six days."

"But my job . . ." she was protesting.

The man who was talking smiled pleasantly. "Let's just consider this part of your job. Your department head will be told when you get back." And he continued to smile as he led her back into her apartment. "Don't worry about the mail or the milk or the newspaper."

She started to protest once more, but now the smile was gone and he was telling her, "The plane is waiting for us at Andrews."

The two men watched her pack a small suitcase.

"Can I call a girl friend?" she asked.

"Something went wrong with your phone a while ago," one of the men said almost sadly.

Though they were aware of her dazed expression and her fear, the two men could not do much to make her feel more comfortable. They only knew that they had orders to see that she did not talk to anyone but themselves for the next six days. Both of them were old hands and assumed that Betsy Lou Hogan had been exposed to information that was going to be kept a secret whether she liked it or not. No one was consulting her, any more than they had consulted the two men from CID.

Breakfast had been over for an hour and LeGrande, in shirt sleeves, was pacing the sitting room. MacWolfe sat on the sofa looking at both his friend and his watch. Janet stood out on the balcony staring down at the river below. Two small sailboats were racing toward the turn of the river to the south, and she could make out the first tourist boat of the morning pressing downstream, its railings lined with passengers in bright dresses and sports shirts. She wished she could go inside and say something to put LeGrande at ease, but there was nothing to be said or done now. She believed that Barney Fannin would appear, because there was no coherent reason why he should not. But he continued to baffle her by his seemingly erratic actions. She had said he was not a Don Juan, and yet he had gone off to spend the night with a woman who was fifth on his list. Barney Fannin was either confused or merely confusing. She was thinking that perhaps this was the baffling part of the man—the tendency to confuse others while he himself had a rationale for his actions which made sense in the context of his own ideas and beliefs. She thought she might be able to come to some conclusions which would surprise both herself and the General if she knew just a bit more about Barney. There was one obvious person who could tell her.

When the doorbell chimed, she had already made her mind up to find out. She did not bother to go to the door. The General would open it, and for reasons she could not explain, she knew that Barney Fannin would be standing there. He would need a shave. He would need to change his shirt. He would like a drink, but he would not take one because he had a busy day ahead of him. He would make a snide remark to Hyde Mac-Wolfe, who disliked him and whom he disliked. He would find something unkind to say to Richard LeGrande, whom he liked and who he knew liked him, oddly enough for the same reason that he would make the snide remark to MacWolfe—his need to be apart. She heard the conversation in the sitting room and smiled to herself. She had been right. By the time she entered the room, Barney had already disappeared into the guest room and the General was looking at MacWolfe.

"You're coming with us this morning?" It was as much an invitation as a question.

The Old Gray Wolf smiled. "You are either mellowing, Dick, or you are looking better by contrast."

Puzzled, the General waited for an explanation.

"Usually, when I want to know what's going on, I have to invite myself."

Janet laughed softly and both turned to her. "He has you there, Dick."

"Not really," LeGrande was explaining. "This entire day is going to be spent in a briefing session. Hyde and the Pentagon are going to have to pick up the tab on expenses and equipment and transport and communications and backstop the operation, because it is far from any base of operations I have. And because I need the Pentagon's help, he has to be kept abreast from this moment on as much as I do."

MacWolfe looked at him in surprise while Janet smiled. "Yes, *mon général*. But this isn't the National Security Council, and all you really needed to do was say Hyde's coming because you're going to need some help."

Both Generals laughed loudly. "She doesn't let you get too stuffy, Dick," MacWolfe said appreciatively.

"Too bad there isn't someone to do the same for you, Hyde."

The three turned to see Barney Fannin tying his tie, his suit jacket over one shoulder. For a moment LeGrande thought he might have to step between the two as MacWolfe came out of his chair, but the Pentagon officer shook his head sadly and turned to Janet. "Now that kindergarten's out, we can get started."

An hour later, the Pentagon sedan dropped the three officers at the safe-house and proceeded to GENOPS Headquarters, where Janet notified both the General's secretary and Harry Fuller's that she wanted their calls routed through her for the day.

At the safe-house, Harry had already called the team together. He had introduced Hac Quan by name, but made a point of not being specific about the qualifications or background of the Annamese engineer. The responsibility had to be the General's. The men were all sitting in the large living room, except Harry, who sat behind a table which he had pulled out on one side of the room. Before him in folders were the maps he knew would be needed for the briefing, as well as the other data he had gathered from the area specialists. LeGrande joined him at the table while Barney Fannin shook hands with each of the team members. From what the General could see, the men were genuinely fond of the Colonel. He waited a few minutes for the cordialities to end and then said he would like to speak with them himself.

Sprague seated himself on the sofa beside Fannin, while Miller and Brodsky took chairs nearby. Only Hac Quan remained alone and unintroduced to Fannin. MacWolfe looked about the room and then settled down in a chair in a corner while Le-Grande spoke.

"Some of you know what this is all about. Some of you know a few pieces of the details. Today we are going to be as specific as we can. But first, and before I begin, I want all of you to know that if you want out now, all you have to do is walk out of that door and down the street, where I'm sure you can find a cab. From there you can go to General MacWolfe's office at the Pentagon, where there is a check waiting to cover your expenses home. If you don't leave now, there is no leaving until the mission is completed. If you survive, all I can say is thanks. There won't be any headlines. If you die, your names will not be engraved for posterity. You fight in darkness. You will be stateless. Your country disowns you, disavows you, will not come to your help if you are taken prisoner, and insists that you dispose of yourselves in that event so there will be no world-wide circus trials."

LeGrande's hands were folded in front of him on the table, and he waited a moment for the others to absorb what he had just said. Then he looked at Zing Miller. "Mr. Miller, are you with us?"

A pause, and then the thin face of the carnie barker bobbed back and forth. "Yes, sir," was all he could bring himself to say.

"Private Brodsky, are you with us?"

Surprised that anyone was really asking him, and at the same time impressed with the appearance of Lieutenant General Mac-Wolfe seated behind the man in mufti who he had been told was an authentic hero and also a general, Joe Brodsky tried to speak and then merely nodded. He could see that the General was not satisfied and forced himself to say, "Yes, sir."

The General smiled as if to put him at his ease and then turned to Carl Sprague, who sat on the sofa, his legs crossed and his hands opening and closing in front of him. "Mr. Sprague, are you with us?"

Sprague smiled. "Yes, General." He knew who LeGrande was and what agency was involved here, though MacWolfe, who had been famous as a tank commander during the Second World War, seemed out of place. Sprague felt for the first time that what was going to happen was important because these men were important and would not be spending their time on the project if it was not. The Williams woman had told him the night before that even the President was involved.

Now the General was asking the stocky, dark-faced man who sat upright in the straight-backed chair in the corner, "Mr. Hac Quan, are you with us?"

But before the stranger could answer, Barney Fannin was on his feet, looking from Hac Quan to LeGrande and asking, "What kind of crap is this, Dick?"

The others in the room could see MacWolfe lean forward as LeGrande sat back in his chair and spoke. "Will you please sit down, Colonel Fannin."

"Hogwash." Fannin was angry to the point where the others could see his fist clenching at his side. "You told me, Dick, that I was picking this team. It is my back that's going to have to be protected out there, and I picked these men because I could trust them."

Very quietly, MacWolfe said, "Colonel Fannin, I think you might permit General LeGrande to explain."

There was a long silence during which LeGrande realized that he had not handled this as well as he might have. He rose to his feet and waved for Hac Quan to join him in the center of the room, wishing all of the time that the others were not watching.

"This is my fault," he said. "Colonel Barney Fannin, Mr. Hac Quan."

Then, as the engineer extended his hand, LeGrande saw that Fannin was not going to shake it. Smiling, the General said, "In that hand, Barney, lies much of the balance of your mission. Hac Quan knows the countryside and the language. If you find your targets, it will be with his help. If any of you survive, it will be because of him." He was glossing over what he did not know about Hac Quan and at the same time trying to make the others accept the stranger.

Fannin merely nodded. "I am in command of this mission?" he asked.

"From the minute it leaves the plane over the valley," Le-Grande assured him.

"Sprague is my second."

The General nodded, seeing Sprague's surprise from the corner of his eye.

"In that case," Fannin said bluntly, "I'll use this man as a pair of eyes, but I'm not trusting anyone I don't know to help get us through." He looked at the other team members. "This isn't a Sunday-go-to-meeting affair. I've got these men to look out for."

"Now, if both of you will sit down." He waited until Fannin returned to the sofa and Hac Quan to his chair before he snapped, "You don't have anyone to look out for, Colonel."

He looked at the team, including Hac Quan. "You have only a mission to concern yourself with from this moment on. If any one of you lives, I shall be pleased, but not if it is at the cost of a single part of your mission." He was taking his seat now and looking at them when he added, "Gentlemen, you have already been written off." He reached out and took the newspaper he saw on the table in front of Harry Fuller. Holding it up so that the others could see the headline about the 707 crash in the West Virginia mountains, he read the list of the dead. When he had finished, he set the paper down. "The names on that list that were not yours were fictitious." He smiled, "As you know, it will not be difficult to explain your survival."

Several in the room laughed nervously. Then, to the surprise of all of them, the General repeated his question which had not been answered earlier. "Hac Quan, are you with us?"

The dark, round face with the slightly slanted eyes was very still for a moment and then the eyes seemed to half close. "I am with you, General." Hac Quan was now looking at Barney Fannin, who was staring at his fist resting on the arm of the sofa.

"I am glad," the General said for the first time. And then he turned his attention to the man on the sofa. "Colonel Fannin, are you with us?"

There was a pause as Fannin's rutted face seemed to expand while he exhaled heavily. "There are some aspects of this you and I will have to talk about, General, but the answer is yes."

LeGrande shoved his chair back and crossed his legs under the table as he rubbed his chin with the back of his hand. "There isn't anything more I'm going to say now because Mr. Harmon here," and he indicated Harry Fuller, "is going to brief you until lunch. After that we can go over every question and detail." He gestured for Harry to begin, and the operations specialist pulled himself to his feet and started to explain what had to be done and why.

It had been Janet's intention to call Lil MacWolfe for lunch. But to her surprise, one of the first calls routed from the General's office was from Lil. Before the other woman could ask any questions or blurt out anything that Janet did not want to hear over a phone, Janet said sharply, "We will talk at lunch, Lil."

A moment's pause. "Can we meet earlier?"

Janet half suspected now why the call had been placed to the General. "Don't talk to anyone," she warned, "and I will pick you up in front of the Hilton in an hour."

"You know what's wrong?" Lil asked.

"An hour in front of the Hilton," Janet repeated firmly.

There was a long pause, and then, "All right."

When the General's sedan pulled up in front of the Hilton Hotel, the doorman opened the rear door of the car and Lil MacWolfe stepped in, holding a copy of the Washington *Post* in her hand. Ordering the driver to take the road to the Potomac Towers, Janet sat back to wait for Lil's reactions to the headline and was surprised when she said, "It isn't true, Jan. He came to see me this morning."

Very slowly, Janet drew a cigarette from the package in her handbag and, lighting it, tried to understand just what this might mean. What other security had Barney Fannin blown? He had been told of the fake crash story that would be released. He had been warned against seeing anyone whom he knew. Janet was aware that Betsy Lou Hogan was on her way to Fort Huachuka. But what she did not know was if there were any other Betsy Lou Hogans or Lil MacWolfes. And she did not know what she would be able to do with Lil.

"What's going on?" Lil demanded, and Janet knew she had the right to an answer, but she questioned whether or not she was the one who should give it to her. She had arranged to meet Lil in the car so that they could talk without being heard by anyone except the sergeant, who she knew was cleared for security. Leaning over, she tapped the sergeant on the shoulder. "Pull up at the first gas station and check the car," she directed.

The sergeant understood, and several blocks later he drew up at a gas station, stepped out and asked the attendant to check the air in the tires. Twice Lil started to speak and both times Janet shook her head, "Not yet." The sergeant dropped down on his knees and checked underneath each fender, the back of the bumpers, under the hood, in the trunk compartment, and finally along the sealed bottom of the car. The attendant was puzzled to find the tires needed no air and accepted the fifty-cent tip. Returning to his place behind the wheel, the sergeant opened the glove compartment and ran his hands under the dashboard. Then he leaned over and felt along the underside of the seat. As he did this, Janet checked the rear seat. When both of them were satisfied, the driver nodded to her and started once more for Potomac Towers.

A startled Lil MacWolfe had said nothing until they were on the road again. Then she asked, "What was he looking for?"

"Tape recorder. Radio," Janet explained.

Lil started to laugh. "You aren't serious?"

Somewhat disappointed at the naïveté of a woman who had spent her life among the military, Janet nodded. "We aren't playing games, Lil." Then she realized that whatever the newspaper headline meant to her, it must have had a completely different significance to Lil MacWolfe. "What does this"—and she pointed to the article in the paper—"mean to you?"

"It doesn't mean anything, because I know Barney's alive."

"And if you did not know that?" Janet asked.

There was a long silence and Janet watched the other woman fold the paper and refold it as if the condition were important. "That's a funny question," Lil finally said.

"It was not intended to be funny," Janet assured her. Then to approach the subject so that the other woman could talk about it and at the same time she could learn what she wanted to know, Janet said, "Why don't you tell me about Barney Fannin?"

Lil sat back in the sedan, unaware of the traffic or the fact that they were about to cross the Potomac. "We met when my father was commandant of the Academy. Maybe you don't know what this means, but for Barney the Academy was like the beginning— the beginning of—well, a new way of living. He had been away from Texas only a year then. His father was a wildcatter and Barney had won his appointment by saving the life of some men when a well blew. He was a combination hero and bright boy. Barney was shy then. He wasn't, later. When he graduated, we got married. Life was one army post after another. Barney was a second lieutenant and then a first lieutenant and everything was, as we used to say, coming up roses." Then she stopped talking and shook her head. "You don't want to hear this."

Janet disagreed. "I've been trying to understand Barney Fannin," she said. "I don't."

Lil put one hand on the window of the car as she looked out and away from Janet. "I don't either," she said.

"And after he made first lieutenant?"

Lil turned toward her. "That was it. I don't know what happened, but Barney didn't make captain when the others did. Dick made it. Hyde made it. The others did. The build-up started for the war, and they went on to major and light colonel and Barney was a first lieutenant. Dick got a regiment and Hyde got a tank battalion. But Barney stayed an adjutant to a regimental commander. He pushed paper, and no one would let him do anything else. We moved from Fort Sam to Fort Lewis. From Lewis to Wood. Barney remained a lieutenant. He started to get careless. Make mistakes. Quarrel." She paused to think, and then she admitted, "I called my father and asked him to look at Barney's efficiency record, thinking that someone had done Barney dirt. But my father said that I should forget it, and he wouldn't explain."

The car sped down King Street southward and Janet lighted another cigarette with the one she had been smoking.

"Then the war started, and Barney went to Africa a captain. Three years later he came home a major. Dick was a brigadier then. Hyde had a star. And I knew and Barney knew that neither one of them had anything that Barney Fannin didn't have. I asked questions at the Pentagon, because I had friends there. No one would talk." She laughed, humorlessly. "And then, my God, they gave Barney Fannin the job of closing out an ordnance depot in the Dakotas. He made every mistake in the book, fought with everyone he met and a good many he never met. Another job like that one and another and then he got sent to Korea as a light colonel. Barney Fannin," she said bitterly. "He came home with an eagle on his shoulder, but whatever had been eating at him from the time he was named an adjutant finally destroyed his insides. He gave up fighting it. He just didn't care." She looked at Janet defensively. "That was when I left him. When he didn't give a damn any more." Both of them were silent, and finally Lil explained, "If he had continued to try for a good efficiency report, for a promotion, for a break, for the affection of the boys . . ." She paused and then added, "If he had even tried just to keep up appearances for me, but he didn't. Barney lay down and quit."

"Barney Fannin lay down and quit?" Janet did not believe this, because if it was true the General was in serious trouble.

"In his way," Lil said, "in his way. He made a point of fighting with everyone. It was no longer an accident or something that needed provoking. Barney Fannin quit by walking away from everything he knew would help him. He set out to lose whatever it was that had made him the young man I had met at the Academy—brave and bright. He hated being either one."

Janet tried to understand just what this meant. "He dissembled?" she asked.

Lil nodded. Then, as if she had finally made her point, "He went into hiding. He plays at being a fool or making a fool of himself over his work or . . . or women."

Recalling her earlier notion that Barney Fannin was deliberately confusing, Janet smiled. She had been right. But just what this meant, she was not certain.

"The article," Janet finally said, pointing to the newspaper, "is there because we are trying to cover up something Barney is going to do. He shouldn't have blown that cover." She considered this. "Maybe he was doing it to play the fool, but he picked you to do it with."

"He's going to be all right?" Lil asked.

Deciding that there was no reason for telling the truth now, Janet lied. "I am sure of that." Later she would have to face Lil, but for now there was no reason for Lil to worry. The General and Hyde and she would worry enough when they sorted out Barney Fannin.

The team and others at the briefing session ate the lunch brought in by Cliff Carter and continued to work through the afternoon. It was almost five when the General excused himself and asked Barney Fannin if they could talk together for a few minutes. After both of them were settled in the den and Le-Grande had closed the double doors, he waited for Fannin to speak. When the Colonel remained silent, he reminded him, "You said there were some aspects of this you wanted to discuss with me."

"This Hac Quan, Dick, you were keeping him a secret. Why?" Fannin rose from his chair and poured himself a Scotch.

"Because you couldn't find anyone who could do what he has

to do for you, anyone who would be acceptable to me and to Hyde."

"My team has to be acceptable to Hyde?" Barney was angry now, and LeGrande knew it.

"I don't give a damn about your sensitivities to him and vice versa. But if you are going to get in and maybe get out . . ." he paused while Fannin chuckled, ". . . and maybe get out, then we have to count on the Pentagon's help. But we were talking about Hac Quan."

Fannin swirled the drink in the glass and stared at it for a time. "You think I'm gook-minded?"

The General shook his head. "I've always said you were all kinds of a damned fool, but I've never accused you of lumping all of the non-WASPS into one bundle and labeling that bundle bad."

Barney seemed to relax. "Then you know we are only talking about this man?"

LeGrande agreed.

"In that case, let me explain my reservations. I don't know who he is, what he is, and why he is coming." Before the General could interrupt, Barney's hand went up. "I know why you think he's coming, but I don't know why he thinks he's coming, and this bugs me."

Both of them were silent for a moment, and then Barney asked, "Have you checked him out?"

"Polygraphed him."

In a gesture of disgust, Barney threw back his head and swallowed his drink. "Polygraphed! For God's sake, Dick, that's kids' stuff today. I wouldn't trust even you—noble and upright Dick LeGrande—to flunk a polygraph if you tried."

The General was listening with care, because he was hearing for almost the first time the kind of thinking he had hoped for from Barney Fannin. The chips were being tossed on the table and the dice were going to be thrown soon, and because of this Barney was showing more logic than he had in two days. Le-

Grande had his own reservations about the polygraph, though he knew there were many who swore by its accuracy. What it could not tell him were the answers to the questions he had not asked. This was its biggest flaw. There was no way to know what would be the question to trigger a special response. In the case of a crime, a specialist could ask questions about the crime, but in the case of Hac Quan, what questions did one ask? The fact that Barney was sharp enough to see this difference pleased Le-Grande, but he knew it could not change his mind.

"Accepting all the reservations you have, Barney, you must have someone who knows the language. He does. You need someone who knows the countryside because you can't ask directions like a tourist. He can. In fact, let me explain the worst part of your mission from an intelligence point of view. In any European country your team could walk through any city, and if it kept its mouth shut and wore the right clothes, no one would notice you. You could even walk through any English-speaking country and fumble your way through with your mouths open slightly, though I am not always sure what language Zing Miller speaks. But in an Oriental country you cannot only not walk down a street, you cannot be seen—period. Let someone get one look at you and you are in trouble. You don't have to have a cover. You have to be completely hidden. I don't know from here how you'll manage that, but I'm counting on Hac Quan to help you." He paused to think about the problems he had outlined and then added, "You have to count on him and I'm not going to give you the onward-and-upward speech. This damned mission is important even if it's being jerry-built because of time."

Fannin rose and poured two glasses of Scotch this time; handing one to LeGrande, he raised his glass, "To the irrefutable fact." LeGrande was about to smile when Fannin continued, "The fact that this mission is jerry-built." Then with a wry smile, "From top to bottom and outside."

"From the top," LeGrande agreed, to Barney's surprise. "Only a damned fool would have seen Lil this morning, knowing all the time that the newspaper would carry the story of your death."

Fannin swirled his drink as he considered this. "You learn things fast here."

"Lil talked to Janet and Janet called me."

A broad smile and Barney asked, "Well, what else would one expect from Barney Fannin?"

LeGrande put his glass down on the end table beside him as he snapped, "That's almost exactly what Janet said you would say." He could see that this made Barney nervous, and he knew that somehow even though he was not becoming any clearer about the personality of Barney Fannin, Janet was.

"Isn't it time we were breaking that meeting up?" Barney asked, changing the subject. LeGrande pulled himself out of the easy chair and nodded. "You're going to give us an inspiring speech, aren't you, Dick? Something for us to take away believing we can walk on water."

Ignoring him, LeGrande entered the living room. MacWolfe had sat in the back of the room and said nothing through the entire briefing, but he had made notes. LeGrande nodded to MacWolfe and then said loudly, "I've a couple of words of warning and advice." The men in the room turned toward him and he could see Barney, who was walking over to the sofa, smile.

"This mission means something to all of us. That's corny, but it's true. You must follow instructions. You will drive from here to the plane that will take you to our air base near Saigon. You will remain in that plane until all of your gear is shifted to the plane that is going to drop you. You will speak to no one." He smiled, "In fact, for your own safety, General MacWolfe has been kind enough to offer us MP protection to see that no one approaches you anytime between now and the time you step out of that plane." He watched MacWolfe make another note of something he had to take care of. "I have promised to have a plane at the point located on your map. It will be there for ten minutes unless it is shot at. If it is, then I shall assume you've been taken and the location has been revealed. General MacWolfe will arrange to have a number of air passes made at various other fields in the vicinity of the valley so that their radar will reveal all the passes and they won't be sure where we are bringing you out. Remember that the completion of the mission is more important than your coming out." He looked at MacWolfe, "Is there anything we've forgotten?"

The Pentagon officer shook his head. "You have discussed five targets. A dam, a bridge, railroad tunnel, an air base and a tank farm. All I can ask, gentlemen, is that you understand that every one of them has to go."

LeGrande nodded and turned to Barney, "Anything, Colonel?"

A moment's pause and Barney shook his head. "Clothes and equipment are on the plane and I think that's where we should be."

The others waited for LeGrande to break up the meeting. "You have ahead of you the labors of Hercules. Everything I am and everything I believe in counts upon your success. For myself, I'm saying my thanks in advance."

"I'd like to add mine," MacWolfe said. "It's very old-fashioned and very Victorian, but I've been told that's about all a run-down tank commander really is; accepting that as a fact, if General Le-Grande does not mind, I'd like to drink a toast."

Taken aback at MacWolfe's parlor manner, which so rarely came into view, LeGrande nodded, while Cliff Carter poured drinks and handed them around. LeGrande waited for Mac-Wolfe to propose the toast, "This is your doing, General."

Raising his glass and feeling almost foolish at the pomposity of the act and yet at the same time believing that somehow it was appropriate under the circumstances, LeGrande listened.

"To the brotherhood of arms in defense of the brotherhood of man."

The others started to drink, but LeGrande added, "May you all be as Lazarus, risen from the dead." They were smiling now.

An hour later they stood beside the C-135 at the Andrews Air Base north of the city. Each man stepped forward and shook MacWolfe's hand and then came up to General LeGrande. Joe Brodsky was the first, and LeGrande said, "Do it well, son, and you'll know that you've never done anything more important if you live to be . . ." a grin ". . . as old as I am." Then Zing Miller was standing in front of him and shaking his hand. LeGrande winked, "I'm counting on you to see we get a big bang out of this."

"I'll try to arrange for you to hear it from here, General."

And then Carl Sprague was standing before him. "I feel like someone who's stumbled into a kid's birthday party, sir, but I'm going to put on a funny hat and do my best."

LeGrande smiled, but Sprague worried him even though Janet and Barney were satisfied. He was thinking of only five days of action when he answered, "I'm sure you'll do your best, Carl."

Then there was Hac Quan. "You've never jumped, have you?" the General asked.

The Annamese engineer shook his head. "I feel confident that I shall come down, General."

Both of them were smiling, but again LeGrande had fears. He disliked working without knowing everything, and at this moment there was too much about Hac Quan he could not know. "I'll have a first-class job for an engineer for you when you get back," he promised, knowing that in the vague event that the man did return, he would owe him this much.

Surprised, Hac Quan said, "I'll come back for that, General."

Then Barney Fannin was standing in front of Hyde MacWolfe, and LeGrande saw that they did not shake hands. Even though this was probably the last time they would meet, they would not be hypocrites or liars. To LeGrande's surprise, he heard Barney say, "Tell the boys kind lies about their father." He moved on to LeGrande, smiling wryly. "I'll hear from you while we are in the air?"

LeGrande nodded, "Explain jumping to Hac Quan and see that Brodsky checks out that radio a few times en route."

"Yeah." Then bitterly, "I'd never have thought of that."

"I'm sorry, Barney," and LeGrande found he actually regretted having underestimated the man.

"As you said the other morning when I apologized, 'Don't be, we're happy.'"

They shook hands and then, to the surprise of those in the plane and on the ground who were watching, the General stepped back and saluted. Barney lost his bitter smile as he returned the salute. Mounting the steps of the plane, he looked back toward the city. He seemed to smile and then he looked back at LeGrande and MacWolfe at the base of the steps. "I'll be in touch," he said.

The two generals nodded, and Barney Fannin disappeared into the plane. The flight sergeant pulled the heavy door shut and the ground crew wheeled the steps away. A few minutes later the plane was airborne.

Walking back to the sedan that was waiting for them, Mac-Wolfe said, "We'll be able to follow their progress through the air pics."

LeGrande nodded. "Once they go in, they couldn't be farther away than if we'd sent them to the moon."

"It's about as safe a journey," MacWolfe added.

They were standing by the car now. LeGrande was staring at the trail the plane had left behind which was breaking up now as the breeze caught it. He looked up, and beyond the smoke he could make out a few stars. "One thing you can thank me for when this is all over, Hyde."

His friend looked at him, questioning.

"I'll probably have killed Barney for you." Both men were silent as they stepped into the car. Only when they were in the city once more did LeGrande ask, "What are the chances of getting a promotion for Barney?"

"Not in a hundred years, Dick."

When MacWolfe dropped LeGrande off at Potomac Towers, the two agreed to meet the next morning at the Pentagon to discuss any loose ends which might have been left by the team's departure. Nodding a greeting to the doorman, LeGrande took the elevator and went to his apartment. Only after he stood in front of the door did he recall that Barney had forgotten to return the key. He wished he were not thinking of Barney Fannin.

Janet was already in her robe, listening to a late newscast. The General stood for a moment in the doorway listening as he took off his coat and tie. There was nothing he did not already know that meant anything to him. Over the years he had learned to tune out the local news, the crime news, the unusual occurrences to individuals who were not otherwise news. He had enough trouble keeping up with international affairs without getting bogged down in small details.

Janet turned off the television and asked if he had eaten.

"We ate together and then they left," he said, standing over the coffee table and pouring a drink.

She watched him staring into the glass, and after a moment noticed that the glass was not steady in his hand. "You wish you had gone?" she asked.

"As Barney would say, 'Yeah.' " Then he emptied the glass and touched her hair with the tips of his fingers. "The Old Man said it was time I grew up and let other people do things like this, but I'm not sure that he was right. At what point does a man become so important he can let other people get killed for him?"

Janet reached up and, taking his hand, drew him down to the sofa.

"There's nothing you can do about that decision now," she said. "But there may be something you had better look into tomorrow."

He cocked his head to one side and waited for her to explain.

"There's a tape in that machine," she said, pointing to a tape recorder on the sideboard. "You'd better listen to it."

The General shook his head as he opened his shirt cuffs and drew his sleeves back. "Do I have to?"

She nodded. "It's Lil on the subject of Barney Fannin."

There was a long silence and LeGrande shook his head in disapproval. "You sneaked a tape on her?"

"Listen to it," Janet said, neither in justification nor in apology. Both of them knew what her job was and that she had done it.

Pulling himself off the sofa, LeGrande wearily approached the tape recorder and pressed the button. For twenty minutes he listened to the tape. When he was done, he pressed the rewind and listened to what he had selected a second time.

That was it. I don't know what happened, but Barney didn't make captain when the others did. Dick made it. Hyde made it. The others did. The build-up started for the war, and they went on to major and light colonel and Barney was a first lieutenant. Dick got a regiment and Hyde got a battalion. But Barney stayed an adjutant to a regimental commander. He pushed paper, and no one would let him do anything else. We moved from Fort Sam to Fort Lewis. From Lewis to Wood. Barney remained a lieutenant. He started to get careless. Would make mistakes. Quarrel. A pause. I called my father and asked him to look at Barney's efficiency record, thinking that someone had done Barney dirt. But my father said that I should forget it, and he wouldn't explain.

Pressing the rewind again, the General listened to that portion a third time. When he was done, he pressed the erase and cleared the tape. Janet sat on the sofa watching him. She did not approve of his wiping out the record, but she did not argue because she knew he was deeply troubled. When he turned to her, he asked, "Did you send for Barney's 201 file?"

Janet nodded. "I called G-1 and acted as if it were a routine request because he had been assigned to us."

"And?"

"It's been stripped."

LeGrande waited for her to continue.

"There's a summary sheet of promotions and assignments, but none of the usual papers for a man who's been in service as long as he has. No letters of recommendation or condemnation. No efficiency reports. No comments by anyone for over twenty-five years of service."

"Nothing but the summary sheet?" LeGrande found this hard to accept.

"Nothing," she said.

A low whistle, and he shook his head. "Lil seems to have spotted when things began to go wrong, but she stops there."

Janet nodded. "What about the Old Gray Wolf?"

"Maybe," LeGrande said. "Maybe. That's what we'll be talking about in the morning." He shook his head as if to clear it of the thoughts he did not want and, crossing over to the sofa again, leaned down and kissed her. When they separated, he smiled, "I don't know about you, but I'm ready for bed."

Rising, she leaned over to turn off the light. "I don't know if that's a compliment or if you're just tired." The only answer she received was a sharp swat on the bottom, and when she turned to protest, he kissed her.

The General's driver dropped him off at the Pentagon and drove on to GENOPS headquarters with Janet. LeGrande stood for a moment on the steps of the Mall entrance looking back at the car. Others passed him on their way into the building. Some knew who he was, others did not recognize him in mufti. Looking up at the clear sky, LeGrande knew this was going to be a warm day, and he wished he could go fishing or out on the Cape with Janet. But he strode up the steps and, entering the building, walked past the large counter that stood just behind the door. He continued down one corridor and up a ramp and a change of the colors of the walls until he approached the offices of the Deputy Director of the Defense Intelligence Agency. He paused to look at the framed blue card with white lettering that identified the office. Hyde MacWolfe was going up in the world. LeGrande was about to enter the office when he realized he should have been stopped. Slowly turning about, he saw that two junior officers and two sentries were watching him. Beckoning one of the officers over, he asked, "Is this a security area?"

"Yes, General."

Satisfied that the man recognized him, LeGrande asked, "Then why wasn't I challenged?"

"There were four of us, sir, and we all knew who you were." It was obvious that the young captain was pleased with his answer.

"Do your orders tell you to pass persons you recognize?"

"Not really, sir, but it has become practice."

LeGrande nodded. It was not for him to discipline someone else's command, but he did not approve of the laxity. "Recognition can get a man past?"

"Yes, sir."

"Do you know what Chou En Lai looks like, Captain?"

A long silence, and the young captain admitted, "Yes, General."

LeGrande turned on his heel and entered MacWolfe's office. There was a large reception room with two desks and two couches set against the walls, one to his right and one to his left. Beside each leather couch was a magazine rack. LeGrande glanced at the names he could read from where he stood: *The Army Times, The Armed Forces Journal,* and *The Command and Staff Quarterly.* He wondered how much these would relax visitors to the Defense Intelligence Agency, and as he thought about this, he wondered who would visit the DIA. They bought very little, and that meant they were out of the mainstream of influence where money was important—no salesmen, no lobbyists, no congressmen pressuring for constituents. LeGrande smiled; it was almost as remote as GENOPS, and that was as far removed from the sources of power as he could imagine.

A lieutenant colonel rose from behind one desk. "Can I help you, General?" He was holding out a register, and LeGrande initialed it.

"General MacWolfe is expecting me."

The lieutenant colonel asked if LeGrande would be seated and then he stepped into MacWolfe's office. The General remained standing as the office door at the opposite end of the reception room opened and the Director of Defense Intelligence emerged, looked at LeGrande and nodded. "Something we can do for you, Dick?"

Lieutenant General Martin Brown was almost ten years Le-Grande's senior and a man under whom he had served in Africa as chief of staff. Though they were friends, there was an element of personal respect on LeGrande's side which he would not have granted a contemporary.

"I'll bother Hyde, sir. If he doesn't shake loose, I'll come banging on your door."

The older man smiled, "Fair enough." Then the smile was gone and he said, "The Gray Wolf tells me that your team is on its way."

Not certain just what was expected as an answer to what was not a question, LeGrande said, "Yes, sir."

There was a silence as General Brown picked up some papers from his secretary's desk. He held them in his hand for a moment while he seemed to be trying to make his mind up about something. "I knew Lil MacWolfe's father," he finally said.

Knowing that this had to lead someplace, LeGrande nodded.

"He was a great soldier." It was obvious now that whatever the older General wanted to say, he was finding it difficult. "I had a lot of faith in his judgment."

"I can appreciate that, sir." LeGrande could only wait until the Director fumbled through.

"He didn't think much of Barney Fannin."

And there it was. In a way, LeGrande realized this was an implied criticism of his own judgment. And because it came after the older man's comment that he knew the team had left, he must have been aware that even if LeGrande wished to change the structure of his team, there was nothing he could do about it now. "I have heard that, sir," LeGrande said, believing that this committed him to no position except that of a man who did not accept the wisdom of his elders. He had been in this position in the past and it did not disturb him.

Brown shook his head. "I understand that the Chairman asked you if you were acting for sentimental reasons and you said no." Both were silent as LeGrande considered the fact that the Chairman of the Joint Chiefs as well as the Director of DIA had discussed his selection of Barney Fannin. He wondered where this conversation had led.

"I believe you made a serious error in judgment, Dick," Brown concluded, and then without waiting for any comment, he disappeared into his office.

LeGrande turned back toward MacWolfe's on the other side of the room. He was trying to figure out why General Brown had come out of his office to pass judgment on his decision. As far as LeGrande was concerned, it was no accident that Brown had stepped out of his office just as the spear carrier had disappeared into MacWolfe's. Believing that he could be reading more into what might have been a casual meeting than he should, LeGrande smiled to himself. The Balkan mind was at work, tracing down the reasons why a man cocked his head, smiled or did not smile, coughed, said hello instead of good morning—the basic set of suspicions which turned one upon another and back again until relationships became impossible and a man could not trust even himself.

The spear carrier emerged from MacWolfe's office and said, "The General is expecting you, sir."

LeGrande looked at the man and shook his head. "I told you that five minutes ago, Colonel." Impatiently, he entered his friend's office. It was heavily carpeted and had all of the status symbols, including the flag behind MacWolfe's chair spread to reveal the three stars—white on red. There was a carafe of water with four glasses on a silver tray, telephones in several colors indicating direct lines to important places, four heavy leather chairs and only one chair with wooden arms. The waste basket matched the light gray of the room and the furniture. LeGrande chuckled as he said, "Hyde, you will have to go—you don't match the decor."

Rising from behind his desk, bare except for an in-basket and a small plastic model of a tank, MacWolfe said, "Just jealous. There's always someone who thinks that the brass doesn't work and doesn't deserve what it gets."

"That's right, Hyde. And I'm one of those someones."

Both men were smiling as LeGrande dropped into one of the leather easy chairs.

"Are there any particular problems we can help with at this stage of the game?" MacWolfe was asking.

Very slowly, he nodded. "Tell me what happened to Barney Fannin in 1938."

MacWolfe's head dropped back as if he were trying to see Le Grande from a distance. "I don't get it."

"Nor do I." Then, picking the tack he hoped might work, LeGrande began to press casually, "Is Barney officially assigned to us now?"

"You know that. You asked for the orders to be written that way —Temporary Duty, Detached Service."

"Then can you tell me, Hyde, just why the hell his personnel file was only a summary of posts and promotions?"

There was a long silence as MacWolfe digested what he had just heard. "That's all you got?"

LeGrande nodded. "That's all of it."

The Old Gray Wolf weighed the significance of this and LeGrande could see that he was equally confused. Picking up the phone, MacWolfe snapped, "Get me the AC/S G-1 and not some damned outside man in the skunk works." The two generals stared at each other as they waited. Then MacWolfe was speaking into the phone, "Will, this is Hyde MacWolfe. Colonel Barney Fannin was put on TD with GENOPS and assigned personally to Dick LeGrande. Am I right?" LeGrande recognized the Will as the nickname of the AC/S G-1. "Then why did the 201 file sent there include only a summary of posts and promotions?" LeGrande wished he could hear the answer as he saw MacWolfe look across the desk while he listened and nodded. "That's it? Okay. That's it, then. Thanks." He cradled the phone and continued to stare at LeGrande.

"Will Eberts says that was all they had. The 201 was lost twice." A pause, and then he added, "A long time ago and then again recently."

LeGrande weighed what he had just heard with care. He did not believe it, but he could see that MacWolfe was prepared to accept the answer he had been given. He was trying to decide if he should press MacWolfe to help him break through the obvious cover-up or if he should let his friend off the hook and go elsewhere for help. "Did Eberts know that we had asked for that file yesterday?"

MacWolfe nodded. "He seemed to."

Now LeGrande was more convinced he was being fed a story; it had to be something out of the ordinary for the AC/S G-1 to even be aware of the transfer of the personnel records of a colonel, and especially one who was on the way down. His thoughts drifted back to his conversation with General Brown, and he was more than ever convinced Brown had tried to tell him something. Or had he? Disapproval of Barney Fannin by Brown, by Lil's father, now retired, and of course, the interest of the Chairman in Barney. Knowing the Chairman as well as he did, LeGrande wondered if he had not been warned again to lay off pushing the subject of Barney Fannin and to live with what he knew. The summary 201 had been sent with the knowledge of the AC/S. Had the Chairman known about this also? LeGrande thought that conclusion reasonable if one took into account the fact that the assignment of Barney had been a subject for discussion on policy levels.

"Why were you curious about 1938, Dick?" MacWolfe asked, and LeGrande wondered if he could tell his friend that his interest was predicated on a covertly taped conversation with the Pentagon officer's own wife.

"It's when he started falling behind in promotions. From that year on the summary shows he was promoted each time he was due to be dropped as over-age in grade. He's just hung on by his teeth since '38, and I want to know why." Pulling himself out of the overstuffed chair, LeGrande said, "I'll be talking to you later."

"Wait a minute," MacWolfe said. "There were some things we were going to go over this morning."

"They'll keep until I get this one settled." Then LeGrande walked out of the office, aware that he had left a startled and puzzled MacWolfe behind. He believed that MacWolfe really did not know what he wanted to find out but that his own manner of leaving would make those who did know aware that he was not yet accepting the story of the lost 201.

In the reception room of the DIA directors, LeGrande paused at the desk of the lieutenant colonel. "May I see your copy of the phone book?" he asked as he picked up the long yellow book listing the Pentagon officers. Flipping it open, he quickly found the number he was looking for. He turned the phone around so that it was facing him as the lieutenant colonel asked, "Can I dial it for you, General?"

LeGrande shook his head, brushing off the obvious attempt to learn whom he was calling. Always checking up. With his face set and his jaw muscles tight as he weighed what he was doing, he dialed quickly.

"This is General Richard LeGrande. I am in the building. May I see him now?" Then he listened to what seemed to be a reasonable excuse. The Old Man was at the White House. "Can you tell me when I can see him?" And he was being told that no appointment could be made before the next morning. "Will you tell him that I have asked for an appointment and that I said I believe it is important." He was informed the message would be delivered and he hung up. MacWolfe was standing in the doorway looking at him.

LeGrande nodded sadly, "Some days you can't make a dime." They walked out of the office together and down the long corridor. A young messenger on a three-wheeled bike almost bumped into them and LeGrande was tempted to eat him out when he remembered that he was not a Pentagon officer, but rather a castoff, one of the least of humans around this oversized and uniquely shaped outhouse.

"Barney in '38. What do you think it'll get you, Dick?" MacWolfe asked.

It was a reasonable question, and if there had been a lot of time to pursue his goal, it would have made sense. But with the time left to him before his team jumped in, and with the radio his only contact, any explanation made little sense. "I'm trying to get a better understanding of the team and how it may or may not function."

"Doesn't make complete sense when you realize that once they leave the joe hole of that plane . . ."

"Joe holes are passé. They walk out the door these days."

"Don't get technical with me. Once they've jumped, there isn't a damned thing you can do."

They were in front of the snack bar now and both stopped to buy coffee. They remained silent until they had left the group around the cash register and those who were eating breakfast or drinking coffee at the stand-up tables.

"I'm not giving up all contact," LeGrande said, "but even if I were, I have to know what I can expect in case I must shift my tactics and come up with something else."

MacWolfe crushed the empty coffee cup in his hand and dropped it into a waste basket. "You won't have time to do much more than blow your nose if this team falls on its face."

Tossing his cup after MacWolfe's and missing the basket, LeGrande shrugged. "If I've only got time to blow my nose, I've got to be ready to."

"And knowing about something that happened in '38 to Barney Fannin, boy FU who went from riches to rags, will help you get ready to blow your nose?"

"I don't know if it will or it won't, but with what is facing us if this team fails, can I leave a single turn unstoned?"

They were at the Mall entrance now and standing on the steps leading down to the street. MacWolfe watched two cars with diplomatic license plates drive up and he looked at LeGrande. "Play it out to the end of the string, Dick. I hope you don't find anything there, but you've got to play it."

Both of them were watching the two ANZAC representatives mount the stairs of the building, and they knew that the implications of failure were greater than they wished to contemplate.

THE WESTERN PACIFIC •

THE GIANT SILVER JET raced through the night toward Clark Field in the Philippines. To Barney Fannin, sitting alone in the back of the darkened plane, staring out of the window into the night, Clark was a field of memories. He could recall that day when a sentry dashed into the small wooden house at Fort Leonard Wood and stammered that the Japs had attacked. Lil had shaken her head in disbelief and then turned on the radio with the comment, "They wouldn't dare." But they had dared. Barney recalled the impact of the radio reporter from Clark Field describing the first bombing in detail as the Japs strafed the helpless crews trying to climb their outdated planes into the air. He recalled his own anger as he had picked up the phone and spilled his orders as adjutant to the duty officer. Double the guard. Cancel all leaves. Stop all discharges. Then he and Lil had settled back to listen to the rest of the news. Hickam and Clark. Old memories. Scarred and deep. A light beyond the plane, and he realized he was staring at a star. There were very few visible. Ahead of him in the front of the plane, he made out the figure of Zing Miller playing cards with Joe Brodsky and winning fanciful millions from the innocent young private who did not know that Zing was a professional. Hac Quan lay sprawled across several seats, his eyes closed. Fannin stared at the man for a long time. Twice during the day he had been tempted to talk to the Vietnamese engineer. He knew he should try to learn why the man was along, what his motives were in coming, but somehow, Barney did not want to think of Hac Quan until he had to.

A light behind him, and Carl Sprague emerged from the lavatory. He stood beside the Colonel's seat for a moment, looking out of the window. "Miller asked me if I'd write him a policy—life insurance. I agreed for a joke, and then he said he didn't know who he'd leave it to." To Carl Sprague there was something inordinately sad in being as alone as Miller.

Barney merely nodded because he felt much as Zing. The boys would be taken care of by Lil and Hyde, and his insurance would help them further if they needed it. But he was not fool enough to believe that anyone really needed Barney Fannin. He looked up at Sprague. "His name's Zing, Carl. I don't think a man should go out as just another Miller when he's at least earned a nickname."

"Zing," Sprague repeated. "I'll remember that, Colonel."

Sprague walked down between the seats to the table where Miller had just won another million dollars in gold payable on demand from Joe Brodsky. Joe tossed out the cards for a third hand without comment. From the rear of the plane where he was watching, Barney smiled as he heard Zing explain the stakes. He looked once more out at the far sky as the conversation drifted to the back of the plane—"payable on demand."

There were very few stars in the sky.

WASHINGTON, D.C. ●

THE CHAIRMAN of the Joint Chiefs of Staff was a short, stocky man, broad-shouldered and gray-haired. His strong hands closed on the handle of the briefcase which rested in his lap and he stared straight ahead in the car. Only half an hour earlier the older man's secretary had called to tell LeGrande he might drive the Chairman home.

Suddenly, without looking at his companion, the old General snapped, "I was told what you wanted to talk to me about was important, Richard."

Relaxing now, LeGrande said, "I think it is, sir." He paused to consider how he should best begin. "I am not hedging that statement, sir, when I say there are those who would not agree with me."

The older man was growing impatient. He spent much of his day being briefed, and the one thing he believed he had the right to expect of his subordinates was a clear, concise statement of any problem. It was the difference between a good staff officer and a poor one.

"I have been told, sir, that Colonel Barney Fannin's 201 file has been lost twice. Once before the war and once since. I do not believe that, and I believe that I have the right to know what is in that file because my decisions in the next few days must be made with full knowledge of anything that may have meaning to my assignment."

There was a long silence as the car inched through traffic, and the sergeant driving rode his horn for half a block, trying to clear a path. The Chairman shook his head, impatient with the intrusion on his thinking.

"G-1 told you that file was lost?"

"Yes, sir. General MacWolfe asked and relayed the information to me."

"Then you walked out of his office as if nothing else was important and you did not even bother to return to your own office to place your request for a meeting with me. Instead, you showed your petulance by phoning me from Hyde's outer office."

LeGrande understood that he was being told that no detail had been overlooked before he had been granted this interview. "I do not agree with the description of my action, sir. I have the right to know the details about Fannin or he should not have been assigned to me at all."

There was another silence, and the older man continued to stare straight ahead of him. Finally he said, "You may be right, Richard. But I am curious. Would you have insisted upon assigning Colonel Fannin to this important mission if you had known that his file had been lost?"

Realizing that a trap door had just been opened under him, LeGrande debated his answer. If he said "no" then he was admitting that he had been wrong in the first place because he had acted without full knowledge of Barney Fannin and his past. If he said "yes" then he would be admitting that he did not need that file.

"What you are asking is if I have stopped beating my wife, sir," he said softly.

A grunt as the older man appreciated the fact that LeGrande had seen the trap.

"Do you really believe that this file is important, Richard?" backing away from his own question.

"Something happened to Colonel Fannin about 1938 which changed his entire career, sir. It must have been significant because he was the most promising junior officer I ever met. I want to know if it will in any way affect what he is about to undertake."

The older man's head nodded almost imperceptibly. "You are right. The file is not lost. The orders to say it had been lost were placed in the file itself, so no one has done anything other than what he was told to do."

"I understand, sir."

A snort. "No one asked for your understanding, General." A silence and then the older man shook his head. "The file was closed by General Rhode to protect his daughter. I shall ask his permission to open it to you because I believe he has the right to be consulted." A moment of silence and the Chairman added, "There is nothing in the file which would have hurt anyone but Colonel Fannin, and that would have embarrassed those near to him."

About to say that he understood, LeGrande remembered in time that he had just had his hand bitten off for saying that.

"You may say that you understand this," the older man continued, "because this warrants your understanding."

"Yes, sir." And LeGrande was smiling. And even though the Chairman was not, he believed that somehow he was aware of the humor of the situation.

But what the Chairman said next indicated he was not thinking of anything funny. "A tragedy: Fannin. The effort to save him may have been wrong. Perhaps he should have been spun off into civilian life."

"Perhaps into an independent agency," LeGrande added.

Slowly the old General turned and looked at LeGrande. "Purgatory is a place or state of temporary punishment. There are those who would define it as a pause while waiting for expiatory purification."

Unable to control himself, LeGrande laughed loudly. "How long, Oh Lord?" But he stopped laughing when he realized that the Chairman was taking his question seriously.

"When the purification has been completed. Both personal and professional."

The younger officer nodded, knowing he had been put in his place. He could start up the ladder again when he separated from Janet and when he was prepared to give up his fight for an independent agency to control irregular warfare. The quarrel between the two Generals on this issue was much too deep to be discussed at this moment, when both of them had other responsibilities, but both were aware that it was Richard LeGrande as director of an independent agency who was keeping guerrilla and sabotage operations out of the Pentagon's cold, formal and unimaginative hands.

They were pulling up in front of the General's home at Fort Meyers. The Chairman brushed aside their quarrel as the driver stopped the car and opened the door. "I shall call General Rhode at the Cape, where he is living for the summer, and I will let you know his answer."

Both of them stepped out of the car and LeGrande stood back as the other man started up the walk to the house. He paused and looked back. "The Sergeant will drive you wherever you wish to go, Richard." A pause, as if there was something he was trying to say. "Perhaps a man can justify purgatory to himself. I suppose it really depends upon his own evaluation of the venality of his sins." Then he continued up the walk.

LeGrande smiled as he slipped into the car again and the driver closed the door. "Potomac Towers on the Mount Vernon Highway south of Alexandria," the General ordered, thinking of what Janet's reactions would be when he reported his drive with the Chairman.

However, when he arrived home, they discussed her meeting with MacWolfe's aide first.

Janet waited until the General had made himself comfortable, tie off, shirt sleeves rolled up and feet on the sofa. She had poured a drink for him, and now both of them were on their second, waiting for dinner to warm up on the stove.

"The Old Gray Wolf's Indian drove me home," she said, watching him twist about on the sofa so that he could get a better look at her as she dropped another ice cube in her drink.

"What did he want?"

"The Pentagon has received two calls from Columbus, Ohio, asking about Colonel Barney Fannin."

LeGrande tried to weigh the significance of this.

"Mrs. Carl Sprague," she said, placing the calls into context for him. "Sprague told people at his office that he was asked by Mrs. Williams to go to Washington to see a dying Colonel Fannin."

Impatient to see where this was leading, the General snapped, "Well?"

Realizing that he was tired, she went quickly to the core of the problem. "Colonel Fannin was reported killed in the same plane as Carl Sprague, and his wife thinks that something is fishy."

LeGrande watched as Janet settled into an easy chair opposite him. "The cover story that brought him here and the one that killed him . . ."

"Were not too well coordinated," she said bluntly. "I am Mrs. Williams and Harry was given the cover job."

LeGrande sipped his Scotch thoughtfully. "Someone goofed."

"Yes, *mon général,* and his name is LeGrande. He mixed operations and personnel work without letting either one take direct responsibility." She was lighting a cigarette now, and he watched as the match lighted up the flat of her cheek.

"*Mea culpa,*" he said without smiling. "Too fast. We always have to move too fast." Then, before she could comment, he added, "But that does not relieve me of the responsibility."

Again Janet agreed.

"What did they tell her?" He was trying to figure out how to patch a blowout in security.

"They said they would look into the matter and call her back."

LeGrande nodded. "And they expect us to do that?"

"It's your tea party. You invited the guests."

He set the glass down on the coffee table and sat upright. "I have a simple solution."

Janet waited to hear what he had in mind, and after a moment he realized that she was not going to ask him.

"It's a job for personnel."

She stared for a moment at the smoke rising from the cigarette in her hand. "That's your idea of a simple solution?"

LeGrande grinned. "Now the authority matches the responsibility and everything is coordinated."

Softly and with affection, she said, "You are a bastard, Richard."

Nodding his complete agreement, he rose and fixed himself another drink. "And what does the Director of Personnel propose to do about Mrs. Carl Sprague? She has to be answered before she goes to the newspapers."

"Personnel has had Mrs. Williams call Mrs. Carl Sprague and tell her that the Colonel was dying and that Mr. Carl Sprague had asked to take the Colonel home with him for a couple of weeks."

LeGrande shook his head. "Mrs. Williams is skating on pretty thin ice and may land on her cute fanny. Barney wasn't that close to Sprague."

Janet agreed. "But Mrs. Carl Sprague cannot deny that he thought a lot of his old buddy and might have made the grand gesture." She thought a moment and then added, "And if he doesn't return, she will go through life thinking how noble of her Carl, and she will never know how noble he actually was." Janet thought about the proposition and said sadly, "There's a kind of irony in that."

He held out a hand and she pulled herself up from the easy chair. They stood together for a moment, his hand on her cheek as he kissed her. Then she disappeared into the kitchen to check her dinner on the stove. LeGrande looked after her, but he was thinking about Mrs. Carl Sprague and wondering what he would do if the hole in the cover story came unplugged. That was a bridge he would jump off when he came to it.

SAIGON ●

THE SPRAWLING CITY lay impaled by the morning sun on the right bank of the Saigon River for which it was named. Overflowing its southern boundary, the Chinese Arroyo and the Arroyo of the Avalanche on the north, the whole area appeared to be in movement. The large port developed by the French was occupied with naval vessels and supply ships surrounded by small craft of every description plying the muddy waters. Once Saigon had been enclosed by its rivers and arroyos, but in the long years of war, it had been swelled by refugees and foreigners; these came to flee from or to fight its battles, and the city now extended past its waterways. The French arrived in the middle of the nineteenth century and threw out the Chinese, whose hold had always been tenuous. The French in turn gave way in 1940 to the Japanese, who built the large Saigon airport which served southern Vietnam. Then the French returned, only to be hurled out in the bloody war which ended with Dienbienphu. Now there was fighting again. To the Annamese, the Chinese and the Europeans who called the city their home, it seemed as if the fighting had never really stopped. Almost a quarter of a century with small bands of men tearing the villages from the earth and destroying the rice paddies. Few in Saigon could remember when there had been peace. Even fewer were really deeply concerned about the war. Until the bomb burst in the street or the automatic weapon coughed in the night, the war belonged to someone else. Very few bothered to look up as the jet transport passed over the river and settled swiftly and smoothly down on the newly paved runway. Foreign planes came to Saigon every day now. No single one seemed more important than any other.

Inside the plane, Colonel Barney Fannin and the men who had traveled almost twelve thousand miles with him were aware that they were almost at the end of their journey. They had gained a day at the International Date Line, and what was night across the world in Washington was morning now. Their world was somehow upside down.

Soon after they had left Clark Field in the Philippines, the Colonel had gathered his team about him and reviewed the details of a safe parachute jump. He did not yet know the kind of plane they would be taking over the valley to the north, but he assumed they would be using a static line. With care each man tried on the single chute the Colonel had commandeered at Clark. Each man went through the motions—the stomp to the open door, the spring up ten inches and out thirty and the fall from a plane seat to the hard plane floor—until he had remembered or learned for the first time the points of the fall from shoulder to hip to thigh to calf and the roll which kept his legs from being broken. Then he showed them how to open the quick release catch which dropped the harness. Carefully, Fannin explained the count and the sudden shock they could expect when the risers jerked past their heads and the nylon canopy filled with air. He did not explain the need to count from one thousand to four thousand by thousands before they pulled the emergency chute. None of them was going to be wearing an emergency chute; they were carrying too much equipment to waste the chest space on an insurance policy.

Now that they were on the ground in Saigon, Barney shoved the chute under a seat and out of sight from any prying eyes. He and his men were in Saigon and they were going north. Where and when and why were secrets he had to fight to keep until they stepped out of the door of the plane over the valley of the Song Koi.

Sitting back in his seat and watching the military police detachment with its white helmets and belts form about the plane, he wondered if the special security ordered out of Washington was actually security. Looking about, he saw another plane nearby. He called the MP sergeant aboard the plane and a few moments later the detachment took its position around the other plane. Barney did not know if he had set up his decoy too late or not, but there was nothing to be lost by trying.

He told the flight attendant to close the plane door and then he sat down once more. Morning, and he had to wait for darkness. Leaning his head back on the seat, he thought for the thousandth time since leaving Washington of a bridge, an airfield, a dam, a tank farm and a railroad tunnel. A bridge, an airfield, a dam, a tank farm and a railroad tunnel. One a day for five days and a man becomes regular. Then he should taper off with the proper advice of his doctor. If not, the results could be damaging. A bridge, an airfield, a dam, a tank farm and a railroad tunnel. He closed his eyes as he tried to recall the details of each as it had been sketched out from the recon photo. He knew that he could never fully trust a cross-section drawing of an installation which had been photographed from above at a hundred thousand feet.

Some place back in Washington, he knew, more photos were sitting on desks waiting to be read by people who did not need them as badly as he did.

He had thought during the flight of asking for a set, and then he had changed his mind. The only person who was to be told of their mission in Saigon was the pilot who would fly them north, and he had not yet been briefed. To single out a set of photos and deliver them to a plane would mean their being developed in Saigon and passed from hand to hand before eyes which might be curious.

Barney Fannin heard the pilot as he emerged from the flight compartment and started for the door of the plane. "You will remain in the plane, Captain, until I have left it. Then you will take on gasoline and return to Clark Field."

Fannin did not even bother to open his eyes and look at the pilot or the plane crew. He was giving the orders he had agreed upon with LeGrande and MacWolfe and which he knew would be backed to the extent of confining the pilot and crew to Clark Field for five days after their arrival. But he knew he did not have to reveal this surprise now. He waited a moment and heard the captain return to the front of the plane.

Opening his eyes, he took inventory of his team. Carl Sprague was sitting at the table where he had lost five million dollars to Zing Miller. He was writing a letter to his wife which Fannin knew would never be mailed. Zing was sprawled out across several seats telling Joe Brodsky about a broad he had known in KC who had the biggest tits he had ever seen. "She wasn't dressed, she was engineered. Cantilevered. And as an old demolitions man, I felt it my duty to bring all that superstructure down."

Fannin could see the far-away look in Joe Brodsky's eyes as he tried to picture for himself the woman Zing was lying about. Nearby, Hac Quan sat bolt upright in a seat, staring out of the window at the confusion on the airfield: planes coming and going, trucks hauling supplies and gasoline, passengers scurrying under the wings of the big birds, ignited jets flashing as they screeched like scalded ducks. Barney did not know what to make of Hac Quan. He was different from the others. He had come for different reasons. Barney wished he could learn what they were, but he did not think he could learn them here. He would discover them late—he hoped not too late. He had enough ahead of him that he did not want surprises. Hac Quan. Engineer. French-educated. Hong Kong-trained. He said he had never jumped before, but he had slipped the chute on with an experienced hand. Either he lied well or he learned fast—Barney Fannin could not be sure. He would know more when he transferred their supplies to the other plane and broke open the crate of weapons. Barney was sure he could tell a man's training by the way he picked up a weapon; he would either do it confidently, or diffidently because it was not something he had slept with and lived by. Barney smiled as he considered the difference between the way most men handled their wives or someone else's. It all depended on what you had slept with and how comfortable you felt with it.

Behind him he heard the door of the plane open and he sprang to his feet toward a middle-aged man in fatigue clothes, wings on his chest and a silver oak leaf on his collar. Before the man could enter the plane, Fannin was blocking his path.

"I'm looking for Colonel Fannin," the pilot explained.

"Why?"

Shoving his hand into his pocket, the Lieutenant Colonel pulled out a mimeographed sheet and handed it to Fannin. Quickly unfolding the paper, Fannin read the man's orders. Cursing the damned fool who had made them so specific, he handed them back after a second glance to see the name—Maynard. "You found Colonel Fannin." He looked about. "There's a flight crew up front there. Will you lock them in and see that they have their listening gear off?"

Colonel Maynard, a red-haired man, nodded. He did not know what he had been assigned to, but he was willing to go along for the time being until he knew more. He had been told he was volunteering, but even the General who told him admitted he did not know what it was all about. Some damned-fool business cooked up in the Pentagon that could only end in a snafu. Assuring himself that the crew was excluded from the cabin of the plane, Maynard ambled back to Fannin. "You are all buttoned in, Colonel."

Fannin nodded. "You bring a map with you?"

Maynard shook his head. "No one suggested I might need one."

For a moment, Fannin considered the problem. "Pick up a set of maps for Laos, a set for Cambodia, for North Vietnam, for Hong Kong, for Burma and for good measure a set for the Philippines. When you have them, we can talk."

Slipping his hand inside his fatigues, the officer scratched his stomach. "That's a hell of a lot of maps."

"We're going on a guided tour," Fannin informed him, and then he concluded the meeting by sitting down in his seat and closing his eyes. He knew that Maynard was not a fool. The maps obviously were to cover some specific area. But so long as the full list was drawn, no one would be able to pinpoint that area. Barney smiled to himself. Another few days around Dick Le-Grande and Harry Fuller and he would not have been able to think straight. Thinking of the days he had spent at GENOPS, Barney was pleased that he was half a world away. Almost there. A bridge, an airfield, a dam, a tank farm and a railroad tunnel. He almost smiled. It had the touch of a ballad if he could think of any more lines.

An hour later, with stacks of maps beside them, Barney Fannin pointed out the drop zone to Colonel Maynard. The Air Force officer looked at the spot, noted the broken country leading into the valley and the place where the Army officer wished to be dropped.

"Any problem?" Fannin asked.

There was a moment of thought and then Maynard shook his head. "Not for me."

"And for us?"

"I can't promise to drop you on a dime."

The two were apart from the team, speaking softly so that they would not be overheard.

"Lay it out neatly."

"I'm flying at several hundred miles an hour at night over a spot on a map that I have never seen before. I will be going in a straight line, and at the right second you will all have to bail out. If I've drifted a minute or two off course or if you delay a few seconds, you are not on the spot you want. Maybe miles apart."

"Can't you circle and drop us?"

"If this was a tactical jump with a company or a fighting unit, there would be no need to keep it a secret, but if I circle—radar. You'd be pinpointed before you hit the ground." Then he added, "There's a moon, you know."

"We didn't pick this schedule, but we'll have to live with it. As a chaplain once told me before a jump—you do the best you can and leave the rest to God." Then he started to laugh, "Barney Fannin, Chaplain Corps."

WASHINGTON, D.C. ●

CHARLES BOYER had almost made up his mind to kiss Bette Davis when the telephone rang. A moment and it rang again.

Janet reached out and picked up the small crystal-encased clock on the end table beside her chair as the phone rang a fourth time. "It's almost midnight, *mon général,* and you have a mission in the field."

The phone had just rung a fifth time when LeGrande answered it and identified himself. Janet watched as he sucked in one cheek and considered what he was hearing. "I'll be home," he said, concluding the conversation. Slipping back onto the sofa, he asked, "Did he kiss her?"

Deciding to ignore the question, Janet asked, "Which blonde was it this time?"

Without taking his eyes off the small screen where Charles Boyer's insane wife was threatening Bette Davis, LeGrande explained, "That lost 201 is on its way over now." Then Charles Boyer was attacking his wife, but the action was off screen.

LeGrande looked at Janet as she sat with her feet curled up under her, the blue silk negligee he had bought her for Christmas pulled tight as if she were cold. Her hair seemed almost auburn with the soft yellow of the lamp shining on it. From were he lay sprawled on the sofa, he could barely make out the first few flecks of gray in her hair. She was smoking a cigarette.

"They are only bringing over one document," LeGrande told her.

She nodded. "That means the Chairman called General Rhode, who probably couldn't care less about Barney Fannin's career now that Lil is married to Hyde."

LeGrande was not so certain. "If that were the case, then why wasn't the file brought up to date and completed?"

At times Janet thought she showed great patience with the General's naïveté. "Because," she explained as if to a child, "General Rhode classified that material years ago and no one ever pressed for it until now." She smiled as she added, "Like too many other things in this big and wicked city, nobody gave a damn."

Bette Davis was now being arrested with the warning that she say nothing that could jeopardize her own defense. No one was telling her what she had done wrong, and she looked so very sad. Fifteen minutes and two commercials later, Charles Boyer died ever so nobly of poison he had taken to save Bette Davis's good name. Then the man she had met in the first reel was proposing to her as she sailed away from wicked France. The doorbell chimed.

LeGrande turned off the television with a sigh. "The Late Late Movie has a John Wayne war picture." He crossed to the door and opened it. A middle-aged general staff major in uniform stood at the door, his garrison cap in hand and an attaché case under his arm.

"I believe G-1 called you, sir."

Nodding, LeGrande stepped aside. The Major entered, introducing himself. "I'm Major Salvador Keen of G-1."

LeGrande introduced Janet, who remained where she was. At

first the Major seemed embarrassed, and then Janet saw that the flush on his face was normal, his jowls heavy and his bull neck squeezed by a tight collar.

Keen placed his hat on the coffee table and, setting the attaché case beside it, flipped open the lid and handed LeGrande an envelope. "If you will sign this, General."

The General turned the envelope over and noted the curious classification—*For the eyes of General LeGrande only*. Reaching for his pen, he found he did not have it in his shirt pocket and accepted the one proffered by Keen. Initialing the envelope, Le-Grande opened it and quickly turned to the last page of the document. Twenty-five pages, single-spaced.

"I have orders to wait for that document, General," Keen informed him.

LeGrande nodded and smiled at Janet. "Will you offer the Major a drink, dear, while I see what dire doings we have at hand." With that he opened the French doors that led to the balcony, and sought the light switch. Stepping out, he closed the door behind him and sank into the iron-framed chaise.

The document was dated 18 September, 1938. Looking back to the end, LeGrande read the signatures of the Board of Inquiry. Three of them meant nothing to him. One who was then a colonel had gone on to earn five stars, while another who was then a major had been killed in Normandy, a brigadier. Honorable men. Settling back in the chaise, LeGrande began to read.

Lieutenant Barney Fannin—and all of the identification—had been brought up on charges. On a stormy night in the Mississippi Delta, the platoon under his command had lost the raft it had built and was marooned on a silt and quicksand island near the river's mouth. Flood time and the river rising. Convinced his men could cross, Lieutenant Fannin had made them tie their belts together and form a chain, passing one companion on to the next through the swift current of the rising river . A man slipped loose and was lost in the darkness. And then another. Names given and serial numbers. Finally, Lieutenant Fannin had his men secured on land again. A quick reconnaissance of the spot revealed that instead of reaching the mainland he had led them to a second silt island, more unstable, with the water rising in flood stage. Another hour and there would be no island. Lieutenant Fannin decided that he would form another chain. Man linked to man and passed once more to what he was convinced had to be the shore in the distance. Five men refused to attempt the crossing. They could not swim. They had seen the loss of their companions. Lieutenant Fannin had argued with them, pleaded with them, threatened them. But the men were afraid. Each deposition made at the inquiry revealed that the five men were afraid. They refused to try crossing the river a second time. Finally, leaving the five behind, Lieutenant Fannin had made the crossing with the remaining eighteen men. The river had risen. Four of the five bodies were never recovered. The fifth was found bloated and dead downstream three days later.

The conclusions were simple and obvious. Lieutenant Barney Fannin had been in command. He had been armed. He had not been able to lead his men to safety. He had not been able to bring them out of their panic. He had not shot one as an example and driven the others off the island. Instead, he had abandoned them to the river, the storm and their fears.

Before he even looked at the defense's summary, LeGrande closed his eyes and tried to reconstruct the circumstances. 1938. Army Regulars. Depression men swept into uniform by legitimate hunger. Possibly one real soldier among the five. He looked once more at the serial numbers. Two of the five had been in for more than twenty years, if he could recall the time schedule of issuing numbers. The night—dark. The storm—high, and the roaring river devouring the edges of the island that was not really an island. Maneuvers to train when there was not the proper equipment or the noncoms to instruct. Barney Fannin recently out of West Point where he had been a football player and a scholar. The Man Most Likely to . . .

LeGrande wondered what he would have done that night had he been the lieutenant. Hoping he could find something to assure himself he would have done what Barney did, he read Barney's defense. If he had remained, he would have endangered the lives of those who wished to be saved. He had chosen what he thought was the best for the most men.

Whistling softly, LeGrande shook his head. He did not even need to read the rest of the hearing. Barney Fannin had not assumed that he was responsible for all of his men. One of those lives he had saved at the cost of five others was his own. American military tradition will not allow an officer to abandon his men. It is not in the rule books, but it is understood wherever men gather who have held command. The commander's word is absolute in action. It is his responsibility to see that it is obeyed. LeGrande knew that there were no alternatives to this. Nothing Barney Fannin said would ever change the fact of what he did. Nowhere did the investigation even question the deaths of the two men swept away in crossing. But five men who had been abandoned by a commander had died and he had lived.

Having read the transcripts of a thousand hearings, General LeGrande knew the rest was formality. He had found the core of it, the flaw in Colonel Barney Fannin. As he held the document in his hand, Richard LoCrando somehow wished he had never read it. An old line of sentimental poetry came back from the fringes of his mind—*nor all thy tears wash out a word of it.*

Barney Fannin who knew and understood battle. Barney Fannin who could plan and fight. Barney Fannin who was not afraid of anything alive or dead. Barney Fannin could not lead.

Sighing, LeGrande crushed the document in his hand. Lil had said melodramatically that Barney could lead men to hell and back. With his own modification, Hyde MacWolfe had said the same thing. LeGrande agreed that Barney could travel the road to hell, but he had no assurance that anyone would follow.

For a moment LeGrande tried to recall the assignments that Barney had held after 1938. The adjutant. The troop commander who never brought his men into battle. The staff officer who hated paper work. The retreat in Korea. The depots and the training commands. Barney Fannin knew and Barney Fannin could teach. Only Richard LeGrande had thought he could lead.

Rising from the chaise, the General thought of the men who had shaken hands with him as they boarded the plane for Saigon: Joe Brodsky, Zing Miller, Carl Sprague and Hac Quan. He brushed away their faces because he realized that he was not focusing on what was really important—a bridge, a dam, an airfield, a tank farm and a railroad tunnel. Suddenly, as if he could hear the loud, shrill sound of a diesel engine, LeGrande's hands went up to his ears. He closed his eyes and tried to block out the night and the lights on the river below. When he opened his eyes again, he could barely see the few stars to the east. He had to make a choice now. He looked at his watch. Two in the morning. Two in the afternoon in Saigon. Barney Fannin would be curled up in the plane waiting on the apron for darkness. Colonel Barney Fannin.

LeGrande looked at the file crushed in his hand and for a moment was tempted to throw the papers into the river and tell himself they never existed. But he knew they did, and so did too many others, men who hated Barney Fannin, and men who had brought him along slowly as if he were a cripple who needed a hand, promoting him each time he would have been retired because of his age. Barney Fannin. The General cursed aloud. Barney was not a cripple. He had made his decision. He had lived with it. And he had never had a chance to redeem himself. This was what LeGrande wanted to believe, but he had difficulty telling himself that this was true. From where Richard LeGrande stood, from what he knew and what he believed, Barney Fannin had been wrong that night on the river. His judgment had been faulty or flawed. But it had been his judgment. What LeGrande had to live with or reject was the fact that Barney Fannin would have to make decisions and that those decisions would affect the operation in the valley of the Song Koi. If they were wrong there would be war. But the General had to decide it his way and the way of the Army was the only way. He knew what the Chairman would have said. He knew what Hyde MacWolfe would have said. In fact, they had all said it in one way or another already. Now, with all of the facts before him for the first time, he had to make up his own mind if there was more than one way in which a man could command a mission.

LeGrande opened the French doors and stepped into the living room. Janet and Major Keen were sitting with drinks before them.

Keen came to his feet when he saw the General.

"Thank you," LeGrande said, as he placed the Court of Inquiry Report back into its envelope and, sealing it, handed the envelope to Keen.

The staff officer accepted the envelope and waited. "General Eberts thought you might have some orders, sir."

LeGrande shook his head. "I have none that concern G-1 at this time." Then he smiled, "Thanks for bringing the file over, and tell General Eberts I am pleased he was able to find it again." Seeing that Keen obviously was not in on the secret, LeGrande said, "Just tell him that."

"Yes, sir," and the Major left LeGrande alone with Janet.

For a long time neither of them said anything. Then Janet knew that he did not want to talk about what he had learned.

"It's getting late," she said.

He crossed the room and extended a hand, helping her to her feet. When he kissed her, she could see that he was sad. A moment later, he turned off the television and said, "I'll be with you in a minute." She watched as he walked out onto the balcony again. She could make out his tall figure in the darkness, the white of his shirt in the shadows. He was leaning with his elbows on the railing and staring at the stars. She left him that way and went into the kitchen to make a pot of coffee. When he wanted to talk, she would be waiting for him.

SAIGON •

SHORTLY AFTER DARK, Barney Fannin and his team moved from the large jet transport to a C-123 seated nearby on the runway. The weapons crates were opened and each man took the one he had selected back at the safe-house in Virginia. A side-arm and a carbine or submachine gun or automatic rifle. All of them carried knives, and Barney Fannin placed a garrote beside his other weapons. It was obvious that each man knew the weapons he had chosen. Barney noted the assurance with which the Annamese selected his, and when Hac Quan saw the American watching him, he smiled.

"It's only hardware."

Then they changed their clothes, leaving behind them all personal effects—rings, wallets and even money. They had selected black jackets and dark wool trousers. The last case was opened and each man took the seventy-five pounds of plastic explosives he was going to jump with. Zing Miller carried a small bag of primer cord, short fuses and two electric igniters. The bazooka was handed to Joe Brodsky, who would carry it down strapped to his leg. His radio was strapped on his chest.

Then Barney Fannin opened the bottle of rubber-covered pills and passed two to each man. Kept in the mouth, they could do no damage. If swallowed intact, they would pass through the system and out. If bitten, the glass beneath the rubber would scratch the back of a man's throat and he would be dead in seconds. "No world-wide circus trials," LeGrande had said. And they had agreed. "Only a dead man does not talk," he had explained. "No man can resist drugs." And they had said they understood. Now each put his two pills where he could best reach them—in the upper pocket of his jacket. "From the time you hit the ground," Barney said, "remember that pill." Then he opened the second bottle and passed a handful of pep pills to each man to dump into his trouser pocket. After that he passed out plain wrist watches, small compact food bars and the food capsules. Five days on two pocketsful of food.

They were ready now. There was nothing more they could do in Saigon. None of them had seen the city. Each of them knew he probably never would. Lieutenant Colonel Maynard, who had watched the preparations in the belly of the plane, handed each of the team a parachute. None put it on yet, because they had a long flight before them and Maynard agreed to give them half an hour's notice before the jump. He went forward to receive his orders for take-off and start the engines.

Barney signaled for the team to come in close so that he could talk to them for the last time before they jumped. "No fancy speeches," he said. "You heard those in Washington. I want you to remember two things: that pill in your pocket and the place where the plane will pick us up five days from now. In the butt of your guns you will find your compasses. You all know how to use them. That plane will be there for ten minutes. Not eleven. That's the taxi home, the last car on the line. You all know the signal for assembly on the ground. If you fail to make that or get separated later, you are on your own. Five nights from tonight for ten minutes."

Anything else he might have said was drowned by the roar of the plane. His hand came up and he formed a circle with his thumb and forefinger. He looked at Brodsky, who nodded. At Zing, who nodded. At Carl, who nodded. And at Hac Quan, who nodded. Then Barney raised his hand in a half salute and lay back on his chute. A few minutes later the plane raced down the runway and rose into the darkness.

WASHINGTON, D.C. •

THE EARLY MORNING staff meeting was completed and General LeGrande had already returned to his office at GENOPS. He was just settling down to read the Overnight Reports which his secretary had set on his desk when the intercom buzzed. Turning it on, he identified himself and waited. General MacWolfe was on the phone. Picking up the phone, LeGrande listened to the report from the Deputy Director of the Defense Intelligence Agency. The transport had spent the day in Saigon on the landing strip. The transfer to the second plane had been accomplished.

"So I've heard, Hyde," and as he held the phone he wondered why MacWolfe was bothering to inform him of routine data.

"And by the way, Dick, that 201 you were looking for, did you ever locate it?" He realized that MacWolfe was not in on the secret and was now on a fishing trip.

"The 201?" LeGrande played stupid for the moment while he considered what he should say.

"The Fannin file."

LeGrande laughed, "The way you put it, it sounds like a mystery story. Barney's file. If it can be located, I will be shown it." The only lie here was in the tense and not in the fact.

LeGrande looked up to see Harry Fuller and Janet enter. He had come to expect a worried expression on Harry's face, but Janet's troubled him. "I'll call you back, Hyde," and he hung up.

Both his deputy and the Director of Personnel approached the desk. It was Harry who held out the newspaper. Puzzled, LeGrande accepted it and glanced at the story which had been encircled with a red marking pencil. *Czech envoy declared persona non grata and shipped home.* Shrugging, the General looked at the other two.

"Saw that this morning. Routine. Got caught with his hand in the till." At the moment, LeGrande felt better. He had feared some news break about the story that planted the deaths of the team in the airline crash. Mrs. Carl Sprague may or may not have been satisfied by Janet's call. The entire business of a coffin that could not be opened always smelled to a wise newspaper reporter, a breed that LeGrande did not underestimate.

Then Harry was handing him a file. "This came in as routine from the FBI."

Waving both Janet and Harry to seats, LeGrande opened the file and started to read it. Harry was correct. It did appear routine. The persons met by the Czech embassy official. A fascinating circle of friends. An envoy from Mali. A UN representative from Colombia and another from Chile. An American enlisted man who was assigned to Cape Kennedy. It was the EM who had blown the whistle on the Czech. A meeting in Lafayette Park shortly after midnight three days before. Contact unidentified. LeGrande turned the page to find a Xeroxed copy of a taxi driver's daily report. Picked up two passengers at airport and took them to the Willard Hotel. Eight thirty. Picked up a woman at the Willard and took her to Georgetown. The address set down in what was almost an illiterate hand. And the time. Glancing down the copy, LeGrande saw the pickup of a man at Lafayette Park, driven to Alexandria, twelve fifteen A.M. The General started to turn the page when he looked at the address a second time. He had never seen it before. Then very slowly he set the file down and came to his feet. "Two doors from the safe-house." It was not a question, but Harry and Janet nodded.

"Dropped off two doors away, in front of the school," Harry pointed out.

"Has anyone spoken to the cab driver?" LeGrande was pressing now.

"I called the FBI," Janet said, "but they have no further information. A man dressed in a suit, and it was dark in Lafayette Park, in the cab and on the street in front of the school."

"Was there an accent?"

Janet shook her head. "The FBI says the cabby does not recall. There are so many accents in this town that no one notices them any longer."

What she was saying made sense. But LeGrande had to assume that someone on the team—anyone on the team—could have talked that night to the Czech operator. "It was the night before they were briefed," he said, thinking that whoever was involved had known only a limited amount of information.

Harry shook his head. "But the man in the dark could have brought home a bug and set that living room up in five minutes the night before the briefing. The bug could have been removed after we left."

There was a long silence and LeGrande realized that the clandestine mind of Harry Fuller rarely made mistakes in evaluation.

Harry did not say that what he described was what had happened, but they knew they had to work on the assumption that it had.

Still standing behind his desk, LeGrande picked up the phone and snapped, "Get me General MacWolfe on the phone at once. Tell his aide it is an emergency." Then he set the phone down. "Has either of you any bright ideas?" he asked.

Harry shook his head.

Janet smiled wryly. "Was there anything in the file you read last night?"

Startled that she would even think that Barney Fannin could be involved, he snapped, "Nothing." A pause as he thought. "What about Hac Quan?" he asked Harry.

"I've checked the polygraph report. He was asked if he had ever worked with the Communists and he said no. Came off clean."

"Do you trust the polygraph?" LeGrande asked.

"On a thing like this it's hard to say, Boss Man. The DIA and the CIA are living with it. It could be one of the other three. Two of them were pretty hungry."

The General nodded.

The phone rang and LeGrande had MacWolfe on the other end of the line. "Hyde, can you get your commo section to contact Saigon on priority. That plane carrying the team is not, and I repeat *not,* to drop it." He was looking at his watch. Ten in the morning meant ten at night over Vietnam. He set the phone down and sat down himself. "He will call me back and verify."

None of the three said anything as Janet lit a cigarette and watched the smoke climb slowly. Harry opened his hands and closed them. He wanted to say something about mounting operations too rapidly, but LeGrande had said it himself so many times. Besides, the schedule was not of their making. The pieces of construction in the valley of the Song Koi had all come into focus as they neared completion. It would have been nice to have had people in the valley who could have given CIA a report. There might even have been such people there then. Might even be now. But Harry was recalling the weeks and weeks that frequently passed before informants could pass their messages from hand to hand to mouth to dead drop to live drop to a border and a sampan and on through enemy waters to a place where someone could pick it up and hope it had not been garbled in the transmission. Even then there was no real way of knowing how well the informant had been able to evaluate what he had seen and how reliable he was—no way to evaluate it from a distance of weeks and months and a strange mind trained in different patterns of thought.

"Always jerry-built," he said half aloud and half to himself.

LeGrande looked at him and nodded. "The only hope is that the other side is moving as vaguely through a dark and half-seen maze as we are."

The phone rang. LeGrande picked it up. "Yes, Hyde?" A long pause and, "Thanks." Then with a bitter smile, he said, "I'll tell you about it later. Here or at your place? Fine. I'll wait for you." Then he hung up and looked at the others. "They've already jumped," he said.

THE VALLEY OF THE SONG KOI •

THE LARGE CANOPY of the parachute drifted down through the darkness. Dangling loosely, his hands on the risers and his eyes on the faint horizon, Barney Fannin listened to the drone of the plane. After a moment there was total silence and total darkness. Then he knew the earth was just below him and, drawing on one riser and then another, he slowly let the air escape from the canopy so that he came down on his feet. A half stumble as the chute collapsed behind him, and he struck the quick release button at his waist and dropped the harness. Swinging the heavy package of explosives off his back and the automatic gun from his shoulder, he set them on the ground at his feet. Looking up, he could not locate any of the other chutes. He had been the last to leave the plane, and he assumed the others were already down.

Rolling up the chute, Fannin shoved it under a rock and, taking his sheath knife from his boot, cut some brush to cover it. Finished, he looked about for the landmarks he had spotted on the map. He could make out the edge of a scrub forest ahead. If the maps were accurate, the forest was rimmed by the river. As far as he could see in every direction there were no lights. He was north of the activity. Crossing over the broken ground he made his way toward the river. There was an overhang of rocks and he scaled it in the darkness; once again he slowly turned around, trying to make out some light. Darkness. Above were a few scattered stars and clouds. The moon would be out soon and the land flooded bright.

He pulled a lighter from his pocket and, kneeling to make as small a silhouette as possible, flicked it on in his cupped hand. Once he opened his hand. A second time. Then, beside the river, a light appeared briefly. A second time. He shoved the lighter into his pocket and, picking up his load, moved off toward the light. A copse of trees rose up in the darkness, and his gun came to hand as he heard a sound.

"Here," he heard someone say, and he moved closer to the voice. In the dark he could make out the figures of two men, musette bags at their feet and submachine guns in their hands.

"Who?" he asked.

"Sprague, Colonel."

"Miller, sir." And then, softly, "Glad you dropped in."

Fannin did not feel ready for humor as he scanned the area around him. "Brodsky? Hac Quan?"

"Nothing yet," Sprague said. He was breathing heavily, and Fannin wished there had been time to take off some of the overhung gut. Then, some distance away, he saw a light. A second time.

"Answer," he told Miller.

A few minutes later they were joined by Hac Quan.

They waited. Barney sent Miller to the river's edge to make sure they were not surprised. A minute. More. Three. The sound of planes overhead, and Fannin told Sprague and Hac Quan, "They spotted something on their radar, but they can't pin it down."

Silence now and five minutes passed. Then, as if from a great distance, they heard a cry, vaguely lost in the slight rustle as the wind brushed leaf against leaf. The cry again, like an injured animal.

"Wait here," Fannin ordered Miller, and he moved out with Sprague and Hac Quan. From the way the Annamese engineer moved through the darkness with a sure foot, Barney knew the man had been in danger before.

The cry again. Closer, but softer. They moved in toward it, their guns in hand, their steps shorter and more certain now. Then, beside a tree they made out the writhing figure of a man. Approaching with care, Fannin clamped a large hand over Joe's mouth as he ran his other hand down the young soldier's body. He touched the right leg. It was twisted grotesquely behind the boy's back. The other seemed to be bent forward at the knee. Fannin realized the bazooka strapped to Brodsky's side must have caused the bad drop. The soldier's rifle lay under him. Barney pulled it out, his hand still over Brodsky's mouth. Then Barney shook his head. He knew Joe was staring at him, but he dared not remove his hand from the boy's mouth. They were silent for a long time, and then Barney reached into the soldier's jacket pocket and pulled out the two capsules he had handed him only a few hours before.

Hac Quan knelt down at the other side of the boy and waited for the American colonel to decide.

"Can't we take him with us, Colonel?" Sprague asked.

Fannin remained silent.

"Can't we, Colonel?"

Suddenly, Barney jammed the capsules into his own pocket. Removing his hand from Joe's mouth, he struck the youth across the jaw as hard as he could. The eyes closed. The head went limp.

Quickly they removed the chute, cut away the risers and strapped the two legs together with the stock of the carbine, making a single splint with the weapon. When they were done, Barney told Hac Quan, "Get Miller."

This was the first order he had given the Oriental, and for an instant Hac Quan hesitated. Then he rose to his feet and trotted off in the darkness while Fannin gathered the ripped chute and hid it as he had hidden his own earlier. He was already cutting the limb off a nearby tree when the rest of the team joined him.

Barney glanced at his watch. It was already two in the morning. He had about four hours to take his first target and find a place to hide. Looking down at the still unconscious body of Brodsky, he asked, "Where's that bridge from here?"

The Annamese thought a moment. "A kilometer south, where the Song Koi bends."

Fannin accepted the information. He had no choice. "Let's get this gear buried by the overhang back there," he ordered, "and then you," pointing to Miller, "and you," pointing to Sprague, "will come with me." To the Annamese, he said simply. "You will keep him quiet if you have to cut his throat."

Hac Quan's face was hidden in the night, but Barney could see the slow bob of his head as he indicated he understood the order.

Fifteen minutes later, they had moved Brodsky to the overhang; they buried the bazooka he had brought down as well as the explosives they were not taking with them and the radio. As Barney set it in the earth, he wondered if it was usable and, if so, who could use it.

Rising from the ground where he had smoothed dirt over the cache, Fannin swung his weapon onto his shoulder and his musette bag onto his back. "Let's go." He moved out without waiting for the others. Zing Miller picked up his gear and followed. Carl Sprague looked at the limp body of the boy lying in the shadow and up at the sky where the moon was emerging from behind a cloud. A half nod to Hac Quan, squatting beside Brodsky, and Carl trotted after Fannin, who was setting a fast pace.

Barney knew that he did not need specific directions to find the bridge. It crossed the river, and he was walking the river bank southward. Miller came up to his side, and a moment later, Carl Sprague. The insurance man was breathing hard again. Fannin thought about slowing his pace, but he knew that he could not if he was to get his job done and his men into hiding. For fifteen minutes he walked through the valley of the Song Koi. There were fewer trees now. The moon was lighting the landscape like a giant torch, and Barney took what cover he could. Once he thought he saw a light ahead. But he did not pause. The light seemed to move away, and then he heard the sound of trucks and he slipped into the shadows cast by a large tree. Carl and Zing blended beside him into the darkness. A moment to listen, and they realized a road ran not far from the river. This had not been visible in the photos. It might have been new or it might— as was more likely—have been well hidden by the foliage. Barney knew that a road went to the bridge or there would have been no bridge. But he had not thought he would be moving so close to it. Walking quickly to the Song Koi, he decided to take advantage of its banks, and he stepped into the water, remaining close to the bank. Carl and Zing followed in silence. The only sounds now were the frequent trucks which appeared to be riding in a spaced convoy and the nearer sound of their own sloshing in the cold river.

Then suddenly the river bend, and a large bridge was revealed before them. It looked bright in the moonlight, and as they knelt in the river to stay within the shadows, Fannin thought how far wrong the drawings had been from the actual object.

A low whistle beside him. He looked at Zing, who was shaking his head. "It's a biggy, Colonel."

Fannin nodded. "Can we take it?" He was pulling his field glasses over his head and passing them to Zing. The carnie man alone could decide.

Staring at the bridge through the high-powered glasses, Zing looked at the abutments and the tall and almost gleaming shafts of concrete that seemed to be feeling for the river bottom. He tried to calculate the height of the bridge. Fifty feet above the river. This was not important. The posts were. They appeared to be several feet across and arched under the spans. He assumed that the concrete was reinforced. Quickly, he tried to calculate the distance between posts. Long—perhaps fifty yards. That made for the impressive sweep and the beautiful lines. But Zing did not think it made for strength. Here, he thought, was the weakness of the bridge. He looked at the thickness of the spans and saw that the road across the river was at least two truck-widths wide, perhaps twenty feet. There was no walk as far as he could tell, which meant that any marching troops would use one of the two truck lanes. It meant, too, that the spans were not re-inforced by high sides. As far as he could tell, only a single cable stretched the length on each side of the span. He wished he had a pencil and paper and a chance to make measurements. He also wished he had time, but as he lowered the glasses, he could see Fannin glancing at his watch.

"It's a bitch baby, Colonel. A three-winged bitch." He was speaking softly because he knew how far sound traveled over water at night. Fannin nodded and started away from the bridge to the shelter of a large rock, which rose as part of a hill between them and the road and from which they could hear trucks com-ing. Zing counted softly, "One, two, three, four." And he waited, but there were only four trucks. Crawling out of the water, Zing dropped to a prone position and scanned the road. Four small vehicles. Troop carriers. Weight about a ton and a half each at most, if he knew European trucks. Ten men at two hundred pounds. Add a ton. It was not enough. Edging himself back, feet first, he rejoined the others. Sprague had pulled the musette bags open and set the seventy-five pounds of high explosives on the ground. He was already taking out the primer cord and the det-onator. But Zing stared at them and shook his head.

"Can you?" Fannin was asking. "Just make believe it's a blonde whose superstructure you want to bring down."

In the darkness, Zing half smiled. He wished it were a blonde. No matter how he calculated it, they had all underestimated the bridge.

"Can you bring it down?" Fannin asked again.

"With luck, Colonel. With all kinds of luck." Zing knew he was committing himself, because he knew that Fannin was not listen-ing to the limitations of his promise.

Before Fannin could say anything, Zing picked up the charge

and looked it over. Three twenty-five pound plastic elements.
The primer was in perfect condition and the small electric detonator alive. He knew that he had to control the time. That was
the only way it could work. The only way. Moving out toward
the river, Zing let Fannin and Sprague haul the charges and cord.
As soon as he could see the bridge clearly again, he raised the
field glasses. Shaking his head in disgust, he knew he need not
have looked. Two men paced the bridge from the ends toward
the center. He waited as they came together and held his breath.
They were stopping and talking to each other. To the surprise of
Fannin and Sprague, Zing sat right down in the river, keeping
the glasses on the sentries. He was counting. Finally, they parted
and he swept the glasses from end to end, counting again under
his breath. Then he started counting again as they moved toward
each other. When they met, they stopped to talk. Again Zing
started his counting. When the men separated, he knew how
much time he had to reach the point of the post he wanted, just
below the arch, fifty feet from the water. Though he could not
see them from where he stood, he had to assume that there were
rungs—steel rods—set into the concrete posts so that the underside of the bridge could be checked against cracks. He had to
assume that. Handing the glasses to Fannin without even looking at the Colonel, he set his gun on the bank, picked up the
musette bags and moved out into the river.

Fannin motioned for Sprague to put away his guns and follow
him. The three walked to neck depth and then started toward
the bridge. Anyone looking down would have seen three heads
and a hand holding a large package out of the water. Barney
knew they were unarmed, but he knew, too, that a man does
not gun down a bridge. Slowly, silently, and with the advantage
of the moon hidden behind a cloud, they approached the post
Zing had selected. He waved the other two aside and moved into
deeper water, dragging the waterproof musette bags with him.
Where the footing of the bridge reached the river, he slowly circled the post. The darkness had been deceptive and the post was
thicker than he had thought. He spotted a steel rung and, slip-

ping the explosives over his shoulder, listened for the footsteps
above. The guards were separating. He started to count as he rose
from rung to rung. Though he could no longer hear the men
above, he knew when they should have reached their farthest
point of separation and started back. When he thought they were
within a few feet of him, he paused. They would be talking now.
Now they would be separating and walking away. He moved up
again. Three meetings above and three pauses based only on his
count, until he came to the base of the arched concrete at the
head of the post.

Suddenly he heard a shout above him and he froze. More
shouts. Two men, and as the moon came out from behind the
clouds, he could see two silhouettes reflected in the river almost
directly under him. There was silence now, and Zing knew that
all he could do was wait. If the moon disappeared before the
men, he would have no way of knowing if they had remained
alert. Then they were gone and it was dark again.

Carefully, he set his charges tightly against the thinnest point
at the apex of the arch. With deft hands, he shaped his charge,
forcing the plastic into the crevice. "With luck," he had told Fannin. "With luck." Now, as he felt the unseen power of the charge
under his hands, he knew that it would take all of the luck he
could muster. One end of the cord was in place with the detonator, and he quickly lowered the other end to the river below. He
could see Fannin come out of a shadow and take the end, leaving
enough slack so that it could not be seen from above. Fannin
waved to him in the semi-darkness, and Zing started down the
steel rungs. One after the other. Quickly. Silently. Without the
load of charges, he believed he could make the descent unno-
ticed. Then he felt the bridge shake and smiled to himself as he
moved even more rapidly under the protective sound of a small
convoy. A strange shudder of the bridge and he paused until
he realized troops were crossing in route step. Then he was in the
water, swimming toward Fannin. Waving for Fannin and
Sprague to follow, he moved along the bank as far from the
bridge as the length of cord would allow. He calculated fifty feet

up the bridge and a hundred feet from it. Then he secured the cord to a rock and motioned for the Colonel and Sprague to come closer.

"I'm going up on that rock," he explained. "And I'm going to wait. When I fire my gun, Colonel, you twist that damned igniter. Not one second before, or we've come a long way for nothing."

"Will it work?" Carl asked, and Zing smiled wryly, his dark eyes appearing even darker as he ran his fingers through his short, black hair. Then with a patient look, he shrugged.

Zing picked up the glasses, retrieved his forty-five and submachine gun and crawled up the rock toward the road. He was alone again. He could see the moon coming out and the strange twisted black line that emerged from the distance—the road. "Wait," he had said. "Wait." But he did not even know if he had the patience himself. He lay on his belly with the glasses tight against his eyes until he could barely see from the moisture forming. Darkness again as the moon was lost, and the road seemed to shorten as he could see less distance.

Maybe he should have flattened his landlady in Keene and forgotten that he did not have a job. Maybe he should have told Barney Fannin to drop dead. Maybe he should have found some other job when the war was over. Maybe he should never have been sent to demolitions school and worked at the one thing he seemed to be able to do best. Maybe he should . . .

And then he saw the headlights. Counting under his breath, he held the glasses on the road ahead. A turn, and he could see a long row of double lights. He sighed as he tried to calculate how they bounced over the road. They seemed higher than the weapons carriers he had seen earlier, but he hoped he was not fooling himself. The tall general in Washington had stressed that this was important. There were so few things that Zing Miller had been involved in that were important. He had to be right. He could con everyone else, but he was praying that at this moment he was not conning himself.

The first truck passed. Small. A half ton. He almost swore aloud. The second truck, and he wanted to scream. Ten tons if it was one. The next was ten tons. And the next. He swung his glasses toward the bridge and waited. The half ton was on it. Then the first heavy truck, and his forty-five was in his hand as he counted truck after truck, closing up on the bridge as they slowed down. Twelve trucks. Thirteen, and he fired.

There were still trucks on the road near him, and he knew he had to get out of there. Scrambling back on his belly, Zing leapt from the rock and was in mid-air down toward the river's edge when he heard the explosion. He could see the sky become bright and hear the rifles start firing at the point where he had been. The bridge appeared intact, as if nothing had happened. Then suddenly it canted to one side, buckled, and he could see the headlights of trucks falling into the river. There were screams and shouts and the crash of trucks falling one on top of another and the splash of water. He could see a truck come over the edge riding on nothing and then disappear. He felt Barney Fannin grab his arm to pull him away from the bridge and north up the river again as he heard shouts back at the rock. Then they were moving along the bank in the darkness. Zing glanced back once more to see the twisted bridge lighted by headlamps and flashlights and what appeared to be a fire. Perhaps a petroleum truck had rammed into another. Perhaps . . . but it did not matter.

Half a mile away, Zing collapsed on the ground beside the river and rolled over onto his back, staring up at the other two. "There had to be weight enough to bring it down," he said. "There had to be. Thirteen trucks carrying ten tons and the trucks weighing three, and I had a hundred and sixty tons."

"One hundred and sixty-nine," Carl corrected him.

And all three of them chuckled as Zing said, "I always knew I needed an education."

They were wet and cold. There were four more nights and four more targets, Joe Brodsky to be hidden and the days to survive. Barney reached down and helped Zing to his feet. "We've got a ways to go," he said as he squeezed Zing's arm affectionately. Slapping Carl on the back, he said, as they pressed on in the darkness, "I hope he was able to keep that boy quiet."

Carl nodded.

What none of them said, and what all three of them knew, was that their arrival in the valley of the Song Koi was no longer a secret.

Fifteen minutes later the team reassembled at the overhang where Hac Quan had remained with Joe Brodsky. They had two hours in which to hide before dawn, but as they stood over the limp body of Joe, Barney knew he had not the vaguest idea where to go. Originally, he had planned to remain hidden near the river. He and LeGrande had talked about a crevice, a cave, a hole in the ground. They had taken for granted there would be someplace they could hide. Now, as Barney looked down at Joe, he knew he had only two choices—get away from the river and then find a place where they could shelter the young soldier, or kill him now.

"You had to hit him again?" Carl asked Hac Quan, and the Annamese nodded.

"I hit him."

Carl looked at the Oriental, not quite sure how he had felt about striking the youth.

Barney checked his watch. He could not waste any more time. There was the river beside them and the rustling of the water against the banks, and he was hearing another river, angry, tumultuous and long ago. And the decision waiting. He felt his stomach muscles tighten and he tried to shake his head as though to brush something away, but he knew he could not brush it away. "Carl," he said, "do we kill him and stay here or look for a place to hide him until we leave?"

The others were surprised at the question, at Fannin's asking anyone what should be done at this moment.

Somehow, though he could not say just why, Sprague knew he had to make the decision. Maybe he was being tested. Maybe Fannin doubted him. He did not know. Turning to Hac Quan, he asked, "A place? Is there somewhere we could hide during the day? Not here—we'll have to be able to come back at night to the river."

"A place for the boy?" the stocky engineer said.

Fannin moved into the discussion. "Yeah. For the boy."

Pointing farther up river, Hac Quan said, "There's a village there. A town, really. The French built it as a resort."

Barney shook his head. "We can't go into any strange town now."

"It isn't strange to me." Then, hesitantly, Hac Quan added, "My wife lives there. It is my home."

Suddenly, Fannin grabbed the smaller man by the front of his jacket and half lifted him off the ground. "You've been using us to get back here." His fist rose and he was ready to strike when Carl Sprague intervened.

"Didn't you and the General plan to use Hac Quan?" the Oriental gasped.

Trying to pull Barney's arm off the smaller man, Carl Sprague said, "He's right, Colonel. He's here because the General asked for his help." And as Barney almost threw the smaller man from him, Sprague continued, "We need that help now."

For a long moment, Barney considered killing Hac Quan. Then he knew that if he did, he would have to kill Joe Brodsky, who was lying on the ground looking up at them.

"All right," he agreed. "Where's this damned village?"

"A kilometer and half, that way," pointing.

Barney nodded. Then to Zing, "You bring up the rear and keep your gun ready." To Sprague, "You walk right behind this . . ." —with an indecent gesture he indicated Hac Quan. "If we're going into a trap, I'm holding you responsible for killing him." He looked around, "Everything we'll need for tonight is buried, and so we'll have to come back here." Bending down, he half smiled at Joe. "Come on, son. We've got a ways to go." And he picked the boy up in his arms and then carefully swung him so that he hung over one shoulder. With his free hand, he picked up his automatic rifle. "Let's get the hell out of here."

The moon was gone. There were few stars in the sky. The countryside was still and only an occasional bird made any sound. They walked for almost an hour near the edge of an old road, Hac Quan leading the way, Sprague behind him, followed by Fannin and Miller. They were all tired now. Once Carl Sprague reached into his pocket and swallowed a pep pill. Maybe the effect would wear off in time to let him sleep, if they ever found a place to sleep. They passed two houses near the road. A dog barked once when they came too close to a small farmhouse.

Then they were at the edge of the town. More buildings, and to the surprise of the Americans, they were almost modern. The French had built them for themselves when they had planned to remain a long time. Fannin had heard that Hanoi itself was a modern city in spite of its age. He smiled wryly to himself at the delusions of empire. No one should build in another man's country with the intention of remaining. When Barney looked up, he could no longer see any stars. It was nearing the edge of morning. They were passing through a narrow street now. There were no lights in the windows. Anyone coming outside would immediately see that these men were intruders, and Barney snapped at Hac Quan, "Get moving."

Each man had his gun ready to fire. Each was more frightened at this moment than he had been with the darkness for protection. Another half an hour and they would be trapped with no place to run except back to the river, and they had not taken the time to locate a place to hide there.

Finally Hac Quan paused in front of a house. The others melted into the darkness of a large doorway of what appeared to be some kind of official building nearby. The Oriental moved back to speak to Barney. "I will ask her," he said. Then, as if by way of explanation, "I haven't seen her in six years."

Barney did not know what he was supposed to say. He was angry at being caught in this trap. He believed now that he should have killed Hac Quan and then Joe Brodsky. He was tired. His shoulder ached from the weight of the boy he was carrying. The jump seemed like something that had happened to someone else and in another world. The destruction of the bridge was even a thing of the past. Now he merely nodded to Hac Quan. "If you don't come back, I'll come in after you."

The smaller man nodded, accepting the implications of the threat. Then he went to the house where he had paused a few minutes before. It was a small house, Oriental in design, but better built then most, partly because some Frenchman who had been killed in the war had built it for himself, and partly because Hac Quan's family had had the money to maintain it. The engineer struck the door with his open palm and waited. A moment, and he slapped again. From where he stood in the entrance down the street, Fannin saw a light go on in the house. There was electric power here. The town was close to Hanoi, and the engineer had been able to afford power. Then Fannin's gun went up, as did those of Miller and Sprague. The door opened and they could see a woman standing there. The light from behind silhouetted her, but when she turned her head from side to side in disbelief, Barney could see that she was pretty— middle-aged but pretty. Her black hair was piled high on her head and she was wearing a white robe. He wished he knew what was being said at the door, and then Hac Quan disappeared inside.

There was a noise down the street and the three men whirled. A dog wandering. The animal stopped to sniff the air and then moved away. Looking up, Barney could see the first traces of dawn. He looked at his watch. Five minutes. He would wait five minutes and take the house. He thought of all the bad films he had seen about escaped gangsters holding a household at gun point. If he had to . . . Zing went down on one knee as he waited and Barney shifted the load on his shoulder. Joe was stirring now and Carl was afraid that the boy might cry out. Dangling over Barney's shoulder for over an hour must have been misery, but he had been silent. Perhaps unconscious.

Carl Sprague jerked his head from side to side as if to jolt himself awake. The effect of the pill was wearing off now. If he had to move on, he would take another one. His arms were tired, his legs ached. He was a long way from Columbus, and he wished he were back there. He thought of his bed and wished he were in it. His head came up with a jolt as the door of the house opened. Hac Quan looked up and down the street before he joined them.

"Well?" Barney asked, his patience frayed.

"We can't stay there." Then, as if it were an explanation, he added, "She lives with a Chinese captain. He was called away a few hours ago. Someone destroyed a bridge."

The other three looked at him with pity.

"You should have killed her," Barney said.

Hac Quan shook his head. "I was gone and she was lonely."

Seeing that he had been misunderstood, Barney snarled, "She knows we're here." Then he made up his mind. "I'm not taking any chances. She knows we're here." He started to lower Joe to the ground, when Hac Quan said simply, "She was my wife. She will not betray me."

It was with difficulty that Barney held back his laughter. "She already has, Bub. She already has."

"I trust her." Then, firmly, as if he would not discuss the matter further, Hac Quan said, "And you will, Colonel."

Very slowly, Barney pulled himself up to full height as he considered what had been said. The Annamese was letting him know that the team was at his mercy. For an instant, Barney's hand tightened about the rifle.

"The General said your mission was important, Colonel. I'm sure it is more important than killing Hac Quan."

Barney Fannin knew the trap had been sprung, and there was nothing he could do about it. He looked up and then said, "This street will be alive in twenty minutes or I'm crazy."

Hac Quan nodded. Then he walked out of the shelter of the building entrance and back down the street. After a moment, Barney motioned for the others to follow. He shifted Joe's weight on his shoulder and started after them.

A half mile beyond the village, Hac Quan stopped in front of another house. "My sister lives here," he explained, as he gestured for the trio to hide in the brush beside the road. This house was larger than the first. It was older. Less French influence. There were two stories, but the second, set back from the first, seemed very small.

This time Barney could not see Hac Quan when the door

opened, but he could hear the man talking. A woman—no way to judge her age. A noise, and Barney could see a man walk down the road. An old man. A moment later another passed. A uniform. Chinese. He was wearing a sidearm. Staring straight ahead, he did not see the small group. Looking up, Barney realized that it was day. A moment later Hac Quan was trying to attract his attention. Quickly the others entered the house. When they were inside, Hac Quan closed the door behind them. The room was larger than Barney had expected and French and Oriental in decor: two benches on each side of the door, several low tables, a cabinet, two stuffed chairs and a piano. But Barney was not paying as much attention to the furnishings as he was to the young woman who stared at the four Americans.

"My sister's child," Hac Quan introduced them. "In another time my father and her father might have said, 'a girl and therefore a worthless thing,' but she has agreed to help us since her mother is dead and her father has been taken away by the Chinese."

"Yeah," Barney snorted. "I'd like to be polite, girl, but I am bushed." Seeing the puzzled look on her face, he explained, "Beat. Bushed. Done in. Fatigued."

The girl smiled slowly as she repeated, "Fatigued." Then she turned away and led them through the room to the staircase beyond. Hac Quan brought up the rear and joined the others at the top of the stairs.

"Li," he said, indicating the girl, "will take care of Joe. We can sleep in there," and he pointed to the two rooms beyond. There was a mat on the floor of each. Fannin walked into the closest and very carefully swung Joe Brodsky down upon the mat. The boy's head turned from side to side as he tried to keep from crying.

Li knelt beside him and then ran her hands over the two broken legs strapped together and to the carbine. Without even looking at Fannin or her uncle, she loosed the cords which bound the legs. Then she ran her hands gently up and down the legs, shaking her head as she did so.

Staring at the girl, Barney half smiled at his own ignorance. He might have crippled the boy for life by cutting off all circulation. He hoped she had acted in time. Joe's eyes were closed now, and Barney wondered if he were unconscious again. "Can she find some morphine?" he asked Hac Quan.

The girl looked up at Barney from where she knelt. "There is none here."

He was startled at the English and turned to Hac Quan for an explanation. "You were not surprised to find I spoke English."

"That's no answer," Barney grunted. He did not like loose ends.

"My father lived in Hong Kong. My sister and I did. Your Mrs. Williams in Washington knew we lived there once."

Barney nodded, and for a moment he stood looking down at the girl. She was beautiful, if one liked Orientals. Her face was small and round and her eyes were soft. Her dark hair was down about her shoulders and from where Fannin stood, he could see the swell of her small breasts under her blue robe. After a moment he half smiled and repeated, "Fatigue," and left Joe Brodsky with the girl and Hac Quan. In the adjoining room, Carl Sprague and Zing Miller had already removed their jump boots and jackets and were lying down. Zing had taken the mat for himself, while Carl had made a pillow of his wet jacket and was closing his eyes.

Zing looked up at Barney as the large officer swung his rifle off his shoulder and set it against the wall. "The tank farm tomorrow."

This was not a question, but Barney nodded his agreement. He, too, was thinking of the tank farm. Unlacing his boots, he set them on the floor, pulled off his jacket and rolled it, as Carl had done, into a pillow. Then he sprawled out. From the next room he could hear the soft voice of Li as she tried to comfort Joe Brodsky. Barney's hands went to his head—he tried to keep it from shaking as he had seen the boy's shake a short time before. The room was light now. It was morning. When Hac Quan joined them a few minutes later, all three were asleep.

WASHINGTON, D.C. ●

"AND THAT'S IT?" MacWolfe was asking as he stared at LeGrande. It was dusk and they were standing on the balcony of the apartment at Potomac Towers.

"Well, let's just say that's what we think. Someone from the safe-house met someone from the Czech embassy." LeGrande picked an ice cube out of his glass and, dropping it over the edge of the balcony into the river, watched it slip in the breeze and land about ten feet from the spot directly below him. He could not hear the splash.

"You're taking it calmly, Dick."

Behind them they could hear Janet in the kitchen, talking to Lil MacWolfe. Both listened for a moment, and then LeGrande shook his head.

"Calmly? No. I'm trapped, Hyde. I've got to act, and I don't know what the hell to do yet."

"You've got four days left and then, if you haven't done the job, the Air Force will." MacWolfe was not threatening, but rather was stating what both of them accepted as a fact.

Another ice cube bombed its vague target below. Both men watched its course and saw that it was no more successful than the previous one.

"You know if we let them take off from that place, we could lose all of Southeast Asia before we even got into position." LeGrande was tempted to drop the glass, but he knew that Janet would not approve.

"You think the team's finished?"

"No."

"But if the Reds know?"

LeGrande laughed softly. "Depends on who knows and who tells whom." He turned and looked at the stocky sometime tank commander and grinned. "We think—and with good reason—that someone told the Czechs we were moving against the installations in the valley of the Song Koi." He paused and repeated the name again, "Song Koi—sounds like a recipe for chop suey."

Impatiently, MacWolfe growled, "For heaven's sake, get on with it, Dick."

"How the hell do we know the Czechs and Russians will tell the Chinese that we're going hunting in their park?"

MacWolfe considered this for a moment and then shook his head. "If they say nothing and you luck out and get those five targets, then you've prevented a war. Is that right?"

LeGrande smiled. "You are getting warm."

"But maybe they want us to tangle with the Red Chinese so they can sit back and watch. If that's the case, then they'll stop the team by alerting the Chinese and we are left with starting a war we don't want."

Suddenly the tall general in mufti laughed loudly. "You're beginning to think like an intelligence officer, Hyde. That'll ruin you in that rarefied atmosphere you live in at the Pentagon. And besides, think of the image. The Old Gray Wolf, terror of the tank column, picking up a Balkan mind. That will look awful when people start studying your campaigns. Imagine the full-speed-ahead, damn-the-torpedoes, run-'em-down confused with some solid thinking instead of all muscle. It will create havoc with thousands of military historians."

Used to being ridden by his friend and classmate, MacWolfe waited until LeGrande paused and then asked, "All right, Dick. I may be wrong. But how do you dope this race?"

"I don't. I haven't the faintest notion what happened in that park or which man talked with that Czech. The kid we sprung from a military prison? Possibly. There are malcontents in any army, men who can't take the discipline and grow angry at the world. I know he lied about his father. Maybe he came to believe it. The carnie man who jumped his room rent in New Hampshire? Possibly. He was a con man. Maybe he carried it all the way, thinking he could fool us and them. Maybe he thought he found a way to locate that pea under the walnut shell. The insurance man? Possibly. His family could come into some money, and that's better than buying life insurance and taking a bomb aboard the plane. People are looking for bombs on planes nowadays. Then there's the engineer. He checked out so damned well you'd think he'd been raised all of his life for this mission. An engineer. Knows French and the local languages and just happens to know English about as well as you do. And to top it off, he's all fired willing to do and die for dear old Siwash and us not knowing just where his Siwash is really located. Where's his heart buried?" LeGrande reared back and threw the empty glass into the river in anger and disgust.

"Didn't you leave someone out?" MacWolfe knew he had to ask.

"Barney Fannin? The Man Most Likely to . . . ?" LeGrande shook his head. "I don't believe it."

The Pentagon officer shook his head, not as much in doubt of Fannin as in disbelief that LeGrande would go so far with any man under the circumstances; and as the Director of General Operations had laid it out, the circumstances were war. "You're certain you're right, Dick?"

A long silence as LeGrande wished he had something else to

drop in the river. "I have to believe it, Hyde." He shook his head. "For all kinds of reasons, I have to believe it."

"We'll know more tomorrow when the recon pics get here from their first night." MacWolfe was looking for solace, but LeGrande could not agree.

"Not really. Maybe the Russians will be slow passing on the information and will let us get one or two targets. Maybe the person who finked will not have made the contact he wanted as soon as he landed. We might get one or two or even three targets and then find we've just partially damaged them. We won't know if they're willing to risk attack with what's left in the way of supplies and transport."

Again MacWolfe whistled. "What are you going to do? This part of the game's yours."

LeGrande smiled bitterly. "I'm sure I shall hear that as long as I live. Dick LeGrande sent out the invitations and the wrong people showed up to his party." He slammed his fist into the stone railing in anger and frustration. Then he rubbed it against his white shirt as he turned and looked at his friend. "I didn't tell you this for the fun of it. You know me better than that."

Sighing patiently, MacWolfe nodded. As the Deputy Director of Defense Intelligence, it was part of his job to keep abreast of General Operations and learn what he could of its activities, but he could not recall another time when LeGrande had been quite so candid. "What's this going to cost me?"

"I want to be prepared to buy another day or two, if I can." He hesitated and then stated his price. "I want your support for that time."

MacWolfe shook his head. "Hell, no." He paused. "Look, Dick. You are the one who said 'seek out and destroy in ten days or they will move in fifteen.' We can't run the risk that they won't move in less. Whether you know it or not, there are men in the Pentagon who think your five days may be a few too late."

Startled that others were thinking the same thing, LeGrande asked, "Then how the hell did I get the time I have?"

"For reasons known only to God, the Old Man said that you

were to have them. He fought the Cabinet for them even before you walked in with your cockemamy proposal." A snort, and he added, "Barney Fannin. Christ, Dick, you ought to have had more sense."

LeGrande looked at the torn skin on his knuckles and shook his head in annoyance with himself. "And you won't support me?"

"Won't and couldn't if I wanted to. The Old Man bought you five days. He can't buy you any more."

LeGrande was willing to accept the fact that the Pentagon hierarchy had discussed the possibility of his asking for a few more days.

"And, Dick," MacWolfe was warning him, "don't think you can get smart and go cry on some senator's shoulder this time. The President was against this from the start, but no one had any better ideas." He thought a moment and added, "They all stunk."

LeGrande rubbed his chin with the back of his numbed hand and nodded. He knew when he had reached the end of largesse, if that was what one wanted to call it.

"What are you going to do?" MacWolfe was asking.

"Give me five minutes." Then, with an almost ingenuous smile, he said, "They're part of my five days."

MacWolfe laughed. "I'll mix us each another drink." He started toward the living room when LeGrande asked, "Does Lil know anything about this?"

Without looking back, MacWolfe shook his head. "The boy is in Saigon. I'm not going to worry her."

Then he was gone and LeGrande was alone on the balcony. It was dark. Even the lamps from the living room threw no light across the railing. He looked up and stared at the stars. *What are you going to do?* He had been trying to think of an answer to that question from the moment he had set the phone down in his office and told the others that the team had already jumped. He thought he had an answer, but it was going to make many people unhappy. He had kept out of the war in Vietnam because CIA and Defense were playing this as if it were a game for people with only blue chips, and with his budget he could only afford white ones. He did not even have an office there. He had not pushed for one in the past. And no one had missed him because they were all so busy tripping over their own tails. He knew that if he moved in for other than this mission he would be inviting attack from the larger agencies. He did not want to fight with them because he had enough to worry about.

MacWolfe was standing behind him, and he turned and accepted the drink. "Dinner?" he asked.

"They said in a few minutes."

Both of them knew that LeGrande had to make a decision; he could not live with the situation, and no one would allow him to. "Decided?"

"It's going to cost you," LeGrande smiled. "I want to get to Saigon in twenty-four hours so I can move in if the team is stopped."

MacWolfe almost dropped his glass. "The Old Man said you might be thinking that way, and he said that he had warned you not to play games but to grow up. It's time, Dick. Believe me, it's time."

"I'm going to brief the Executive Director of the Security Council as to the situation tonight and leave in"—he looked at his watch—"two hours. You can arrange the plane. If I need anything, I'll be in touch and you can have it ready at Clark Field in the Philippines."

Annoyed, "I know where Clark is." Then both of them were thinking of the implications. "You use planes the way Janet uses cigarettes—often and as if they were expendable. The Air Force has other missions."

"Come off it, Hyde. You know what's important as well as I do."

Sipping his drink, MacWolfe looked at his friend. "Who's going with you?"

"Janet, to handle details in Saigon. I'll arrange to have my own men move in from Berlin and Austria. They know how I work."

"I'll contact them."

Smiling at MacWolfe's attempt to locate GENOPS covert personnel as well as the chance to evaluate them, LeGrande shook his head. "That's Harry's job." He emptied his glass. "I'll want the radio report from you on the progress Barney's making."

"If any?"

"If any. But I'm hoping he's still alive and functioning." A pause and then LeGrande shook his head. "Tell the Old Man that he's right. I shouldn't go in. I won't if I can avoid it."

Both of them were silent as MacWolfe nodded.

"You arrange for the plane," LeGrande said. "I'll go meet with the Exec of the Security Council and make my way to the airport." He thought about what he had just planned and then said with a grin, "You can tell Janet she's to pack a bag and meet me at Andrews."

MacWolfe laughed softly. "Some day you're not going to get out of feeding the MacWolfes."

"I'll owe you a dinner," LeGrande said as he walked through the living room, picked his suit jacket out of the closet and went directly out. The call he wanted to make to the Presidential Assistant for National Security Affairs would be made from a phone booth on the way through Alexandria.

LeGrande was still in the elevator when MacWolfe called the home of the Chairman of the Joint Chiefs of Staff from the bedroom extension. "MacWolfe, sir. He's on his way in two hours." A pause as he listened. "Yes, sir. He will brief the Executive Secretary." Another silence, and he added, "He said nothing about keeping an office there, but she's going. I arranged the plane as we agreed, sir." He hung up to see Janet standing in the doorway. Remaining where he was on the edge of her bed, he smiled. "It isn't polite to listen in on other people's conversations."

"Politeness has nothing to do with our business, as you just proved." He could see that she was not smiling.

"It's all in the family," he said lamely. Then, "Dick asked you to pack a bag and meet him at Andrews. We'll drive you out."

"With you arranging the plane, I wish Sprague were here to sell me some insurance." She was already taking her bag from the closet, though she had not the faintest idea where she was going.

MacWolfe rose and, taking the bag from her, swung it onto the bed. Then he turned to her and put his hands on her arms. "Look, Jan, we're friends. Believe me."

He was relieved to see her smile and nod in agreement, but then she added, "So long as GENOPS and Dick do not get in your way."

THE VALLEY OF THE SONG KOI ●

THE SMALL RESORT VILLAGE near which Hac Quan had taken the team for cover became quiet soon after darkness set in. The trucks and troops which had passed through the streets in the earlier part of the day disappeared to camps beyond. The street merchants sought their hovels. The women who had gossiped by the small stream while they beat their clothes on the rocks smoothed by centuries disappeared into their houses. The children who had squalled and the children who had screamed were silent. To any curious eye the village appeared deserted. The only unusual activity during the day had been the posting of signs by the Chinese soldiers and the news that farther downstream the beautiful new bridge which everyone viewed with awe, appreciation and pride had been damaged by intruders from the south. But no one was worried, because the Chinese officers and those of North Vietnam had assured the people of the village that the intruders would be punished. And so they returned to their homes. And as they had done every night for a thousand years, the villagers ate their dinners of rice and fish and minded their own business.

Barney Fannin and his men waited until almost midnight before they ventured out. They were carrying their weapons and the small map they had drawn for the night's mission. With the help of Hac Quan, they had timed their mission so that they could be assured of darkness on their return. Barney did not want to cut his margin of safety as close as he had the night before. With the advice of Hac Quan, he felt he would not. Each of the men had spent some time during the evening with Joe Brodsky, who remained in pain. Each had assured him that he would be well and that he was not endangering the mission. Each had kidded him that he would have exchanged a healthy leg for the chance to spend the night with the beautiful Annamese girl. And each had left the room hoping that the boy might walk again sometime and that a way would be found to take him back when the group withdrew. Only Barney Fannin had thought instead of the possibility of leaving the young soldier. Barney told himself he was being a realist, but he had trouble believing his own story.

Now, as they passed out of the house into the darkness of the road, Barney glanced up and saw there was no moon. And there were no stars. The door closed behind them and they started to move to the fields beyond. They were passing a farmhouse when they heard a sound, and they all blended into the entrance of a small shed. A young man passed them in a half trot. From their shelter they could see a girl come out of a shadow, take his arm and disappear into a house farther down the road. Zing smiled at the others. But Barney Fannin was not smiling as he looked at a poster on the door of the building where they were standing. Reaching up, he ripped off the poster and stepped into the road where he could see it more clearly in the light cast from a window of the farmhouse. The others gathered around him as he stared at what was obviously an old photograph of Hac Quan. But the poster itself was fresh. Barney asked the engineer to translate the notice.

Slowly, and with almost maddening precision, Hac Quan read: "Hac Quan. Native of this village. Enemy of the State. For information . . ." He went no further, but shook his head in desperation and bitterness.

"Judas," Fannin said softly. "Just a damned Judas. At least we were anonymous before."

The Oriental ran one hand over his forehead as if to brush back his hair and continued to shake his head. Without a word he started down the road toward the village where his wife lived. The others watched him for a moment. Then Barney Fannin realized what was about to happen. After several quick strides he caught the short man's arm and swung him about. "You kill on your own time. I can't afford the luxury of your revenge. You thought she would not betray you to the Chinese. Well, she did. But if you were going to kill her you should have done it before she turned your name in."

Hac Quan half closed his eyes as he seemed to be considering what the American had said. "Are you telling me that you need me, Colonel?"

Barney's hand went back as he prepared to slap the round and taunting face. Then he dropped his hand and, still holding Hac Quan by the arm, pushed the smaller man ahead of him. "Call on me when we've time and I'll kill her for you."

Turning their backs on the village, the men retraced the path they had taken the night before to the cache where they had buried their explosives. Picking up three twenty-five pound charges, primer cord and detonator, they set out for the tank farm with Hac Quan in the lead, Zing behind him, Carl following, and Barney bringing up the rear. They moved swiftly through the rice paddies onto a small road that led north. Twice they hurled themselves down into the brush beside the road as trucks passed. Once they almost bumped into a Vietcong sentry posted at a crossroad. Hac Quan moved out into the road and asked directions, and while the sentry pointed east, the team crossed the road behind him. A few minutes later, Hac Quan joined them and they moved on once more. They topped a small hill, and below them lay the tank farm, protected by bright spots bathing each huge petroleum storage tank with light. The tanks were lined up like soldiers in ranks, stretching two abreast for what might have been half a mile or more. Dropping to their bellies, the four men scanned their target. Ten thousand-gallon tanks. Enough fuel to launch an attack across most of Southeast Asia. Fuel that must have been brought from Baku and Bahrain. Fuel in tankers across the Red Sea and the Indian Ocean. Fuel pumped out of Malaysia and Indonesia. Fuel piped from the coast and hauled in barrels and tank trucks. Fuel carried by ox cart. Fuel enough to start the fire of a large war.

From where they lay just behind the lights, the team could see sentries walking their posts. Fannin pulled up his field glasses and counted. Five guards and then five more. Ten men coming together in groups, each patrolling the closest approach to the tanks. Watching with care and trained eyes, he could see that the sentries were careless. They were looking at each other or the ground before them. They had probably walked the post for weeks without anything but tired feet to show for their efforts. He handed the glasses to Zing Miller at his side, who took a close look at the tanks. Routine. Thin metal sheeting. Close enough together that a single ring main could do the job. When he was satisfied he knew what his problems were, he motioned for the team to fall back. Very carefully they withdrew and planned their strategy. All agreed there was no subtle way to make this strike. It had to be done with a shock and head on. Zing took the charges out of the bags and prepared his primer cord for a ring main. Then he gave the instructions he had to give, and Barney gave his. Hac Quan listened to what was expected of him and nodded. He would do what he had to do. Barney smiled, knowing that if they were at the mercy of the Oriental, he, in turn, needed their help now.

Carefully they moved forward into position. Barney, Zing and Carl each carried his submachine gun and twenty-five pounds of high explosive. Barney settled back on the knoll, looking down at the sentries and the target. He waited until he could see the others were in position, and then he brought up his submachine gun, braced his elbow in the ground before him and selected his sentries, making certain all ten were visible at the same instant. Then with great care, he squeezed off a burst of five shots. Two men fell. Another burst dropped a second pair of sentries as they came together. Zing took out his pair and Sprague his. One Vietcong soldier whirled and started to fire into the darkness; Hac Quan pressed off a burst, hurling the man backward. In an instant all was silent. Barney rose from the ground, threw up a phosphorus grenade which lighted the sky and dashed forward as Carl and Zing, seeing his signal, did the same. Each man set his charge on a rung of one of the small ladders which led to the top of the tank he had selected. Then each fell back with the piece of primer cord he held and tied it to the one tossed to him by the others until the primer cord was tied in a large circle making a single charge of the seventy-five pounds of plastic explosive.

Around them they could hear the warning sirens go off in the night. In the distance they could hear the approach of trucks and the fire of guns by confused men striking at shadows beyond the range of the spots. Suddenly a truck appeared in the lights and Vietcong soldiers spilled out, firing into the darkness.

From where he lay on the knoll, Hac Quan pressed off burst after burst in an effort to protect the team. Zing jerked the six-second fuse and waved for the others to fall back. Barney waited a moment and then, firing as he withdrew, brought down two Vietcong charging at him. The field of fire increased, the noise became deafening. From what appeared to be fright or incompetence, Sprague seemed to panic. Leaving his end of the ring main untied, he fled past Hac Quan into the darkness beyond. Barney did not see the cord come apart as he stood his ground long enough to get off another burst, but as he whirled for a final look, he saw Zing dive back on his belly to hold the primer cord together.

The blast was enormous. Sudden. Frightening. Barney was hurled to his face on the ground; then he rose, running away from the flames which climbed the sky. When he glanced back over his shoulder, he could see nothing of Zing Miller. Another tank burst, hurling its contents over still another until the remaining tanks burst in unison like linked firecrackers. A truckload of soldiers disappeared into the inferno. Then another. As he passed Hac Quan, Barney pulled the engineer to his feet and dashed on into the darkness and away from the confusion behind them. They ran together until they approached the crossroad where the sentry had been pacing earlier. Then they collapsed in the middle of a paddy. A moment later Carl Sprague joined them, his gun in hand, his face smeared with dirt. Slowly he sank down in the mud beside Barney Fannin.

For a long time the old soldier stared at Sprague. Then he said softly, so that his voice would not carry beyond the three of them,

"I didn't expect it. Not you." He wanted to weep as he said, "I trusted you. I believed in you." Then in cold anger, "Did you chicken or betray us?"

Sprague was silent for a time as he shook his head from side to side. He looked at the submachine gun in his hand in complete disbelief. "This is for kids. I've a wife, a family." Then he confessed sadly, "I want to get home."

"Oh, my God," Barney said. "Oh, my God." He felt almost beaten as he evaluated his situation. "A cripple, a coward, and . . ." with a gesture toward Hac Quan, he added, "him." Each man was silent for his own reasons. Then the other two were surprised to see Barney Fannin raise his hand in a half salute into the darkness, a gesture of respect to Zing Miller. He brought his hand down and pulled himself to his feet in one movement.

Then to Hac Quan: "That sentry out there on the crossroad. If we kill him, they'll know which way we went. Just take us around him."

The Oriental nodded. He did not like this large man with the angry manner, but he was trying to understand him. The man who had died meant nothing to Hac Quan. He had barely known him and he knew that, like so many others he had seen killed in battle, the face would become dim and confused with other faces. It was the nature of war, the sudden throwing together of strangers and the sudden wrenching apart. If he felt sorry for anyone, it was the heavy-set civilian who had talked about returning to his wife and family. Hac Quan had held that ridiculous notion not so long ago himself.

The three men rose and made their way back toward the small house near the village.

In the house, Li stood waiting at the window. She had not expected these men to come. She did not know why she had let them use her house. She owed her uncle nothing. As a child she had known him, but that had been a long time ago. She could recall very little about him. In the months since her mother had died, she had survived. The Vietcong had not bothered her. The Chinese soldiers had come and gone through the town, and she had learned that if she kept off the streets during the day they would not discover she lived near the village. Her mother's friends knew. Her uncle's wife knew but did not care. She had her Chinese captain, and before him she had had the Vietcong major. But Li had had no one except the neighbors who brought her food or went walking with her when she shopped. Now, as she waited for the strangers to return, she wondered what her neighbors would think if they knew she was harboring the intruders. Earlier in the day she had seen the poster in front of the mayor's house. The picture of her uncle was an old one, but it did not matter. He could be recognized, and the price the Chinese and the Vietcong were offering was high. Li thought about her small collection of North Vietnamese coins and the two jade rings her mother had left her. There was nothing else she owned except the house, and soon the men of Ho Chi Minh would come to take her house as they had taken all the others. They would tell her the house was too large for one small girl to live in alone. They would offer to find her a place to live in Hanoi. One of the soldiers would offer to share his bed with her. Another would say he knew of a place in the fishermen's mart she could work. And he would smile and say she could stay in the house of his mother. She knew, because the same offers had been made to her friends, and one by one, when they no longer had anything left but the offers, they had gone to the bed of a Vietcong soldier or to the fishermen's mart. Li thought about the large sum of money offered on the poster which described her uncle as an enemy of the state.

Behind her she heard the sound of the young American soldier who was rolling over and over, twisting his broken legs. She tried to shut out the sound of his crying because it was not a very brave sound and because she did not believe a man should cry. But then she knew this was not a man, even though he had a beard of the kind she had seen on the French and the English. She knew he was not a soldier the way she knew the man with the cold eyes and the thin hands was not a soldier, the one the others called Zing; and as she knew the man with broad shoulders whom the others called Carl was also not a soldier. There was only one soldier among the men: the Colonel. The large man with the face that looked like a weathered rock or the dried hide of a cow. A strange man. The others did what he told them to do, but she wondered if they liked him or were afraid of him. For reasons she could not explain, she was afraid of him. There was something about the way he moved, the way he carried his head. Her father had told her of men who looked like the Colonel. Men who were lost, and angry because they were lost.

Behind her the young stranger, hardly older than she, was no longer crying and she wondered if he was conscious. Part of the day he had been asleep and part of the night he had been awake. But she had never really been certain if he knew where he was or what was going on about him. The other strangers had come in and talked to him; sometimes he appeared to know what they were saying and other times he seemed to be looking for something far away.

Leaving her place by the window, Li crossed to the mat where the young soldier lay. His eyes were open in the darkness. She reached out and touched his shirt to find it wet. He probably had a fever, but there was nothing she could do about that any more than she could do anything about his legs. Kneeling beside him, she did the only thing she could to help him: she smiled.

"Have I been here long?" he asked, and from the way he turned his head from her, she knew he did not believe she understood him.

"Since last night," she said.

She could see the surprise on his face, and the lines about his mouth seemed to disappear as if he were able to relax with someone who could talk to him.

"The others?" he asked.

"They went out."

He nodded and, reaching down, touched his legs. "They're numb now," as if he had to explain why he was not crying. Then he seemed to remember his question. "Are they coming back?"

Li nodded. "The large one said they would be back before morning."

"The Colonel," the young man identified Fannin for her. "If he said he will be back, he will be." Brodsky said this partly to assure her and partly to show that he believed that nothing could stop Fannin from returning if that was his intent. "Did they get the bridge last night?"

Looking away toward the window where she could see a piece of the moon, Li nodded. She did not want to tell him that because they had blown up the bridge there were more soldiers patrolling the roads now.

"I was supposed to help," he said, as if his presence needed an explanation.

She nodded. There was a noise below and then she heard footsteps on the stairs. There was no place to hide, so she remained where she was. The young man tried to reach for his gun, but it was resting against the wall, and when he appealed to her for help, she shook her head. Then the door opened and the large American stood in the doorway. Behind him she could see the man called Carl and her uncle. A wry smile spread over the rutted face of the old soldier as he saw the girl kneeling beside the young man. Then the door closed and Li could hear the men going into the next room, the guns being set on the floor, the boots coming off and a man dropping down to sleep. She reached out and touched the young man on the pad as if to comfort him and then left the room, closing the door behind her.

When Barney Fannin looked up from the floor where he was loading his automatic rifle, he saw the girl standing in the doorway. "How is he?" he asked.

Not knowing what she was expected to say, Li smiled. The man called Zing was not with them, and the man called Carl looked very sad and was sitting cross-legged on the floor next to her uncle.

"I'll talk to the boy in the morning," the Colonel was saying, and she knew he meant for her to leave. She bowed slightly and backed out of the room as she had seen her mother do when there had been guests in the house. When she closed the door of the room and stood at the top of the steps, she thought again about the poster with her uncle's picture and of the boy lying on the mat where she usually slept.

In the bedroom, Barney Fannin flung himself back on his jacket and stared at the ceiling. Beside him, Carl Sprague closed his eyes in pain. Hac Quan sat up slowly and looked at the two.

"I know how a man feels about his wife," he said, as much to explain his own return as to tell Sprague that he understood what had happened to him. "I don't think it is a wrong thing for a man to think of his wife. I often thought of mine."

Carl Sprague rolled over and faced the wall.

Hac Quan looked at Barney Fannin, who was shaking his head and saying, "Blow it out. Tomorrow we've got a dam to go, and how the hell we do it without Zing is more than I can figure now."

Hac Quan nodded. He had not thought of the dam, but he could not tell this American colonel with the angry look that what he was really thinking about was his wife and the Chinese captain. Even when he lay down to sleep, he kept thinking of his wife and the captain instead of the dam.

THE WESTERN PACIFIC ●

THE PLANE carrying General LeGrande and Janet Garner to Saigon was three hours out of Clark Field. Both of them had slept through most of the Pacific crossing and had remained in the cabin when the plane put down in the Philippines. Here they were joined by a young major from DIA with a summary report of the activities of the team in the Song Koi valley. There was nothing in it that LeGrande did not already know.

Now, as the plane sped toward Vietnam, the General stared at the bright sky beyond the window. He was in his shirt sleeves; his tie lay folded on the small table between him and Janet. She was watching his eyes scanning the scattered clouds as if he expected to see something. To most people Richard LeGrande gave the impression of great control and poise, but Janet had learned over the years that his eyes tended to give him away. He could control their restless scanning if he thought he was being watched, but if he was alone and worried, he seemed to take in everything quickly time and time again, as he was doing now.

Without turning to look at her, he asked, "Team Two?"

She rubbed an open palm over her cheek for an instant as she tried to understand what he was talking about, and then she realized he had just designated the group that she had radioed from the plane—the GENOPS staff members who were being rounded up as a second choice if the General should decide to commit them to the Song Koi.

"Jeff left London, picked up Max at Templehof, and they collected Leon at Calcutta." She had checked out with the radio operator only a few moments before.

LeGrande looked at her and smiled. "So damned efficient and beautiful, too. Disgusting combination." Then he was serious. "They should arrive in Saigon . . . ?"

"Five hours after we do."

The General nodded. "I don't want to see them," he said. "They can get off the plane and hole up someplace. I don't want them linked with me until I call on them." He was trying to protect his men, not reject them, because he was aware that his presence would be known to the enemy as soon as he stepped out of his plane.

"Until you call on them?" she asked. "Am I to gather that you plan to join the fun and games?" She was not smiling now; and as he stared at her across the table, he stretched his legs under it, touched hers, and, turning his hands palms up before him, said simply, "I don't know."

Then Janet asked the questions she knew he would have to answer to others, though she felt he had an answer that would satisfy her. "Team Two, as you so aptly just named it, why didn't it go in first?"

A bitter smile as LeGrande shook his head. "Get off my back, lady. You know as well as I do that Barney Fannin wanted his own team. He had the right to pick the men he wanted to die with."

It was Janet's turn to smile now. "That's a bit melodramatic for you, *mon général.*"

He framed the word *bitch* with his lips and then said, "That's what it comes down to."

"I hope not until after he becomes a hero."

Pulling himself to his feet, LeGrande reached into his suit jacket for his pipe, which he filled as he stood staring down at her. "If I've learned one thing about Barney Fannin these past few days, it is that all of the hogwash people conjure up about a death wish, not caring, to-hell-with-it—you name the attitude —well, they don't wash. There was a time when Barney wanted to live more than anything else."

Janet was silent for a time and then asked, "Is that good or bad for GENOPS?"

To her surprise, he started to laugh, but Janet knew him well enough to know that what she had said was not humorous. He was not laughing at her question, but rather because, as he said a moment later, "How the hell would I know?"

"I could say that's what *Das Wunderkind* gets paid to know. But I won't, because so many people in Washington will be saying that."

He took the pipe between his lips. "Thanks for not saying it." He started to walk away down the length of the plane, but after a couple of steps he swung back and faced her.

"What's wrong?"

"Wrong?" she asked, one hand going up to touch her hair as she leaned back in her seat.

"Yeah. Wrong." He wanted to be angry with her but he rarely could be. Now, as her face seemed tense and the skin came tight over the flat of her cheeks and the morning sunlight cast its shadows over them, he knew he would have been furious with anyone else these past ten minutes.

Janet's hand came away from her hair and she rubbed her shoulder as she thought about his question. "You're thinking of going in there. The cavalry charge in the nick of time." Then her hand fell into her lap and she was looking at it. He was patient. He waited for her to continue. "I'd like to quote a certain general who will remain nameless. 'Caution and reconnaissance come before an attack.' Or, as he has said many times, 'Don't commit your troops until you know what you are committing them to.' "

The pipe was cold in LeGrande's mouth. Very slowly he reached up and held it in his hands; and as he did so, she wondered how often she had seen him fumbling with a pipe when he did not know what else to do with his hands. "It's the first time," he said. "The first time. The Old Man. The Gray Wolf. You never agreed with them before. And now you are on their side. All of you knowing what I should do and telling me."

Janet did not know if she was supposed to explain her change of allegiance or not, but she knew that she had to say something because General Richard LeGrande suddenly looked as if he were alone—and in a way he was. "Something is not *ipso facto* wrong just because they said it." She was out of her seat and standing up beside him, her head tilted because he was so much taller than she. "I'm sorry, Richard, but I think you would be a fool to play hero now."

He reached out and touched her cheek where the sun had struck it only moments before as if he wanted to reach that spot of sun. Then he half closed his eyes and shook his head. "Doesn't anything ever go the way it should?"

It wasn't a question, and as his hand dropped, he half smiled. "Will you ask the sergeant back there if he can find us some coffee?"

It was a moment before Janet nodded. She knew he had not resolved the matter of his going into the valley of the Song Koi. When she reached the back of the plane, she told the sergeant that the General wanted coffee. Then she looked down the length of the plane at Le Grande, who stood with one hand against the side of the plane, leaning over his seat and staring out of the window, his eyes restlessly scanning the nothing beyond.

THE VALLEY OF THE SONG KOI ●

IT WAS LATE in the afternoon when Barney Fannin rolled over and looked out of the small window. One large hand rubbed over his stubbled beard and he pulled himself into a sitting position. Hac Quan lay asleep beside him. The dark face of the Annamese engineer appeared tense even in repose. Barney wondered about this man. He had come back because of his wife, and yet he had made no move to see her since the night they had arrived. If he planned to disrupt the mission, he should have acted by now. The bridge and the tank farm were large enough targets to warrant action. Ever since he had met the stranger, Barney had wondered just whose ball club Hac Quan was playing for. Maybe—just maybe—he could be trusted. But Barney was too far away from victory or support to trust anyone. He closed his eyes and thought about victory. If he was lucky he would go home, or he would not go home. He was not certain just where his luck lay at this moment. Behind him to the south was Saigon. Somewhere in that sprawling unkempt confusion was the American advisory group. Among them was his son. He leaned back on his elbows and thought about the boy. What would Janet Garner have caught on a tape if the boy had been asked about his father? Barney shook his head. Opening his eyes, he glanced at Carl Sprague, who lay on the floor staring at the ceiling. Their eyes did not meet.

"You bastard," Barney said softly so as not to wake the Annamese. Then he knelt down and, picking up his boots, moved quietly out of the room. He paused for a moment and then closed the bamboo door behind him. There was very little light in the hall that came from the room where he could see Joe Brodsky asleep on the floor. The girl sat beside Joe, her knees pulled up under her chin. She stared blankly at the American officer as if she were not aware that he stood in the doorway, but when he jerked his head toward the staircase, she rose to her feet and for a moment looked down at Joe. Barney watched her. She was smaller than he had thought. Her light blue *cheung san* was slit at the calf, and he smiled to himself thinking that poor Joe Brodsky was not going to get anything. Not here. Then the girl was in the hall beside him and was leading the way down the steps to the room below.

There were several pieces of European furniture—a sofa, two chairs and an old piano. Barney assumed the house had once been furnished by the French. Had the girl's mother slept with the Frenchman then the way Hac Quan's wife was sleeping with the Chinese officer now? The soldiers came and the soldiers went. Barney almost laughed as the lesson of history ran through his head. Sitting down on the piano bench, he pulled his boots on and laced them, knowing all the time that the girl was waiting for him to say something. If nothing else, she would want to know why he had asked her to join him. When he was done, he looked up at her.

"That sign?" he said. "The one with your uncle's picture."

She nodded, puzzled by what he had said and at the same time wondering why his voice was so harsh.

"How much are they offering?" he asked.

Li looked at him and shook her head. She knew how much was offered for Hac Quan, but what she did not know was why this American wanted to know. He certainly was not planning to turn her uncle in.

"How much, girl?" Fannin snapped.

She thought a moment and then explained. "To an American it would be nothing. To one of this village—all he could earn in a year."

Fannin nodded. The girl made sense. "And to you?" he asked.

She hesitated and he came to his feet. "Come on," and his hands were holding her arms. "You've thought of it."

Slowly, almost embarrassed, she nodded.

"And what did you decide?"

Then he saw that she was looking at his heavy fingers digging into her arms, and he dropped his hands.

"I don't want to draw attention to myself," she explained, and ho looked at her with surprise.

"And if you did?"

"I don't know," she said.

Fannin reached one hand behind her head and gently tipped it up so that he could look into her face. It was small, round, with dark eyes framed by black hair. "I'll buy that," he said, and when he saw that she did not understand what he had said, he explained, "I believe you." Then, almost as if he were feeling foolish, he added, "I'll make that loss of reward up to you. That's a promise."

The girl's voice was soft as she looked at this man who had revealed himself more than he knew. "I did not ask for anything," she said.

Fannin chuckled. "If you had, Li, you'd be dead right now. I don't think people who have been bought can stay bought." He reached into his pocket and drew out a chocolate bar. It looked wilted in its dark brown wrapper. With a slight smile, he tore it in two and handed her half.

She looked at it a moment and then, smiling, took what she believed was a peace offering. They both stripped away the wrapper and settled down on a pair of cushions on the floor, watching each other dubiously. After a time, Fannin smiled and then the girl did.

"Li," he said, "that boy up there. I brought him here. He could be home now and be well, but I brought him here. Anything you can do to help him . . ." Then his hands went wide as if to indicate the breadth of his appreciation.

The girl nodded. "The other one?" she asked.

Barney shook his head and believed the girl understood.

"How long will you stay?" She had the right to know.

"Three more nights." Then he shook his head. "No, we'll leave at the end of the third."

There was a sound above and both of them could make out Joe Brodsky's voice as he called for someone. The girl was already on her way up the stairs before Barney was on his feet. He was staring at her ankles as she disappeared. He rubbed his beard and shook his head. He had lied when he said she would be repaid, and though he had lied to women most of his life, he wished he had not had to here, in this place and to this girl.

It had been dark for two hours when Barney and his two companions edged out of the brush on their bellies, their weapons cradled in their arms. Before them rose the dam. "Jesus," Barney said as he tried to measure its height. It was neither Hoover nor Shasta; it was probably even jerry-built, but he was not going to bring it down with the explosives he carried. Not with twenty-five pounds or five times twenty-five pounds of explosives. Near the base of the dam was a road, and he could make out the lights of passing trucks. They would not be of any use as they had been with the bridge. He looked up again. Near the top he could see that water flowed evenly through a spillway and crashed into the river below. The Song Koi was not a great river or even a very important one, but it had been built up here and was furnishing power to the city at its mouth as well as the small towns along its course. Barney did not know what the power was being used for, and at this moment he could not have cared less. The fact of it crossed his mind and he shook it off.

Rolling over in the darkness, he stared at Carl. "Miller could have found a way. I can't." Then pointedly, as if to show his contempt, he asked, "Any bright suggestions?"

Carl scanned the height of the dam, then shook his head slowly.

"Given enough explosives, a man could smash the spillway up there," Hac Quan suggested, his hand pointing toward the narrow place through which the water flowed.

Barney rolled back onto his belly and stared at the top of the dam. Then without turning to look at the Annamese engineer, he asked, "Can we get up there?"

Hac Quan shrugged before he realized Fannin was not looking at him. "Let us see." He crawled back into the bushes, hauling a bag of explosives behind him. Barney waved for Carl to follow and then brought up the rear after taking time to glance once more at the dam.

An hour later the three were standing on the edge of the lake created by the dam. Barney remained covered by the shadow of a tree, his companions at his side. One large hand clutched the automatic rifle slung over his shoulder as he tried to calculate the size of the lake in the darkness. In the distance—he gauged it at two miles or more—there were lights. A control house for the spillway? He did not know. The only other lights he could make out were nearer—about a half mile away toward the southern shore of the lake. A camp? A sentry post? A power station? Without turning around he asked Hac Quan, "Those lights there" —and his hand came up as he pointed—"what are they?"

He heard the Annamese trot off in the darkness. The lake looked black. Barney's head went up and he searched for a star. There were none to be seen. He tried to recall if there had been clouds earlier in the day, but he could not remember. Maybe it would rain. As he knelt and drew his rifle across his knee, he wondered if rain would make any difference. He could not see that it would. The river would swell, but the dam had been designed to control that.

For the first time he turned to look at Carl Sprague standing beside him, the explosives at his feet. Barney looked up at the insurance salesman and down at the explosives and shrugged. "Miller would have known what to do," he said again.

Then as if he had to be heard, Carl Sprague dropped to one knee and thrust his face into Barney's. "You bastard. I didn't ask to come. I'm doing the best I can. If it isn't good enough, drop dead. But believe me, I'm going on to the end of this because I said I would."

Barney's head cocked to one side. "And because if we flub this duck, a lot of kids'll get killed, and maybe yours." He rocked back on his heels as if to get a better look at the other man. "Don't get noble on me, Carl. It isn't fitting. Not now. Just hang on tight and maybe we'll get you back to Columbus, O-Hi-O." Then without waiting for Sprague to react, Fannin came to his feet.

The other man remained kneeling for a moment as one hand reached out and grasped the long grass. Jerking off a handful, Carl stared at it as if to find an answer there. Then he asked, "Did you ever flub a duck, Barney?"

Both the question and the familiar name struck Fannin instantly. He wanted to reach down and grab Sprague by the collar and tell him that he was talking to his colonel. He wanted to shout that a man could not afford to flub a duck, not now or any other time. He wanted to say he knew. He knew. But instead, he reached down and pulled up Sprague by the shoulder strap on his shirt, held his hand on the other man's shoulder and shook his head. "You ever call me Barney again and I'll smash your face in." But when his hand came away and he turned to listen to Hac Quan coming through the brush toward them, both Carl Sprague and Barney Fannin knew the question had not been answered.

For an instant Barney wondered if the Oriental had heard the exchange between himself and Sprague.

"What's there?" he asked.

"Two small boats and some sentries. One of them was standing by the boats. The other was asleep inside one of them."

"That's all there are?"

Hac Quan smiled wryly. "Let us just say that was all I saw."

Barney nodded in agreement. All three were looking off toward the lights now. "How far away?" Barney asked.

"More than a kilometer."

Then the three fell silent as Barney dropped once more to his knee. A kilometer or more. And the spillway was another two kilometers past that. "What kind of boats?" he asked without looking up.

Hac Quan squatted on his heels. "Motor launches. From the look of them, I would say they use them to patrol the lake in the daytime."

"And at night?"

The engineer shrugged. "Maybe they have more boats out now."

Barney looked at the man. This was a notion that had not crossed his mind, but he had to admit that it made sense. He turned and stared across the dark lake. Finally, after what seemed to the other like half an hour, Barney came to his feet. "We need more explosives," he said. "About ten times what we have. I think I know where we'll find them."

Hac Quan looked dubious and Carl Sprague was startled that Barney Fannin believed he knew the terrain so well.

"To get explosives and back to do the job tonight?" Carl asked.

Barney came up full height as he opened and closed his big hands at his side. He had made his decision—and it had not been a simple one. "We'll find our explosives and bring them here."

Without another word, Barney slipped back into the brush along the bank and moved quickly up river. The other two men followed.

•   •   •

Joe Brodsky's eyes came open, and for a time he tried to adjust them to the vague light cast by the oil lamp beside his head. When he could make out the ceiling above, he turned his head and saw the girl staring at him. He tried to smile and failed because his legs hurt. He tried to recall her face. He had seen it someplace before. Somehow it had been running through his head—vaguely at times, more clearly at others. It was a pretty face, full-cheeked and yet fragile. He reached out to touch her. The pain from his legs racked his body, and his hand started to fall short when she grasped it and held it. Her touch was warm, gentle. Now the pain in his legs belonged to someone else and he was only aware of the touch of her. She wore a light blue sheath-like dress, open at her thighs, which allowed her to sit cross-legged on the floor. Joe tried to smile again. This time he fared a little better. "I'm Joe," he said.

"The large man, the one they call Colonel, he told me," she said. "And you?"

Instead of answering his question, the girl asked another. "Do you know where you are?"

The pain was back in his legs again; he could see the sky above him filled with the canopy of his chute and knew that it was open and yet he was coming down too fast. All of the air seemed to be spilling, and he saw that the canopy was really folded in the center, making two large cups—a Mae West. But there was too much air spilling out and the chute was bringing him down too fast. Then he hit the side of a tree and the bazooka kept him from folding his legs under him and so he knew they were broken. But the girl was asking if he knew where he was and he did not, so he slowly shook his head. He thought she was about to tell him when he heard someone knocking somewhere, and he looked at her. For a moment she remained very still. Then she dropped his hand and came to her feet. He was about to ask her something and she shook her head.

Then very softly she said, "I want to live. If you make a sound, I'll kill you."

Startled, Joe watched her leave the room and close the door behind her. Looking about, he saw his rifle leaning near his head, but when he reached for it, he was overwhelmed by the pain in his legs and collapsed on his side.

Li went quickly to the door. If the Chinese or Vietcong were there she would do better with them if they did not have to wait. If it was anyone else . . . but she could not imagine it being anyone else. Not now. She opened the door and in the faint light she could make out the face of Madame Hac, the wife of her uncle. The Madame was a beautiful woman in spite of her forty years. She was taller than her husband. Different, too. Eurasian—the spawn of a French officer and an Annamese bar wench. Even Li admitted to herself that the older woman was beautiful. Without hesitation, Li started to close the door once more, but the woman spoke quickly, "Is Hac Quan with you?"

Puzzled by the question and certain that the police would not send someone else to do their business, Li paused. Then she recalled the reward and shook her head. "You told the police," she said. "Didn't you receive your reward?"

The older woman looked at her tolerantly. "Is he here?"

"He is not here," the girl answered, telling the truth of the moment. She did not trust her uncle's wife. There were few in the village who did any longer because of the Chinese officer.

The older woman kept her patience. "If he is here, tell him to hide. The police are coming to look for him."

Surprised that the woman was giving this warning, Li shook her head again. "Why? Why you now?" she asked.

The older woman drew herself up proudly. "The Captain was promoted to Major and transferred when he informed the police that Hac Quan had returned."

Li looked at the woman, still no less confused and still without an answer to her question. "Congratulations," she said bitterly.

But the other woman shrugged off the bitterness. "The Major isn't taking me with him."

It took Li a moment to grasp what was happening. Then she thought she understood. Madame Hac wanted her small piece of revenge—the woman who had lost her dignity and importance trying in some small and twisted way to retrieve it. For a time Li just looked at her. All of her beauty seemed so pointless in this contorted moment. Then she stepped aside for the older woman to enter. Closing the door, Li stood with her back to it. She had to decide now and she knew there could be only one decision because she was lost in any event. "My uncle was here. He left a friend. A young man. He is injured."

Madame Hac nodded. She did not understand, and she did not care about Hac Quan's friend. But she did want to thwart the Major. "You will have to hide him," she snapped.

Li nodded. "There's no place upstairs."

Madame Hac scanned the room carefully and her eyes narrowed as she stared at the large piano from another world. Li saw where she was looking and said, "You will have to help me." They started up the stairs together and they had reached the top when they heard a crash in the room beyond the door. Madame Hac hesitated, but Li flung the door open. Sprawled on the floor, several feet from the pad where he had been lying, Joe Brodsky lay, his rifle in hand, his head to one side. Kneeling, Li felt under his chin. Then she looked up at the older woman. "He's alive."

But Madame Hac was already thinking of something else. "If you killed him and gave him to them . . ."

Li shook her head slowly. "The piano," was all she said.

The two women looked at each other for a moment and then the older one shrugged. Maybe her husband's niece would tell him who had saved the young American and she would be forgiven and taken to America to live. She had heard that life was good there. Food and beautiful dresses. Maybe . . . Between them, they dragged the young soldier down the stairs, Li carrying his rifle over her shoulder. When they reached the bottom of the stairs they lifted and placed the young man inside the piano, laying him across the strings, which twanged wildly as his weight hit them. The rifle was placed at his side. Then, as she lowered the top of the piano, Li half closed her eyes and prayed to whatever gods there were that the young man would not regain consciousness again that night.

There were sounds in the street and both women recognized the short, quick steps of trotting soldiers. The sound stopped and someone banged on the door. The two women looked at each other, and as Li went to open the door, Madame Hac sat down on the piano bench. Looking out, Li saw the soldiers taking positions about the house. A young officer stepped inside, followed by two soldiers. The officer was Chinese. Li believed he was a lieutenant. She had seen him in the town before. The other two men were North Vietnamese. Strangers to her. The lieutenant reached out and shoved the young girl back as his men sprang forward, their weapons raised and ready for use.

"Girl," the officer snapped, "where are they?"

But before Li could speak, Madame Hac asked softly, "You wanted something, Lieutenant?"

The young officer in the light brown uniform which buttoned to his neck turned to see the Major's woman watching him. "I am sorry, Madame. It was not my intent to frighten you." As he spoke, Li wondered if he knew of Madame Hac's rejection. Perhaps not, and if not, for the moment they might be safe.

"You have come for a reason?" Madame Hac was asking.

"The man who was your husband, Madame. We thought he might be at his sister's house." And as he spoke, Li looked at the older woman. It was possible. Just possible that Madame Hac had come to win back her husband, but only after she had put him in such danger that he would need her help. The girl was ready to laugh at the irony of the beautiful Eurasian's finding herself trapped into helping an American. The lieutenant nodded to his men, who began to walk through the house, their weapons raised as if they were certain they would find their quarry. Li became more sure that her guess about Madame Hac was the right one.

The lieutenant was congratulating the older woman now on the Captain's promotion, and Li was certain that he did not know his superior was moving on alone. Upstairs the soldiers banged from room to room and then clumped downstairs again. The lieutenant looked at them and accepted their shrugs as an answer.

Smiling, he apologized to Madame Hac and said, "Sometime,

Madame, I would like to sit back and listen to you play the piano."

Madame Hac smiled, and her beautiful face was enough to make even Li believe that she was innocent of any deception. "Whenever you can, Lieutenant. Whenever you can." It was an invitation, and the young officer understood what was being offered him. His smile broadened as he nodded and waved his men out of the house. At the door he looked back toward the two women. "I shall find the time, Madame. That is a promise."

Then he was gone. Madame Hac rose from the piano bench and said, "Tell my husband that I looked after him."

Li nodded. The tall Eurasian put out her hand and took the young girl's chin between her fingers and turned her face from side to side so that she could see it better. "You have grown into a pretty thing. There are young officers who would enjoy you."

Her hand came away as she promised, "I'll remember to recommend you. Your American will not get out of here alive. How you turn him in is your own business."

Li nodded, and the other woman left. Li was alone again and she went at once to the piano and opened the top. The pale, partly bearded face of Joe Brodsky was staring up at her. Then she realized that he was conscious and, as she reached out to help, knew that she was not going to turn him in—she had become very attached to this stranger.

After more than an hour's march through the tangled countryside, avoiding lights when they passed them, ducking the sound of passing vehicles and sentries, Barney Fannin led his companions eastward along the river bank. Once, to avoid a road that ran to the very edge of the river, they had moved into the chilling waters. Now Barney raised his hand and the others came to a stop behind him. All three were wet, cold and tired. "We'll find explosives there," he said, pointing toward the silhouette of the bridge they had toppled two nights before. Hac Quan nodded. It was obvious that the reconstruction of the bridge would require the removal of debris, and the quickest way would be to blast off the broken abutments and the tangled steel reinforcement.

Moving forward, the three could make out the small tents of the construction camp near the base of the bridge. The tents had not been there two days before. Barney waved his companions back and started forward alone. Two steps and Hac Quan was at his side.

"Do you want help?"

The tall soldier shook his head. Then, to his own surprise, he clapped the smaller man on the back and pointed to a clump of brush. "Wait for me there." Unslinging his automatic rifle, he handed it to Hac Quan and moved into the river. The cold waters rose above his boots, soaking his trousers and then his jacket. Reaching down, he unclipped his cartridge belt and slung it and the holster over his shoulder. He continued to move through the water. Brush and small trees along the bank cast protective shadows, and when he could, he took advantage of them. A sound on the bank and he paused—a soldier, short and squat, sitting on his heels staring at the bridge above him. Possibly a sentry. Possibly a man who could not rest. It did not make any difference to Barney. The man was there and he had to be removed. Slowly, Barney moved through the water. Then as he was about to close with his victim, the Oriental rose to his feet, stretched and walked away down a small footpath toward one of the farther tents. Barney almost laughed as he looked from the disappearing soldier to his own legs, deep in the frigid water. Waiting a few moments to be certain the soldier had no companions who were awake or moving about, Barney rubbed a wet hand over the stubble of beard on his chin and then moved out of the water onto the bank.

There were five tents before him, square topped and designed for short men. He did not know what was inside them. Possibly sentries. Workers. Supplies. Clipping his cartridge belt into place again, he opened the flap of his holster and removed the piece of coiled wire that he had put there several days before. Reaching up, he slipped the wire around the shoulder strap of his field jacket. Finally, he was ready. There was nothing else he could do

now except make his move. A sound and a sentry. Barney
dropped to the ground and waited, his eyes on the sentry, who
casually walked among the tents and then departed down the foot
path. Remaining on his belly, Barney crawled forward to the
closest tent. He raised a flap and edged in on his stomach. Darkness inside and the heavy breathing of men. Lifting his head,
Barney made out the figures of four men lying on the ground. One
breathed irregularly and then rolled over with his face to the far
wall. Inching backwards, Barney retreated until he was outside
once more. Then he moved on his knees toward the next tent. He
waited with his ear against the canvas. Not a sound. He started to
pick up the bottom of the tent only to find it taut. Angry, he
reached for his knife and was about to slit the canvas when he
heard a sound. Flat again and waiting, the knife in one hand and
his other on the wire coiled about his shoulder strap. A sentry
walked several paces from him, paused in the darkness and turned
around to stare at the river, swelling now from the rain.

Shoving his knife back into his boot, Barney slipped the wire
off his shoulder strap, wrapped the ends about each fist so that
there was a slack of several feet between his hands. Then, in an
instant he rose to his feet, crossed his hands to create a loop in the
slack, tossed the loop over the sentry's head and brought his knee
up into the sentry's back, forcing the man's body away while the
loop closed tightly about his neck. A moment of silent flapping as
the sentry tried to reach the man behind him and then a limp
weight. Barney Fannin lowered the body to the ground. In the
darkness he could just make out the contorted features of his victim.

Turning his attention to the tent once more, he slit the side of it
with two quick jerks of his knife. Inside, he detected the shape of
boxes. Taking a match from his belt, he struck it on a box. Checking them, he saw an odd marking—a house in six parts. He realized this could mean explosives to an illiterate: a breaking apart.
Ripping one box open, he knew he had found what he had come
for. He was standing beside the box when he heard a sound.
Somewhere. Taking a deep breath, he stepped out of the tent,

grabbed one foot of the dead sentry and pulled him inside. A long wait until there was quiet again. Then he lifted the boxes of explosives and carried them one at a time to the river bank away from the cluster of tents. When he had all that he wanted and was sure that he was far enough from the tents, he lifted one box onto his shoulder, slipped into the river and waded back to where he had left his companions.

Very carefully, he set the explosives at Carl Sprague's feet. "There are three more cases back there." He returned to the river, the others following.

Three hours later, as the first streaks of light were tearing away the dark edges of the sky, they had buried the four cases of explosives near the lake up the river. Barney stood for a moment beside the brush which he had spread to cover his cache and stared at the distant spillway and then at the two small craft which patrolled the lake. There was not anything he could do about them before morning, and so they had to flee. Shrugging, Barney started to turn away when Carl grasped his arm. "We still have an hour. If we don't try, we miss the plane."

Barney looked at the man. He did not think Carl Sprague was frightened, but he could not quite explain to himself why the man did not understand they had no choice. With a sweep of his hand, Barney knocked Carl's fingers from his jacket and started toward the house. Carl turned to Hac Quan to protest, but the Oriental pushed him forward after the Colonel.

Inside the small house, Li stood looking down at Joe Brodsky. She had done the best she could for both of them. Joe's eyes were open now and his head rolled from side to side, though he controlled his moans so that only when she put her head down could she hear anything more than his irregular breathing. The young soldier, looking up into the soft round face of the girl, could see the fear in her eyes, and when she reached one hand up to cover her mouth, he could see the trembling. If the night had been painful for him, it had been fearful for her—black, stark, ugly, crawling fear. With all the strength he could muster, he stretched out one hand and took her arm. She yielded to the pressure and came to her knees beside him. There were tears in his eyes and she reached out to brush them away. Then, as if she had suddenly resolved a problem, she pulled off her slippers and lay down beside him, one arm thrown across his chest while the other cradled his head as if he were a child. It was cold, and after a few moments she pulled the blanket over the two of them. Slowly, she rocked back and forth, trying to comfort the youth in her arms. Her eyes were closed and she did not see the first light crawl across the room.

The sun was already up when Barney Fannin returned to the house and found the two of them in the corner of the living room. Fully dressed, the boy and the girl lay asleep with their arms about each other. Standing behind the Colonel, Hac Quan half smiled and then climbed to the bedroom above, thinking about the two young people and recalling his own youth. Carl Sprague, who had waited downstairs to see if anyone had noticed them enter the house, turned from the window and found Fannin still watching the sleeping pair. Barney looked at him and shook his head. He wished he were young again. He glanced outside the window and realized that he had been so busy through the night and so weary before dawn that he had not even noticed the stars. He wondered if there had been any. Now he would never know. He followed Carl Sprague up the stairs, pulled off his wet boots and fell back on his elbows. Another night ahead and then another. He would not finish, and yet he would do the best he could.

As he stared at the ceiling above, he tried to make himself remember the thousands of Americans stationed in Vietnam. They did not know it, but they were depending upon a very tired man. He tried to recall the face of his son and he could not. He was too weary and the boy too far away. His eyes closed and he was almost asleep when he realized that in his exhausted condition he had missed something important. It took all his remaining strength to pull himself to his feet and pad down the stairs again. Neither

Joe nor the girl had moved. Trying to wipe away his fatigue with a heavy hand across his face, he knelt down beside the girl and shook her. After a time she opened her eyes. A moment to realize where she was as she looked first at Joe, whom she was holding in her arms, and then at the American officer. Very slowly she nodded as if she understood the question he had not yet asked. Untangling herself gently from Joe, she came to her feet and retreated across the room with Fannin.

"Why's he down here?" he asked softly.

Li glanced back at Joe and then she told Fannin about the visitors she had received the night before. He listened without a word, and when she was done, he nodded. For a moment the girl thought he had not understood, and then he turned to look out of the window. He tried to recall LeGrande's comments about cover. In a European country a Caucasian could walk down a street. In an Oriental country, he had to remain completely hidden. And with the light outside, he knew that there was nothing he could do, no place he could go.

He looked at the girl once more and then he half smiled, "It's like the old story, girl. When rape is inevitable, relax and enjoy it." Seeing the puzzled look on her face, he explained, "We're here. We'll make the best of it."

"And if they come back?"

He reached out and put a comforting hand on her shoulder as he said simply the words he knew would discomfort her, "If they come, we'll fight. We won't win, but we'll fight."

Li thought she understood now. He was admitting he might be trapped. She watched him. His face looked old in the morning light, and she knew that the days and the nights were leaving their traces.

"They've been here," he said. "Maybe that will satisfy them for now." He thought about what he had said and then added, "We'll be gone soon." He was walking away now and as he reached the stairs, he glanced back at Joe and then at her. "Your uncle," he said, "don't tell him. He'll only get his hopes up and then maybe get all of us killed."

She waited a moment before she answered. "If he lives, will you tell him she helped?"

Fannin nodded. Then he made his way back up the stairs, thinking how simple her request had been to grant considering the condition she had placed upon it. As he fell asleep, Barney told himself that he had to remember that he would not be able to leave Joe again.

SAIGON •

GENERAL LEGRANDE had been in Saigon most of the day. When their plane touched down, he and Janet had been met by a staff car and driven to a house near the outskirts of the city. The entire area had been cordoned off by sentries, and the colonel who took them to the house assured the General that every effort would be made to keep his identity a secret from everyone except those whom he wished to contact. But this was a kind of security for which LeGrande had little respect. Too many Vietnamese worked at the airport for his arrival to have been kept a secret. He knew they would not have recognized him immediately, but once they had described both Janet and himself and been shown photographs, his presence would be no secret. Besides, nothing was more of a challenge to espionage than a house surrounded by sentries. However, the General decided to let the Army play its games so long as they did not get in his way or link him up with Fannin's team.

Le Grande and Janet looked over the small house, nodded to the colonel and waited for him to leave. When they were alone, they wandered through the five rooms, including two bedrooms and a small office. Janet wondered if the house had been selected from Washington by a discreet MacWolfe or ordered by the puritanical Chairman of the Joint Chiefs. It was not important.

LeGrande settled down in the small office. Janet watched a sergeant who brought in their bags. The sergeant informed her that he had been assigned to the house for any duty she and the gentleman wished. For a moment Janet was puzzled, and then she realized that the soldier had not yet met "the gentleman" as he so nicely put it. After thanking the sergeant and telling him that she would call on him for little more than coffee in the next few hours, she joined LeGrande in the study. It was a comfortable room, occidental in its furnishings, and LeGrande assumed that it had once belonged to an unlucky Frenchman. He said as much to Janet, who only snorted, "What's unlucky about being out of Vietnam?"

"We're alone here?" he asked her, and when she told him about the sergeant, he snorted. "That means Hyde wants to know what we're talking about." He thought a moment and then said, "I'll bet you a new girdle that this place is bugged."

Janet shook her head. "My only concern is who bugged it," and both of them laughed.

She crossed over to the easy chair into which he had settled and sat on the arm of it. The General reached out and placed one hand on the flat of her thigh and slowly rubbed it. Both of them were silent for a time. "Now that we're here, *mon général*, what next?"

LeGrande's hand stopped moving and he looked up at her. "My hope was to play it by ear."

"And?"

"I've got to wait to hear from Washington about Barney. It's just that simple. If he's functioning and everything goes as planned, hell, then we fly home and act as if we've never been here."

Janet was not to be put off, because all he was telling her was what both of them knew to be obvious. "And?" she repeated.

LeGrande thought for a moment, glanced at his watch and rose to his feet. He turned and looked out of the window. From where he stood he could see two sentries. Turning to another window he could see three more. Somebody thought he needed to be all buttoned up. He crossed to the door and flung it open and saw neatly trimmed shrubs sliced by the drive. Tilting his head back, he stared at the afternoon sky. It was bright, and he did not know why he should have expected anything else. Maybe because the night had been long. Maybe because he expected bad news. He felt it like an itch and did not know where to scratch. Smiling to himself, he thought that sometime when he was talking about Saigon, he would tell of his itch and how a man should not believe his premonitions. Barney would call them a woman-thing. And his thoughts were back to Barney Fannin. Still seated on the arm of the chair, Janet watched the General as he rubbed his knuckles against the door frame. He was tense because he was waiting. And there was nothing he could do now except wait.

Suddenly, he whirled about and faced her. "I'm going for a walk."

Janet nodded. She had not expected this, and she considered the effects. There was no security against infiltration in this city. No one knew who was friendly with whom. No one knew the locations of the dozen small radios which broadcast in the jungle beyond the fringe of the city. Janet was wondering what difference it would make if the people in the north knew LeGrande was in Saigon. They were aware by now that Barney Fannin was moving among them. If Barney was still alive, they knew that. If he was dead, they knew that, too, because they would have been the ones to kill him. Unless . . . and her mind drifted back over the details of the Czech and the meeting in the park. It was always possible that the enemy still did not know who Barney was, did not know that he had a timetable, a plan of attack. Janet was thinking now because she did not believe that Richard Le-Grande could any longer. She had said so many times that her job and the job of others who worked with him was to let him talk and to react to his ideas. Now she was doing the thinking, because she could not be certain he was.

"I'll be back soon," he said.

And she realized he had been waiting for some kind of an answer to what had not been a question. "Do you want company, Richard?"

He smiled and shook his head. "If you hear anything, I'm sure the sergeant will know where I'm walking."

"What do you expect to hear?" she asked.

"Sometime this morning a plane flew over the valley and brought back a picture. The film went to Washington. Hyde will let me know what was on it." He half grinned. "I'm interested in that picture."

His hand came up as if to salute her and he started down the walk toward the street. Janet went to the door and watched the surprised look on the faces of the soldiers he passed. Then, as he walked beyond the shrubs and into the street and turned down it, she saw a small sedan start after the General. From where she stood, she could make out the face of the colonel who had brought them to the house. MacWolfe must have been very specific in his instructions for DIA to use a full-blown chicken to keep LeGrande under surveillance.

The General walked about a block down the crowded street. Annamese with pushcarts forced him aside twice. Two young Buddhist priests stalked by, their heads up and their eyes angry. The General wondered if these were the zealots who would make torches of themselves. A young woman dressed in a white skirt and blouse walked by, paused and looked back at the tall American. She hesitated a moment while she considered whether or not he was actually lonely. Then she noticed the military sedan slowly following him down the street and she scurried on. LeGrande nodded to two air corpsmen as he passed them. They were young. Their shirts were open at the collar and they wore their caps at a jaunty angle. He smiled to himself. This was Saigon. This was the city in the trap. When all was said and done, when all the accounts were in, a single fact would emerge—the government really controlled little more than the city itself. The countryside belonged to the aggressor, as it always did in a guerrilla campaign. Lawrence had written in Arabia a half century before that the guerrilla could limit the formal military to the main arteries and the centers of command. And here there were no main arteries. The roads were in dubious condition, the sky paths were flown by copters which were easy targets. This was a war, and LeGrande doubted if it could be won as it was being waged. This doubt he knew he could never really voice, partly because there was an aspect of *lese-majesté* in it; but more important everyone knew that Richard LeGrande had been spun out of the Pentagon because he believed that a well-trained guerrilla fighting in broken terrain was unbeatable. He might be limited in his scope, but he could not be completely destroyed so long as he had a neutral base to which he could withdraw and a source of supplies. And in the second half of the twentieth century, he had compact weapons which gave him the strength of many, radios with which to coordinate his operations and unlimited support from friendly nations. Richard LeGrande, in spite of all of his own training and the campaigns he himself had waged, believed such guerrillas invincible; and he knew that any time he expressed himself on the subject there would be those geared to discount his opinions. The battle he was fighting in Washington was being won for him by the enemy. He knew this was true and believed it was tragic.

He paused, a tall, spare man with broad shoulders and the look of the hunter in his eyes. Very slowly he pivoted, as if to gain a better perspective of the city about him. Then he half raised his hand and waved for the sedan, which he knew was following, to pull up to his side. The colonel stepped out and was about to salute when LeGrande shook his head.

"Can you contact your headquarters and find out where Lieutenant Robert Fannin, Regular Army Infantry, is located?"

The colonel looked puzzled for a moment and then said, "Yes, sir." He had orders to help the General in any way that he could, but he had not expected this request. Stepping back into the car, he picked up the radio-phone and placed his call. LeGrande slipped into the rear seat of the sedan, and a moment later when the information was received, asked that they be driven to the Lieutenant's unit. The car wove its way through the crowded streets. As they approached the base, LeGrande leaned forward and tapped the colonel on the shoulder. "Will you go inside and ask Lieutenant Fannin to join me here? You need not tell him who is waiting to see him."

The car came to a halt before a rambling building which LeGrande assumed had once been a museum and which the army had either rented or confiscated for its own use. A few minutes later the colonel returned with a young officer in tow. Lieutenant Robert Fannin was almost as tall as his father. His face was as ruddy, though his hair was more like his mother's— a kind of blond. His face was thin and his jaw seemed to jut out, tightening the muscles under his chin. He was wearing fatigue clothes and a helmet with a single silver bar stenciled on it.

LeGrande slipped over in the seat and opened the door. "Come on in, Lieutenant."

For a moment the young man stood where he was as he recognized the older man in mufti. He started to salute, but the colonel caught his elbow and guided him to the car.

As they drove away from the building, LeGrande said, "I saw your mother the other night. She was well. Hyde was there, too."

"Thank you, sir."

The young officer sat upright, his eyes straight ahead. LeGrande could see that the youth did not quite understand what was happening and tried to put him at his ease. "Came in on some business and thought that we could talk for a bit and then I'd tell your mother I'd seen you."

The younger man smiled. "Most kind of you, General."

LeGrande asked the colonel to drop them back at the house and turned his attention to young Fannin once more. "It's rough here?"

The Lieutenant looked at the colonel in the front seat and half shrugged. "It's no Sunday-go-to-meeting, General."

"Been out there often?"

"Once a week, and sometimes I stay north for a few days at a time. I'm a kind of liaison with the various units along the Mekong."

LeGrande laughed. "Liaison. Now there's a hell of a word for a counter-insurgency soldier." He laughed even louder as he added, "And counter-insurgency is a hell of a word for guerrilla."

All of the men in the sedan were laughing now. And LeGrande thought that young Fannin was beginning to relax. The car swung into the drive that led to the house and stopped. When the driver opened the door, LeGrande stepped out, followed by young Fannin. Then the General waved the car on, knowing it would once again take its place at the end of the drive. He led the way into the house, where he found Janet still in the study, a cup of coffee in front of her and a radio at her side making strange sounds. He looked at her, his head cocked, as he waited for an explanation.

"You don't dig Oriental music, General," she said wryly.

LeGrande shook his head and, reaching out, turned off the radio as he introduced Robert Fannin.

Janet remained where she was. "Robert Fannin," she said, trying to understand the meaning of this meeting. Since the General had left, she had unpacked their bags and been in touch with the safe-house where the members of Team Two were bedded down.

"I remember you, Mrs. Garner," the young officer was saying. It was clear he knew who she was and, being of a different generation from his father, he was not embarrassed.

LeGrande was waving Fannin to a chair as he settled into one himself. After a few moment of talking about the health of the MacWolfes and Robert Fannin's wife, who had gone to Tokyo after the evacuation of civilians, the General asked simply, "Have you heard anything from your father recently?"

Robert Fannin shook his head, "Just lucky, I guess."

Janet firmly held the cup in her hand. "I don't know your father, but I've heard about him over the years. What's he really like?"

LeGrande, who did not fully approve of what she was doing and yet had brought the young man here so that she could do just what she was attempting to do, gave her a dubious look.

Young Fannin rose to his feet and crossed over to the table where the pot of coffee was plugged in. Turning back to Janet, he smiled. "May I?"

"Please do."

While he filled a cup, Robert Fannin began to speak of his father. "I know he was first man in his class, General," he said, with a nod of deference to the older officer. "I was only tenth. I know everyone thought he would go far." Then with a sad smile, "I hope he does—far away."

Janet waited for the youth to say more, and then she asked, "You don't like him, do you?"

Robert Fannin was standing with his back against the table, cup in hand, as he weighed her question. "To be honest, ma'am, I think he is a lousy son of a bitch, and I am not saying anything to you that I have not said to him."

LeGrande came to his feet and was about to cross the room when he caught himself. An embarrassed look came over his face. "I find that difficult to understand, Bob."

The Lieutenant nodded. "I am certain of that, sir. He is your friend. But he is my father." Both men were silent and Janet looked from one to the other. There were questions she wanted to ask, but she hoped the answers would come without the questions.

Slowly, LeGrande lowered himself into his chair again. He did not take his eyes off the younger man, who seemed at this moment to be reassessing what he had said.

"I hope that I have not offended you, General. It's just that I dislike Colonel Fannin. He is a useless, sensual, drunken animal without the courage one admires in most animals, without the redeeming warmth of a dog or the cold and detached self-sufficiency of a cat."

For a time no one said anything, and then Richard LeGrande asked simply, " 'Without courage' you said. Is that what you meant?"

A tautness developed about Robert Fannin's mouth as he turned to Janet to answer the question. "I think you will understand, ma'am. Barney Fannin is afraid to live like other people because that means he has to meet standards and be compared to them. He is also afraid to live the way he wants, so he hides in a uniform and lets his friends take care of him and bail him out of trouble."

Janet nodded. She was not agreeing, but merely indicating that she thought she knew what the young man was trying to say.

"What I mean is, well, he lacks the courage to be either himself or anyone else." Then the words came which brought LeGrande's head up sharply: "And he never had the guts to finish anything he ever started in his life."

Very coldly, LeGrande asked, "Explain that?"

Surprised that this was all the General was questioning, Robert Fannin nodded. "His career fell apart because he lacked what it took to keep it or anything else going. His marriage. His responsibilities as a father." The young man paused a moment, "And there was something else."

Janet looked at LeGrande, who shook his head to indicate she should not speak. Whatever it was that Robert Fannin was thinking about, it was not pleasant. He set the cup down and crossed the room to stand by the window. The light of the afternoon sun slanted off his face and he looked painfully thin and nervous in spite of his control over his voice as he started to speak. "Once, four years ago . . ." Then he stopped and looked at LeGrande,

"You brought me here for some reason or other to talk about him."

The General nodded.

"Do you really have to know?"

"It would help."

The young man nodded. "I hope you have not become involved with him." Then, realizing that he had said something wrong, "But that's the General's business," reverting to the Army's third person usage.

"You were saying about four years ago . . ." LeGrande prodded.

Another nod and the young man half closed his eyes. "I had just left the Point and was assigned to Benning. I don't know why, but I went looking for my father. I found him in bed with some"—an expression of deference to Janet—"excuse me, ma'am . . . some floozy's bed. Both of them there drunk. I'd seen him drunk before." A bitter smile. "It was not rare to find Barney Fannin drunk, sir. Well, for some reason or other he thought he ought to tell me about *it*. What the *it* was he took a long time getting to and me wanting to leave all of the time, but there he sat, buff naked at her kitchen table, with her lying passed out on the bed. He kept stumbling over the *it* and trying to tell me not to do the same thing. Finally, the *it* came out. Some mess he had gotten into before the war. Something to do with his letting some men get drowned to save some other ones and nobody understanding what he had gone through to make his decision."

Janet looked at LeGrande, who was trying to understand what had been said to him. "What was he trying to tell you?"

"His wisdom, sir. The thing he had learned. Don't make decisions, because if you do, people will hold you responsible for them if they don't agree."

For a long time Richard LeGrande compared what he had just heard with the man he had known in his youth and with the man he had met in Washington less than a week before. Barney Fannin, Colonel, U.S. Army, leader of the mission to the Song Koi.

At stake perhaps were forty thousand American lives and national prestige. Someone had said that the Red Chinese could win the war with half a dozen phone calls. LeGrande thought that possible. But he had been given the job of seeing it did not happen, and he had entrusted the task to Barney Fannin. Now here was Barney's son saying his father could not or would not function.

"What do you think he meant?" The General asked the boy.

"Play it safe, sir." A pause and then, "And that's the worst kind of a coward, isn't it, General?" The others were silent for a moment as they digested what had been said, and then the young man added, "Hyde never played it safe in a battle. He may be the original clumsy giant, but he never played it safe."

The young man did not notice the glance that was exchanged between Janet and the General which might have revealed that both of them thought Hyde MacWolfe had been playing it completely safe in the Pentagon.

"You never played it safe, sir," Robert Fannin was saying. "Not from what I've heard of you in battle." Then with an almost boyish grin, "Or since."

With an impatient gesture LeGrande was waving the praise aside. "It all boils down to the fact that you don't have much respect for Colonel Barney Fannin." His words were crisp and cold.

The young officer nodded again. "You said you wanted to know, sir."

Pulling himself out of his chair, LeGrande smiled that smile which Janet recognized as being no smile at all. "You were honest with me, Bob. I appreciate that, even though I might say that along the way you have shown a minimum of charity."

Then to the surprise of both of the men, Janet started to laugh softly. "Charity might have been a lie, Richard, and lies wouldn't do you any good."

The young officer was embarrassed at seeing his superior caught up and laughed at, but LeGrande recovered enough to smile again. "Maybe before I return, Bob, we can have dinner together some night."

"I would like that, sir."

LeGrande was walking his guest to the door as Janet came out of her chair and shook hands with him.

"We will count on seeing you again before we leave." She was making conversation.

Then the amenities were concluded and the colonel at the end of the drive was given his orders to see Lieutenant Fannin home. Alone in the house, LeGrande yelled for the sergeant who was on duty and asked him if he had located any Scotch. When two bottles were brought out, the sergeant withdrew, leaving the General and his lady alone together.

Janet looked up at LeGrande over her glass and said simply, "Don't do anything foolish, Richard. When you selected Barney Fannin, you knew no one was about to pin a medal on him or give him a fifth star for his collar. You picked him because you believed in him or what you remembered of him. Live with it."

LeGrande reached out an open palm and touched her cheek as he tilted her face so that he could see it better. "You're losing your perspective, my dear. The only thing that is important is what is taking place in the valley of the Song Koi. For the next seventy-two hours nothing else matters."

She half turned her face so that she could kiss him and then she smiled. "And for the next seventy-two hours you just remember that you are not an Indian any longer. You are a chief."

THE VALLEY OF THE SONG KOI •

THE TWO SENTRIES guarding the small motor launches on the lake created by the dam on the Song Koi were telling each other delightful lies about the women they had known in the nearby village. One of them was even stretching his story to include an assignation he had had with the beautiful Eurasian who had been the major's mistress but only the day before had moved into the house of the young lieutenant. Both of the sentries were young men. Neither one had ever been in battle, and so they were not in the least inhibited by knowledge of the nature of war. This allowed them to make themselves comfortable, their weapons beside them and their feet dangling over the edge of the motor launch on which they were seated. They were as happy as soldiers who are on duty can ever be, and they were as ignorant of what was taking place about them as they could have been. It was dark except for the light cast by the lantern they had brought down to the launch with them.

What happened to them took place in less than a minute. The shorter of the two was grasped from behind and held long enough for the wire garrote to cut through his windpipe and stop his breathing, while the taller was jerked upward from behind as a long, slender knife slipped up under his rib cage, plunging into his heart and severing the valves. Though both died silently, the one with the wire wrapped about his throat died more cleanly.

When the slaughter was completed, Barney Fannin tossed the body of the garroted soldier into the lake; Carl Sprague withdrew his knife from the other and simply let the body roll into the water. There was little noise and only a small splash. Barney stood where he was for a moment, then whistled softly and waited until Hac Quan came forward dragging a case of the explosives they had cached the night before. Barney grabbed the case, ripped open the top and started placing his charges in the bottom of one of the two motor launches. He had completed his task when Carl and Hac Quan brought him the second and third cases. He placed these in the bottom of the launch with the first case. Though he was no specialist, the technique that he was applying was simple enough and he felt confident that he knew what he was doing. Linking a single charge in each case to a single charge in the other cases by primer cord, he rigged what he thought would be a unified charge. He was finished with the three cases when Hac Quan arrived with the fourth. Stepping into the small launch, Barney started rummaging through the two lockers under the small seats along the side of the craft until he located what he was looking for—a piece of rope almost twenty feet long. With Sprague's help, he tied the fourth case of explosives to the prow of the launch so that it extended beyond and would be the first point of contact should the launch collide with anything. When he was satisfied that his charge was properly located, Barney linked this last case with the other three. There was nothing more than he could do now.

Hac Quan nodded his approval. Though an engineer, the Annamese had a limited knowledge of high explosives, and the efficiency of the American colonel won his respect. Carl Sprague picked up a single piece of fuse, folded it three times and then cut it into three equal pieces. Ducking down into the shelter of the boat so that the light of his match would not be seen, he touched off a piece of fuse and counted slowly from one thousand-one to one thousand-ten. Then he pinched off the lighted fuse. He measured what was left against the other two pieces and cut them to the exact measurement of the remaining piece. Then he threw away the three matching pieces, leaving himself with two pieces that would burn for ten seconds each.

Suddenly, the men froze in their places. From across the lake near the spillway and where they had seen the lights two kilometers beyond the night before, a large searchlight started playing on the water. A slow, easy sweep from one side of the lake to the other and back again. The three men flattened in the bottom of the boat and watched the wedge of light pass over them and move on. Once. Twice. It took almost five minutes to make a full sweep. It did not appear to be searching for anything in particular. A sharp sliver of light cutting the night and moving back again.

Barney rolled over inside the launch and looked at Sprague. "You up to it?"

The younger man nodded.

Looking beyond the American, Barney waited for a reaction from Hac Quan, who said, "If you wish, Colonel."

"I wish," Barney said.

The light swept by again and Hac Quan pulled himself into the launch and took his place beside one of the crates of explosives where Sprague had set a fuse. Keeping low, Sprague took his position on the other side of the launch, the second fuse at his fingertips. He lighted two cigarettes and passed one to the Oriental. Barney crawled across the bottom of the small craft, checking each charge a final time and then the fuses. A grunt indicated he was satisfied. A sweep of light and he lay still. Darkness again except for the lantern and he came up on one knee and started the small outboard motor. It putted and stalled. Another jerk of the cord and again it stalled. The three men knew the sound could be heard across the lake. A third time as the light swept over the craft. Again they lay still, only the motor chugging now.

The wedge of light moved on as Fannin raced the motor, and the small white launch sped forward toward the spillway two kilometers distant. The three men remained in their positions as the searchlight swept over the moving boat and passed on. Water splashed over the side as the charged prow knifed a trail through the lake. A second sweep of the light and then it shifted its pattern and came to focus on the boat, holding on its course, lighting the small craft in a sudden burst of brightness. With no longer any need to hide, the three men rose in their places. Across the shortening distance, they could see activity on the top of the dam and around the control house. The distance became shorter. Bursts of gunfire traced their way toward them. Short but close. Trying rapidly to judge his time and speed and distance, Barney's hand went up and he shouted, "Fire them."

Hac Quan sucked deeply on his cigarette, brightening the tip, touched it to the fuse and watched it start to sputter. A nod from Barney and the Annamese pulled himself up to the side of the craft, waved and rolled over into the water. The gunfire continued, closer now. Splintered wood splashed over the craft. Carl sucked deeply on his cigarette, lighted the fuse before him and waited for Barney to leave the launch. More gunfire from an automatic rifle. Machine gun fire cutting the water and splashing it high. Barney nodded to Sprague and started to move toward the side. In that instant he felt the craft veer away from the spillway and threw himself back toward the wheel. Only five seconds and no more now. The gunfire was heavier and the lights bright on them. As Barney moved to the wheel, Carl came to his feet and with a single swing of his hip, he caught the large officer off balance, dumping him into the lake. Water passed over Fannin's head, and as he came up, he heard, "So long, Fannin."

Carl was holding the wheel; the launch was white with light and a stream of heavy gunfire tore through its sides. Barney, treading water, saw Carl half rise and twist about as he was struck time and time again by machine gun fire. Then the launch crashed into the spillway. A pause. Silence. The searchlight now on nothing but water. Then the craft exploded. Once. Twice. The huge floodgates tore open and water rushed through the gap. Caught in the sudden sweep of water, Barney struggled for the shore. Finally, he reached it, rose and shook the water from his face as Hac Quan joined him. Without a word the two moved toward the edge of the dam, where the water was breaking away its weakened sides. Below they could see a convoy caught in the sudden flood from above. Trucks tumbling into the river. Distant screams half covered by the crash of falling water.

The two men stood silently in the darkness. Then, with a sigh they started back toward the village. At the edge of the quickly disappearing lake, they paused once again to look at the havoc they had wreaked.

"He was a brave man," Hac Quan said.

Barney Fannin wiped his face with a wet hand, nodded, came to attention and quietly saluted the place where he had last seen Carl Sprague. When his hand dropped, the two turned and disappeared into the darkness. Behind them they could hear the sound of white water.

It was only a short time after midnight when they reached the small house. What had seemed to them like months had actually been a few hours. The entire race across the lake could not have taken more than minutes. And as Barney entered the house, he was thinking how many seconds he had erred in his signal for lighting the fuse. The launch had hung up on the spillway for at least three seconds. But he was willing to forgive himself the error because there had been no way to calculate the distance and the speed. What he could not forgive himself was his treatment of Carl Sprague, and what he could not forget was Carl's question of the night before: "Have you ever flubbed a duck, Barney?" Dropping into one of the old-fashioned overstuffed chairs in the sitting room, Barney watched Hac Quan start up the stairs.

"We'll be going out again," he said, and the Oriental paused for an explanation. "Let's talk about it in a few minutes."

The engineer nodded and continued up the stairs. Fannin watched him disappear into the darkness above and he wondered where the girl was. It did not matter now. Nothing really did at this moment, because all he could think about was Carl Sprague. Carl had stolen a second chance to live even if it meant dying. And that was what it had meant. Barney wondered if he had ever shown as much courage. He knew that Richard LeGrande and others would say that he was showing it now, but that was not true. He was fulfilling an assignment, a soldier carrying out orders. Five targets. Five nights. And perhaps as many as three hundred thousand Americans sitting on the rim of a holocaust, none of them knowing someone was set to shove them in.

Barney pulled himself to his feet. He was tired. Damned tired. He was no longer a boy. If the Old Man had told Dick LeGrande that he was too old to play games any more, then someone should have remembered that Barney Fannin was no younger than Le-Grande. Two stars or five do not change a man's age. But it was not his fatigue that was disturbing him. He knew about that. He knew, too, that he had to be honest with himself the way Carl Sprague had been honest. He knew it had not been simple for Carl. "Hold on and we'll get you home," he had told Sprague. But the civilian had wanted more than a journey back across the seas to his desk. Barney hoped in that final moment when the steel-jacketed slugs had jerked his body upright and he could see the dam rising in front of him, Carl had found the more which he had sought.

Barney had not, nor would he ever. Zing was dead and Carl was dead, like those men in the river more than twenty-five years ago. And he was still alive and wandering. Like the story of the Jew who had not allowed Christ to rest against the wall of his house, no one was allowing Barney Fannin to rest. What he was doing was not heroic. It was his duty. He had been paid to be a soldier in peacetime, had drawn his pay, his rations and quarters, his promotions and his fogeys. Now, in war, he was doing what he had agreed to do for money. If he had not agreed, he would not have been in the valley of the Song Koi. If he had personal reasons for being in the valley, if he had patriotic ones, that was fine. Chalk them up as a plus. They were not why he had been asked to volunteer. A hundred million others might have been asked. But those hundred million others would not have—and Barney smiled as he recalled the line—known they fought only for money. Zing had died, and for this men would be in his debt. And as far as Barney was concerned, this was as it should have been. But Barney was a debtor, and nothing that happened to him from now to the end would change that. One thing he could feel comfortable about—and there was almost nothing else—no one would second guess him now. If he came out or if he failed to come out, no one was going to tell him that what he had done and the way he had done it were wrong. If he lived, he would have taken out his targets. If he failed, no one would have time to think about Barney Fannin.

Rubbing a large palm over his scrub beard, he looked out of the window. There were a few stars in the sky. He relaxed. The decisions he made were between himself and the stars. There would be no more hearings. He had once told someone somewhere—and the memory of it was vague, lost in alcohol—"don't make decisions, because people will hold you responsible for them if they don't agree." Well, there was no one to hold Barney responsible for anything now. No one. He would run with his luck until it failed him, and that would be it.

Turning from the window, he saw Li standing at the foot of the steps watching him. "Is Joe awake?" he asked.

She shook her head. "The other man?" she asked.

"There's just your uncle and me now, Li." From the expression on her face he knew that she understood. "Let's go upstairs and hold a pow-wow." Her blank look brought a quick explanation. "War council. Planning meeting."

The girl nodded and led the way. Barney reached the top step before he realized he was still holding his automatic rifle. He set it against a wall and waited for Hac Quan to join him. They went into Joe's room together with the girl. Joe lay asleep on the pad, his broken legs covered with a blanket, his rifle beside him. Barney watched the girl looking at him a moment and wondered when a woman had last looked at him that way, and then he startled the others by chuckling softly. He was envious of Joe Brodsky. So damned envious of his youth and his girl. Abruptly, Barney stopped laughing and looked at the other two.

"We've got about four hours until dawn. Maybe more. I've got to make up a lost day. I want to hit two targets tomorrow night, the airfield and the tunnel. It will take most of the night. There will be no time to come back here and fetch him to the plane." He could see that Joe was awake now and listening to him. "Got some extra guts, boy?"

"Where's Carl?" Joe asked.

To the surprise of the others, the Colonel said simply, "Collecting his insurance," and Joe understood.

"I'm just along for the ride, Colonel," Joe said. "You call it."

Barney reached out, affectionately placed one hand on the young man's shoulder and squeezed it. "I want to take you out to the place that plane's going to come in."

"Now?"

Barney nodded. "That means you'll have to spend tomorrow under a bush someplace until I get back or I don't get back. Either way, you'll be there for them to take you off."

Joe knew the others were staring at him and he wanted to tell them to go away. It may have been rough watching Zing and Carl die, but he had not been swinging on any Maypoles himself. He was silent for a long time. When he finally spoke, he asked, "And what if I make a noise out there?" He shook his head as if to apologize. "I can't help it sometimes," and he gestured toward his legs, "they hurt."

"I'll gag you if I have to," Barney said, and the others saw that he meant it. "No one ever died from a gag in his mouth."

Joe half smiled. "Let's go, Colonel. Nobody's making any money sitting around here."

Barney nodded and turned to Hac Quan. "You know where we're supposed to meet the plane?"

The engineer nodded. Somehow he was impressed with these

two men though he had never expected to be. "I'll show you the way." He thought a moment and added, "And then?"

Barney looked at Li. "We'll come back here and wait for tomorrow night."

The girl looked at him and realized he was going to take the risk of the enemy returning. Then she jumped back as Barney reached out and grabbed the hem of her *cheung san*. She was frightened and Hac Quan stepped forward, but not before Barney had what he wanted: several inches of the cotton hem. He held it up as the others stared at him.

"I thought you'd want a piece of her, Joe," he explained as he handed the cloth to the young soldier with the orders, "Shove it in your mouth because this is going to hurt." Then he picked Joe up Indian fashion and threw him over his shoulder. The young man had no time to put the cloth in his mouth and screamed once before Barney could make him even partly comfortable. Reaching one hand out from where he lay over the Colonel's shoulder, Joe tried to touch the girl's hand, which came up to his. He tried to say something, and to the surprise of the others, it was Barney who said, "There are no words for it. Just remember what you owe her." With that he started down the stairs, followed by Hac Quan, who paused a moment to cast a comforting look at the small figure of his niece.

"We will be back later," Hac Quan said, knowing she already knew that. But as the gruff American had said, there were no words for it.

Leading the way out of the house, Barney paused in the dark road. There were still stars above, but he was not aware of them now. He was even more tired than he had thought. Hac Quan reached out, took the Colonel's rifle and slung it over his shoulder with his own. They walked quickly and silently through the fields. They had only gone a short distance when Barney paused and held up one hand. Hac Quan stopped and listened. Not a sound. They moved on a few more paces and again Barney thought he heard something. Waving Hac Quan on, Barney continued to hold Joe over his shoulder with one hand as he opened the flap of his holster with the other, drew his service revolver and stepped out of the path. A moment later he heard the sound again. His gun came up and he was about to squeeze off a shot when he lowered his gun. The silhouette against the trees was that of a slight girl.

"Li," he whispered and she jumped at the unexpected sound of his voice from behind. Recovering, she moved closer to him and he knelt, lowering Joe to the ground. From the way Joe lay, they could see that he was no longer conscious. The girl's small face was inches from Barney's when he reached up and put one hand on her slight shoulder. "What do you want, girl?" He did not wish to be unkind, but he felt fatigue flow over him and he had a long way to go to the airstrip and back before dawn.

"I can stay with him until the plane comes tomorrow night." It was not a question but a simple statement of fact, and Barney knew that she meant it. "If they come and you are not there, I can signal the pilot."

Nodding, Barney lifted the boy, cradling him in his arms this time, and as he rose, he saw that Hac Quan had returned. "Let's get out of here," Barney snapped, impatient and embarrassed at the debt he was building up.

It took almost an hour to approach the small field which had been selected back in Washington as the landing strip for the evacuation of the team. The choice had been made from a map and aerial photographs. The approach to the field was over level country, though the photographs had revealed a row of trees rimming the end of the field to the south. When General Canby had picked the site, he had made it clear that any plane coming in would have to be a small one, that there could be no pass at the field because the plane would be picked up by enemy radar, and that the pickup would have to be rushed because once the plane set down, the enemy would be on his way to the place on the radar screen where the plane had last been spotted. Barney Fannin had understood this, and Hac Quan had been sure he could find the field. Now, as they neared the row of trees, Barney paused and looked up. He had been fortunate in the absence of the moon. For a moment he was prepared to say this was the only luck he had

had, but then he remembered the men who had been with him. His shoulder was numb under the weight of Joe. At his side Li stood waiting for him to move on. Hac Quan had paused a few paces ahead, wondering what had brought the American to a halt.

Baney flipped open his holster and drew his revolver. It would be the only weapon Joe could use. The rifle was too heavy, and to use it he would have to be propped up or left lying on his belly. Once he had the gun in hand, Barney nodded for Hac Quan to continue. The Oriental had taken only a few paces toward the row of trees when the first burst of automatic rifle fire sprayed over them.

In a single gesture, Barney hurled Joe Brodsky at Li, knocking the girl off her feet as he flung himself onto his belly. Hac Quan dropped like a professional—onto his knees, belly, elbow and rifle butt, facing the enemy. Barney fired twice and then moved quickly to one side and forward, drawing fire away from Li and Joe. Hac Quan remained where he was between the two young people and the enemy rifle which let go a second stream of bullets over their heads.

Barney rose to his knees in the almost total darkness and sprinted toward the row of trees. He had to know what was ahead and whether he could possibily withdraw with the crippled boy and the girl. Fire again, and wide of its mark this time. Then Hac Quan squeezed off three rounds, and Barney's mind clicked with admiration at the control of the trigger. This was a soldier. Another short burst of fire and Barney was moving forward once more.

He was now in the row of trees and beyond he could see the airstrip. No one was in sight and the firing continued. Rubbing the back of his gun hand across his face, Barney stared at the shape of an airplane on the field. He had to get it off that field before he left or his own plane could not come in the next night. He had to get it off. He could hear Hac Quan firing and then the return fire. It sounded like two burp guns. Then there was a third. The darkness made everyone miscalculate, but Bar-

ney's target was large and he could not miss. He rose on his elbow
and sighted in on the plane. He judged the gas tank to be under
the wing. Ignoring the other shots around him and even the
scream of a man somewhere in front of him, he took his time.
Holding his breath, he squeezed slowly; the forty-five jerked upward and another squeeze as it settled back down on its target.

There was a sudden burst of flames and he could hear the enemy
on the field yelling. Only they were not yelling in Chinese or
Annamese. They were yelling in English. A voice Barney thought
he recognized was shouting for the men to keep their heads
down, but as the shout broke over the field, two of the men rose
and moved toward the plane and into Hac Quan's field of fire.
Two short bursts. One figure silhouetted against the burning plane
went limp onto its face. The other ran two steps, reached for
something just beyond its fingertips and then folded double. At
that moment Barney yelled, "Cease firing. Hold it. For God's sake,
hold it."

There was silence except for the crackling of the burning plane.
Then Barney heard someone call his name, and he rolled over
onto his back and stared at the sky as tears gathered in the corner of his eyes. The last, the final betrayal, and by a man who
claimed to be his friend. The one man he had believed would
allow him to fight his war in his way. The name again. Louder
this time.

"Yes, Dick," he shouted. "Yes. Hold your fire and move toward
the plane so I can see you."

A moment and the tall figure of General LeGrande appeared
in the light cast by the burning plane. Another man joined him
and then a second. Barney waited. There were no more. Taking
a deep breath, Barney yelled, "Hac Quan!"

From almost at his side, he heard the Oriental say quietly,
"Here, Colonel."

Barney slowly rose to his feet and walked away from the airstrip, past the row of trees and back to the place where he had
thrown Joe Brodsky and the girl. These were his friends. These
people he cared about. They had not betrayed him. They had not

given up faith in him. The girl was on her knees now, holding one hand against her face where, when Barney knelt down and took her hand away, he could see a bruise. "Are you all right, girl?"

She nodded and then, as if she thought he needed assurance, she said, "Joe is alive."

"Thanks," he said softly as he held out one hand and helped her to her feet while he rose to his own. Then beside him he could see Richard LeGrande, wearing slacks and a leather jacket. There were two strangers with him and behind them was Hac Quan.

The two friends looked at each other in silence. Finally, Barney said, "You're a day early, General."

LeGrande nodded.

"We'd better get the hell out of here," Barney snapped angrily, as he forced himself to keep his hands down so that he would not strike the man in front of him.

"There are two men back there," the General said.

"You want to blow taps over them?"

The General reached out and placed one hand on Barney's shoulder. "Easy, Barney. Easy."

Barney looked into LeGrande's face and said, "Get your hand off me, General."

The hand fell away and LeGrande asked simply, "Where do you want to go?"

Barney shook his head, leaned down and picked Joe up. He could see the boy was conscious now and he cradled him gently in his arms. With a glance at Hac Quan and the girl, he turned on his heel and walked away from the light cast by the burning plane. LeGrande and the two men with him slung their weapons over their shoulders and followed. The small column had gone only a few yards when the plane exploded behind them. The men of Team Two turned to look, but Barney and his companions continued.

"Our explosives," LeGrande explained to no one in particular and then he caught up to Barney. "Let someone else carry the boy," he said.

Without pausing in his quick pace, Barney asked, "Is that an order, General?"

LeGrande did not answer, so they continued to walk as they were, Hac Quan and the girl behind the two American officers and the two strangers bringing up the rear.

Half an hour later they entered a small woods and Barney knelt and placed Joe on the ground. As Barney propped him up against a tree, LeGrande, who had dropped to the ground next to the pair, was startled to see Joe pull a torn strip of cloth from his mouth. His teeth clenched against the pain, Joe asked, "How'm I doing, Colonel?"

Barney nodded, "Fine, boy." Then he looked about for Li, who had moved to his side. "Stick with him," he said.

LeGrande realized they were staying put for a time and, rising to his feet, told his men to take guard positions a dozen yards away. The two slipped into the darkness, leaving the General standing over Barney, Li and Joe. At LeGrande's side Hac Quan leaned against a tree and watched the two American officers.

Barney's hands opened and clenched at his sides. Finally, he snapped, "You gave me five days, General," hitting the rank hard.

LeGrande nodded. "The air photos showed the dam was still there yesterday."

"It's gone now."

The General considered this and then made what for him was as much of an apology as he was capable of. "I had no way of knowing." Then he looked down at Joe Brodsky and the girl beside him and he waited for someone to explain the lost night. When the explanation was not forthcoming, he looked at Hac Quan. "Good to see you."

The Oriental nodded. Uncertain just why the Colonel was so angry, Hac Quan still felt his loyalty lay with the man he had fought beside.

LeGrande looked about, knowing as he did so that there were no others. "The rest of your team, Barney?"

"I didn't promise to bring anybody home," Fannin growled.

For a moment he thought about this and then added, "I was doing fine until I got your help."

Again LeGrande nodded. "You think you can get the rest of the targets?"

Very slowly Barney raised his clenched fist and then, as if restraining himself, rubbed it over his bearded chin. "That was my assignment."

LeGrande looked at the man in front of him, grizzled, weary and angry. He could see the lines of tension on Fannin's face, the lines that came to a man who was keyed up almost beyond his own ability to keep up with his passion and drive. He had seen the driven before in a battle that was not over. There was a look about them they would not lose until they were dead or removed from the scene of combat. And the General knew that Fannin was in a battle, had been ever since his team had left the plane days before. "Your assignment was five targets, Barney. Let's just say that I brought you some extra hands."

Barney laughed grimly, "And took away our escape route." He thought a moment and then asked, "How the hell did you plan to leave?"

A bitter grin spread over LeGrande's face as he looked back toward the burning plane lighting the distant sky. "Your drop gave you the advantage of surprise. Once you took out that bridge, there was no longer a question of surprise, so I thought we'd be bold and use the field a second time." Then as if by way of apology, "We can't do that now."

"The wreckage," Barney agreed. Then with growing disgust, "I didn't put it there. I didn't ask for it. Nor did I ask for your help."

"You didn't ask for it, but you got it. Now what are you going to do about it?"

"Me, General?" Barney was not certain he understood.

"It's your operation, Barney. You give the orders."

"To the end?"

"To the end," LeGrande assured him.

Barney Fannin stared at LeGrande. Then, almost as if he were assuming command of a division, he nodded and started to spill his orders. "First, we've got to get out of this place. With that signal fire, it's going to be quick with Commies. Can one of those men you brought use a radio?"

LeGrande nodded. "One of them is the pilot."

"The other?"

"Leon Bryant. GENOPS Middle East."

Not quite sure what this meant, Barney Fannin asked, "And the other two?"

"GENOPS Europe."

Satisfied he had placed things in some kind of order in his mind, Barney turned to Hac Quan. "Can you locate the place where we buried the radio?"

The Oriental nodded.

Barney glanced at his watch. "Can you take the pilot and get it to Li's before dawn?"

Hac Quan considered the request. "If I get caught by daylight, I could get to the house, but nothing could hide the size or color of one of you. I'll go alone."

Satisfied, Barney knelt beside Li, "Can you lead us back to the house?"

The girl thought about this. "You will broadcast from my house?"

Barney nodded.

Before the girl could speak, Hac Quan pointed out, "Then she will have to leave it."

Putting his hands on the girl's shoulders, Fannin said gently, "Trust me, girl," knowing that she was thinking of the visit by Hac Quan's wife and the eager lieutenant.

There was a moment before she nodded. Barney picked up Joe as Le Grande helped the girl to her feet. "Let's get the hell out of here," Fannin ordered as he started out of the woods with Li at his side.

With a wave of his hand, Hac Quan started off in another direction, and the two men, seeing the others depart, fell into line behind them.

No one spoke until they approached the house they had left hours before. Inside, Barney set Joe down on the floor of the sitting room. The boy was still conscious, and as he settled back onto his elbows, he looked about for Li, who came to his side. Barney glared at the three men with him, and to the two strangers he snapped, "Upstairs and get some sleep." He waited until they were gone and then turned to LeGrande. "Tomorrow night your pilot will ask for a plane at some place Hac Quan thinks one can put down. The girl will lead you there with those two," gesturing toward the stairs which the men had taken.

LeGrande wanted to ask what Barney would be doing, but decided that Barney would tell him if he wanted him to know. He had agreed to ride with him to the end, and until he saw that something was going wrong, he would do just that. There were questions he wanted to ask, but Barney was already starting up the stairs. The General looked at him and then knelt beside Joe Brodsky and the girl.

He wanted to introduce himself, but decided if the girl did not know his name, so much the better for her if she should be arrested. Reaching out, he touched Joe's shoulder and squeezed it affectionately. "A rough go, boy?"

Brodsky looked at the General who had seemed so sure of himself in Washington and now was deferring to the judgment of Colonel Fannin. He wanted to make a show of bravado, but he did not feel like it. His legs were hurting him, and the worry on Li's face was no comfort. "All the way, sir," he said. "All the way. Once I heard someone say that General LeGrande was a genuine hero. Well, sir, not to be disrespectful, Colonel Fannin's my idea of a hero."

Satisfied that he had heard what he wanted to know, LeGrande squeezed the boy's shoulder again. Then he looked at the girl. She seemed very young. He did not know who she was, and no one seemed eager to tell him. "Do you speak English?" he asked, even though he had heard Barney speak to her earlier.

"I lived in Hong Kong with my uncle." Her voice was soft.

LeGrande tried to smile. He assumed her uncle was Hac Quan because there had been no one else to whom she could have been referring.

"There will be danger when we radio," he told her. "But as Colonel Fannin promised, we will make it up to you."

Li did not know what this tall stranger whom the others called General could do to make the loss of her home up to her, but she knew that having gone with these foreigners as far as she had, there was little she could do now short of turning them in to the Chinese. She was thinking about this when the General rose and followed Barney Fannin upstairs.

In one room the General found Leon Bryant and the pilot sprawled on the floor, their boots and weapons beside them. The door to the other room was closed and he assumed that Fannin slept there. "We got ourselves into one this time," LeGrande said softly.

Leon Bryant, a short, stocky man with a heavy mustache and black eyebrows, nodded. "Max and Jeff got into a worse one."

LeGrande nodded.

"You're going to let this Fannin bring it through, General?" the pilot asked.

Sighing, LeGrande sucked in his cheek as he thought about the question. Then he nodded. "As he said, he didn't ask for us." The three were silent for a time and then the General shook his head. "Maybe we should have waited, but if we had, and we had been wrong . . ." He did not finish the thought because all of the possibilities were racing through his mind as they had raced through it the long day and night while he had waited for the air photos which had revealed the dam still intact. Somewhere, for some reason, Barney had lost a day, but he had not made any excuses for that. He had not apologized. And as far as LeGrande could tell, Barney knew where he was going and what he was going to do when he got there. Seeing the other two watching him, LeGrande half smiled. "And as the Colonel said, 'Get some sleep!'"

Then he left them alone, crossed the small corridor and opened the door to the room where Barney was standing at the low window. It was almost daylight now. Whatever stars there had been were gone. Barney's boots were on the floor beside him and his revolver was holstered on top of them.

Without looking around, Fannin said, "There's no getting out if Hac Quan doesn't make it."

The General nodded even though he knew that Barney could not see him. "But that won't keep you from getting the targets?" As he asked he knew he was not thinking of the targets as much as he was trying to decide what Barney Fannin was really thinking about. It could be a way out of the trap they might be in. If it was a way out, whom did Barney want out? LeGrande was remembering a dark night he had read about, a night in a swollen river with men wanting to live and their officer leaving them because he could not lead them out. He wondered if Barney was thinking of his own way out now. Moving to the window himself, LeGrande asked, "Did you see both Miller and Sprague killed?"

Puzzled at the question, Barney snapped, "You'll get my report when this is over. I'll put it down in four copies for you. Meantime, if you want to know if I was shocked to see them die, go to hell." He was looking at LeGrande now. "I might not always act like one, but I'm as good a soldier as you are, Dick." Then, as if to prove his point, "Or you wouldn't have given me this job."

"Easy, Barney," LeGrande said quietly. "I just wanted to know if there was any chance they deserted you."

Swinging toward his companion, Barney shook his head. "They died, if that's what you want to know."

LeGrande nodded, not sure now if he was as certain of the Oriental's return as he had been a moment before. "Someone talked to a Czech attaché the night before you left, then hopped a cab and drove to the safe-house."

Barney turned back to the window. "Zing and Carl died doing what they came to do. It was not them."

"And the boy?"

Barney considered this and shrugged it away. "Broke his legs in the jump and never talked to anyone but the girl and us."

LeGrande nodded. "The boy or the engineer. Take your pick."
There was a long silence as both of them watched the sun appear on the far horizon. "I'm not picking," Barney said as his hand went up and he pointed to Hac Quan walking down the road wearing a peasant's short white trousers and a white shirt, tails out. In one hand he carried a basket out of which a chicken's head emerged as the fowl complained loudly.

Barney picked up his revolver and took it off safety. Satisfied, he shoved it into his pocket and walked out of the room and down the stairs in his stocking feet. He reached the bottom of the steps as Hac Quan entered the house. But it was not Hac Quan that Barney noticed at this moment, but rather the absence of the girl. Joe lay alone on the floor near the door where he had been placed earlier. Nodding to the Oriental, who was setting his basket down, Barney asked Joe, "Where is she?"

The boy shook his head. "I don't know, Colonel. She just got up and went out."

For a moment Barney thought about this. Hearing a sound on the step behind him, he turned and stared at LeGrande, who shrugged almost imperceptibly. There was nothing either of them could do in the event that the girl were to turn them in. LeGrande, knowing less about the girl than the others, was thinking of his own cover which had been blown when Barney had addressed him as General. He wondered what the Red Chinese would be willing to pay for a full-fledged undiluted intelligence chief. And as he thought about it, he knew that whatever they paid would be too much because they would never take him alive.

Barney turned back to Hac Quan and smiled. "That's a hell of a getup," and waited for an explanation.

The Annamese smiled. "I took it from a farmer. I don't know what he will wear," and he, too, was smiling. He reached down, took the chicken from the basket and held it in his hand as he tried to decide what to do with it. Then he grasped its neck and jerked his hand as though to throw the body away, killing the bird in a single gesture. "Dinner," he explained, as he held out the basket to the Colonel. Barney took it and, as he expected, found the small radio in the bottom.

Barney handed the radio to LeGrande. "Will you ask your pilot if he can use it tonight?"

LeGrande accepted the radio and slowly walked back up the stairs with it, though he would rather have remained where he was for the next few minutes. Behind him he could hear Barney asking, "Your own clothes?"

"Under these," Hac Quan said.

Barney Fannin nodded and then gestured for the Vietnamese to join him beside Joe. Kneeling down, Barney waited for the other man to do the same. A baffled Joe Brodsky looked from one to the other as he lay between them. Barney's hand went into his pocket as he spoke.

"The General tells me that someone met with a Czech in Washington the night before we were briefed. That could mean they passed the information to the Russians, who would pass it right on here. Or they could have passed it on themselves."

"What does that mean to us, Colonel?" Joe asked quickly.

Barney shook his head and waited. There was a long silence and then Hac Quan said simply, "Nothing. It doesn't mean anything to us." He could see the other two staring at him as well as the General standing at the foot of the stairs. Taking a deep breath, he continued, "The Czechs contacted me in Paris and warned me that the Chinese held my wife. They told me that when I arrived in Washington I should meet with their man. I did."

"What did you tell him?" Barney snapped.

The engineer seemed to relax as his hands opened wide before him. "What did I know the night before the briefing?"

Barney tried to evaluate this and then he glanced over his shoulder at LeGrande.

Moving into the room now, LeGrande asked, "Did you bug the briefing room?"

"Bug?" It was clear that the word meant nothing to the Oriental.

"Rig it so someone could pick up a tape or broadcast from the house?" LeGrande explained.

Hac Quan shook his head. "I said I was going on a journey, and I even said that I was going home. I promised to let them know when and why when I did."

Barney thought about this a moment. "We left from the house."

Hac Quan smiled. "That's right, Colonel."

"Did you call them?" LeGrande pressed.

Again the Oriental shook his head.

There was a long silence and Barney smiled as he said, "Thanks, that simplifies things." And to punctuate his meaning, he drew the gun from his pocket.

Hac Quan looked at the weapon as the Colonel slipped on the safety. "How did you know it was not him?" he asked, pointing to Joe.

Fannin smiled almost sadly as he looked at Joe. "He isn't bright enough to get mixed up with them and pull it off."

Then all four of the men were laughing. Barney rose to his feet and stood by the door. It was daylight now and there was no sign of the girl. He wanted to ask her uncle if he knew where she was, but he had enough faith in the Oriental at this moment to believe if there was anything the other man thought he should know, he would tell him.

LeGrande saw that Barney was as worried about the girl as he was.

There was movement on the road beyond the house, and Barney stepped away from the door and turned to the others. "Let's get some sleep." Then, to no one in particular, "Before we split up tonight, Hac Quan will pick us a landing strip from the map."

The engineer nodded. Then he asked the others, "Li?"

Shrugging, Barney said, "You heard the boy. She just went out."

No one spoke for a time and then Barney said again, "Let's get some sleep."

Hac Quan moved across the room and waited for LeGrande to ascend the steps ahead of him. The General looked at Barney

Fannin and then shrugged as if the problem at hand was Barney's. He stepped back in deference to the Annamese civilian and followed Hac Quan up the stairs. Standing with his pistol in his hand, Barney watched both of them go. Then he knelt beside Joe Brodsky, "You, too, kid. Some sleep." Sighing wearily, he crossed the room and sat down in a large chair, facing the door. With his pistol in his lap he waited.

Four hours later when LeGrande came down the stairs again, Barney Fannin was still sitting in the chair. His eyes were open and there was an angry look in them. The two friends looked at each other and then at the young man asleep on the floor. Dropping into a chair, LeGrande said, "I saw your son in Saigon."

"And you asked him about Barney Fannin and he told you Barney Fannin was a son of a bitch." There was no self-pity in the Colonel's tone. If anything, LeGrande was surprised that Barney seemed actually bored.

"Why, Barney?"

"Why what?" the grizzled soldier asked as he stared at the weapon in his lap.

"Why do you want people to dislike you?"

Very slowly, Fannin's eyes came up so that he was looking directly at his friend. "I hadn't thought about it that way."

LeGrande wanted to smile, but instead he maintained the dulled tone set by the other. "Hogwash. It's me, Barney. Dick LeGrande. I know you—either you're lying to yourself or you're lying to me. Which is it?"

For a while, Fannin ignored LeGrande, and then he asked, "How's Bob?"

"All right, I guess. I'm not too sure how one judges things like that. He's at war. He's going to be promoted soon. He's a liaison officer." Both men smiled at the designation.

"And his wife?"

"He said she finds the Orient exciting."

"I never met her," Barney volunteered. "In fact, Colonel Barney Fannin was not on the guest list for the wedding."

LeGrande saw that this did not trouble his friend, or if it did, Fannin was not letting anyone else know it. "That's part of it, isn't it, Barney?"

"Part of it?" Fannin asked.

"The *why* I was asking about." The General had made up his mind to probe and he was not going to let Barney off until he either learned something or determined that he never would. He had committed too much to the mission to the valley of the Song Koi to let anything get away from him, and he considered knowledge about Barney Fannin as important as any part of his plans. Only two days before, Janet had reminded him that he often said a commander never commits his troops without a reconnaissance. He had made that error and now the least he could do was rectify his ignorance. "Did you really stop caring what happened after . . ." And LeGrande let the words falter as he sought other ones. ". . . after the war started, or did you just make a pose of it?"

Fannin's face screwed up, and for a moment the General thought he would rise and leave the room. Instead, Barney slipped the safety off the weapon in his lap. "When you meet my son again, tell him his father isn't the only son of a bitch around."

"Am I getting close to the truth, Barney?"

"That line's not worthy of you. You're a bright boy."

Both were silent for a time and LeGrande thought that he had blown this chance to talk to his friend. Then, as if nothing had been said before, Barney Fannin started talking. His voice was low, and if there was any emotion, the General was not aware of it. "A man can stop caring, and then the people around him stop caring for him, and then he's free."

"From what? For what?"

Ignoring the question, Barney asked, "Is Lil happy with that fatuous ass?"

Trying to keep track of the threads of the conversation as they shifted, LeGrande wondered if he should come to Hyde MacWolfe's defense or wait for Fannin to continue. "I hear the movie people use laugh meters. When I find a happiness meter, I'll get a reading on Lil and let you know."

"How would Dick LeGrande come out?"

Sighing, the General said softly, "We were talking about freedom, Barney. From what? For what?"

"The things people expect of you. To be Number One. The Man Most Likely to . . . The helpmeet. The good father bit when you didn't want anything but the chance to be . . ." And Fannin's voice trailed off.

"To be what?" LeGrande asked, thinking he was near the end of his search.

Barney's head went up and he half smiled. "A good soldier. A professional. Fit to kill or be killed. Fit to lead." He paused at the last word and repeated it. "To lead." Then, as if he had suddenly thought of something, "Ay, there's the rub. What qualifies a man to lead? Think back, Dick."

LeGrande realized that Barney's thoughts were moving toward his youth.

"Think back," the man with the grizzled face was saying. "Is the noble leader the man with the good family? The good father? The happy warrior? Is he the boy scout hero like Major General Richard LeGrande, all bright and shiny? Or is he the good-natured slob who plays the game by the rules and polishes his shoes along with his chief's apple? Is he Hyde MacWolfe or Richard LeGrande? Or is he Barney Fannin, wasted and suited only for the final job? The last one. The one where no one's walking out." Fannin was not smiling. He was groping for an answer which his friend knew had been eluding him for years.

"Is the leader the man who has had it easy or the man who has been there and back? The man who has something to lose and therefore shepherds it, or the man with nothing to lose who does not care if he is coming back or not?"

Both were silent for a time. LeGrande knew he should not be thinking of his friend's description of the boy scout hero all bright and shiny, but he was thinking of it. There was a connotation of innocence about the description which disturbed him. Yet, in comparison to Barney Fannin, maybe it was an honest evaluation from where Barney sat. But he himself saw Barney's as an awesome innocence because the man never saw the world as it was, with both LeGrandes and MacWolfes making their way in it. But there was always the chance that it really was the way Barney saw it. He was asking Barney to be honest, and so he had to be himself.

"Free for what, Barney? The chance to find out if you can degrade yourself, disappoint your friends, betray a set of standards by which the people who know you and . . ." Again the General was groping for words. His hand went up in a gesture of futility. "Oh, to hell with it . . . who know you and love you—live. Betrayal. That's what you wanted to be free for?"

Then LeGrande was surprised to see a look of tolerant humor on Barney's face.

"At least it was not an onward-and-upward approach." Fannin chuckled softly, then ceased and was quiet for a time. "There's no neat answer to your question, Dick. If there were, I think you'd be the person I'd give it to. I've got to do things my way. See my" —a shake of his head as he contemplated the next thing he was going to say—"see my responsibilities my way. Lead my way."

Now, as much as they could, the pieces were falling into place for LeGrande. The words Fannin had laid out before him were now part of a larger whole. "To function your way, to be free to do things your way . . . Hell, Barney, you never should have been a soldier."

Fannin's head fell back as he thought about this and very slowly moved from side to side as if he were rejecting what had been said. "You're wrong, Dick. I'm the only one you know who should be a soldier. I'm fit for a war. I'm the mercenary who doesn't want to be told anything more than what the job is and then be paid to get it done. I'm not for garrisons and peacetime. You may be. Hyde may be. I hope to hell Lieutenant Fannin is. But me, I'm what a soldier really is. No frills. No parades. No purchase orders. No scrambled eggs on the visor of my hat. Just a battle. I may be as obsolete as a right flank march, but you called on me because this is my kind of war."

Before the General could say anything, Fannin looked at his watch. "We can't move out of here in daylight and we can't sit here if that girl has gone to turn us in."

LeGrande agreed with what was being said, even though it made no sense and he wanted to pursue the ideas Barney Fannin had thrown at him. He knew Barney had terminated the discussion about himself. Barney was out of his chair now, shoving the forty-five into his belt. "What do you plan?" LeGrande finally asked.

The tolerant look came into Barney's eyes again as he smiled. "Patience and faith, old friend. You don't need a score card to tell the heroes from the villains."

It took the General a moment to determine what Barney was driving at. "And you think this girl is a hero?"

A tolerant smile again. "Noble is the word." He was looking at Joe Brodsky, asleep on the floor with the blanket thrown over him. "Noble, Dick. A quality belonging to the very young and the very innocent." The obvious cynicism was almost more than LeGrande wanted to cope with, but when Fannin chuckled at himself, the General smiled. "And besides," Barney said, "The wench is in love. And as you and I are both young and innocent, we should have great faith in love."

With a large hand, Fannin wiped his face as if to brush something off it, but the fatigue he felt would not leave him. "Too bad you haven't one of Janet's recorders here. You could add the tape to your collection."

Now both of them were laughing softly. There was a sound on the stairs and they turned to see Leon Bryant, the pilot and Hac Quan coming down. The pilot was carrying the radio. Fannin nodded to him.

"That radio, can you operate it?" he asked.

The pilot, a young man in a flight jacket, stood slight and thin before the burly Colonel. Both of them were looking at the small, compact transmitter. "I can try, Colonel."

"What's the range?"

"Not enough to get me south, but one of the fleet off shore might pick it up and transmit it south." The young flight officer was not promising anything, and for this both of his superiors respected him.

Barney picked up his rifle, whirled it in his hand so that it came to rest, butt up; a quick flip of the butt plate and he pulled out a silk multicolored map. Without any formalities he knelt down and spread the map in the middle of the floor. LeGrande joined him there with the pilot and Hac Quan while Bryant took a position near the door. With Hac Quan's help, they selected a landing field. It was shorter than the pilot wanted, but Hac Quan could think of no others he and Fannin had passed in their night journeys which would serve. All had agreed that the field must be one they had seen, because any other might have had a house or other building erected on it since Hac Quan had left the area six years before.

It was almost dark now. LeGrande took several ration bars out of his pocket and passed them to Hac Quan and Barney. The pilot shared his extra bar with Joo Brodsky. The men ate without a word, Bryant remaining on guard near the window and Barney back in the chair where he had spent most of the day. He wanted to sleep now. He almost felt he had to, and while he thought no one was watching, he pulled two benzedrine pills out of his pocket and chewed them with the ration bar.

LeGrande saw him do it and smiled to himself as he did the same thing, making no effort to hide his need for them. He was getting older and so was Barney. He knew this would probably be the last run for both of them. He hoped Barney knew.

Finally Barney pulled himself out of the chair and picked up his rifle. As he moved, he saw Bryant step back from the window, his automatic rifle coming up as he did so. Fannin and LeGrande exchanged glances as they went for their weapons, but Bryant was already shaking his head. "The girl," he explained.

From where he stood, LeGrande saw the smile on Joe Brodsky's face. Youth and innocence, Barney had called it. Then the door opened and Li stepped inside. She saw the foreigners looking at her and her uncle with them. All of the men were armed and none of them was smiling. LeGrande was tempted to say something, but he recalled his promise to Barney Fannin—to the end.

"You went to turn us in to the Chinese, girl." Barney said softly. The girl nodded slowly. "And you decided not to because you could not bring yourself to for reasons you don't fully understand," Barney told her. Again the girl nodded. "Are you with us to the end now or do you want us to leave you alone here?" Barney was trying to give her a choice which he knew was no choice, because as soon as it became dark, the pilot would have to broadcast. Then they would all have to assume the enemy had direction-finding equipment.

"I am with you," the girl said to the Colonel, though she was looking at Joe Brodsky as she said it.

Barney exchanged glances once more with LeGrande and then said, "Your uncle picked a landing field three miles due north of the place where I blew the dam last night. Do you think you can lead these men there after they signal for an airplane?"

Before the girl could answer, Hac Quan spoke to her rapidly in a tongue none of the others could understand. When he was done, she nodded. "I reminded her that it was a pasture where her grandfather used to run horses for the French," Hac Quan said.

LeGrande hoped that Barney was aware that the message could have been completely different; the possibility remained that the uncle and niece had just arranged between them to betray the foreigners. But Barney had already slung his rifle over his shoulder and wrapped the cartridge belt which Hac Quan had brought downstairs for him about his waist. A quick look at his revolver, and he set it back into his holster while staring at the girl. "You will take these men to the field and your uncle and I will meet you there." He glanced at his watch before looking at the pilot. "I've got a lot of work to do tonight." He calculated a moment. "Have the plane on the field at five hundred hours." He was allowing himself the last moment before the first morning light.

The pilot nodded and was about to say something, but Fannin was already speaking to LeGrande. "You'll take Joe with you and take off at five hundred no matter what happens."

LeGrande nodded, understanding that Barney was asking no favors for either himself or the engineer.

Kneeling beside Joe Brodsky, Barney smiled at the youth. "Imagine another night out with a beautiful girl. You get all the luck, boy." Then he rose and walked out of the house and disappeared into the darkness. Hac Quan hesitated a second as if there was something he wanted to say. Then with a shrug, he slung his rifle over his shoulder and followed Barney Fannin into the night.

LeGrande stood looking after them before turning to the others. "We could have helped him with one of his targets, General," Bryant said.

The General nodded. "He didn't ask for any help." Then as if he had to explain, "There is only one way to get that tunnel roof and only one chance at that. He has the right to try it." Then LeGrande turned to the pilot, "You might as well get started, Lieutenant. I want breakfast in Saigon."

It took Barney Fannin and his companion almost an hour to retrieve the two packages they had buried the night they had dropped into the valley for use in their last two missions. One of the packages contained two dozen limpets and the other the bazooka which Joe Brodsky had brought down strapped to his leg. Tossing the limpets over his shoulder, Fannin let Hac Quan carry the larger weapon. This time as they left their cache, they did not bother to cover the hole. No matter what happened, they would not return. As they walked side by side along the bank of the river they had come to know so well in the past few days, Barney asked his companion if he knew what the limpets were and how they worked.

The Oriental nodded. "I fought the French for five years, Colonel. We made our own in those days."

Barney accepted the information, having taken for granted

since the moment he had first handed the Annamese engineer a weapon that Hac Quan was a trained soldier. They walked for a time in silence. Barney's head went back to look at the stars above and then down at the trail they were following. "You grew up here?" he asked.

Hac Quan did not break his step as he glanced at the rugged profile of the American. The question had been a long time coming, but with it came recognition of companionship. Whatever happened in the night ahead, Hac Quan knew that he and this gruff man with the angry manner would be linked together in each other's memories as few men ever are. Hac Quan had fought beside others. He had seen men die before. Some of them had died bravely and foolishly, some bravely and wisely. Some had just died. And as the years had passed after the war against the French, he found increasing difficulty recalling the men he had fought beside. But he did not think now he would ever have difficulty remembering the American Colonel.

"Born here?" Hac Quan said, not so much to ask a question as to give himself time to answer. "About ten kilometers from my sister's house."

Barney paused in the trail, and at the sound of someone coming toward them, the two sought cover in a cluster of bushes. They remained where they were until they could see two men pass. Perhaps they were guards set out against the invaders. Perhaps they were merely peasants going home from work on the bridge. Barney knew only that he did not want to meet anyone this night.

When they were on the trail once more, he asked Hac Quan, "You went to school here?"

"For a time. Then when the French left, the family moved to Hong Kong."

They were passing some farmhouses now and both trod softly, though they could hear a dog barking as they went by. Another hundred paces and Hac Quan continued his story. He did not know why, but he wanted the American to know who he was. "Engineering school in Hong Kong and then back here where we were promised everything." He was silent as he thought about the promises the Ho Chi Minh agents had made to him in Hong Kong. There was need for engineers. Because he had accepted this fact he had readily accepted the promises made to him. But what no one had told him was that the engineers would not be given any more freedom to work where they wanted than anyone else. "What they did not tell me," he said, "was that we would be taxed to nothing and build nothing that was important."

The American was not certain just what this meant, but so long as the man at his side was talking and not thinking of the impossible targets ahead, he decided to let him tell the story in his own way.

"As I think of the war against the French, I realize it was just that—against the French and not *for* very much. And . . ," he hesitated to put his own regrets into words, "and what we got was not very much."

Barney nodded in the darkness. Ahead he could see a bright area against the sky and knew they were approaching some kind of installation. They moved more slowly now, expecting more sentries.

"Finding nothing back here, I left," Hac Quan said, as if this summed up everything.

For a few hundred paces neither of them said a word, then Fannin asked, "And why did you come back?"

Knowing that the man beside him could not see the bitter smile on his face, Hac Quan did not hesitate to let his feelings show. "I left a wife. Her mother was ill and when I had to go . . ." He shrugged. "She could not leave."

Part of this Barney had already guessed, and as he knew what the Oriental had found on his return, he said no more. However, to his surprise, Hac Quan thought he had to explain further. "I don't think I would have remained with you, Colonel, if she had" —and he struggled to find the words which said what he was groping for—"if I had found her waiting for me."

There was an honesty about this that brought Fannin up short and he stopped in his tracks and looked at the man at his side as if seeing him for the first time. The darkness hid their faces even at a few feet, but Hac Quan knew the American was staring at him. "I didn't owe you any loyalty," he said.

"None," Barney agreed. "Then why . . . ?"

They were moving on again. The sky above them was brighter now and they knew they were near their first target of the night. A clump of trees and a knoll ahead. Setting down the bazooka and its two shells, Hac Quan reached out for the limpets that the Colonel was handing him.

"Why?" he said. "You can thank the Chinese for that, Colonel." And there was a twisted kind of humor in the comment which brought a smile to both of their faces.

"Let's," Barney said softly.

Hac Quan nodded, set his rifle beside the bazooka, and together they dropped to their bellies and moved slowly up the knoll, uncertain what they would find on the other side of it and disturbed that the area was so well lighted. When they reached the top, they could see the airstrip before them. The near end of the field was covered by brush to hide its actual length from aerial photographers and perhaps even to fool enemy bombers. But along the field were distributed two dozen planes. Barney looked them over with care. None was new. Nothing here the Chinese had not had in Korea. And he was ready to assume that many of these had flown over his head more than a decade ago. About a third of the planes were bombers and the rest war-weary MIGs. From where they lay hidden, Barney and Hac Quan could make out sentries. Five. Seven. Ten. They were walking the perimeter of the field. Barney relaxed; all he had to do was get through them and inside of the area, and they would not interfere with him until he was on his way out. The lights along the ends of the field posed a problem, but the center area was dark enough to move in without too much difficulty. His hand went up and he pointed to the west half of the field where the bombers were scattered. Then he pointed to Hac Quan. His hand went up again and he pointed to the fighters and then himself. The Oriental nodded to signify he understood.

"They are set for thirty minutes," Barney whispered as he glanced at his watch. "Just break the glass tips."

Hac Quan's head bobbed and Barney pointed to the place where they lay. "Forty-five minutes," he said, and the Oriental looked at his own watch and nodded again. Barney inched back from the knoll, planning to move around the guards to the far side of the field and penetrate the perimeter. He had almost disappeared from the top of the rise when he heard Hac Quan's whispered, "Good luck."

Barney's hand went up and his thumb and index finger formed a circle. He was alone now and moving around the field in the darkness. He made a large sweep, moving quickly because he knew his time was limited. Satisfied that he was where he wanted to be, he moved once more toward the edge of the field. The lights were bright here and he had to do something about them. Coming to a halt, he dropped to his stomach once more and crawled forward slowly. When he saw two sentries directly ahead, he froze where he was until they moved on. But they were not ready to move yet. Instead, they paused and talked. Barney looked at his watch. Ten minutes gone already. He edged back and, rolling over, looked at the skyline. A power wire set against the sky from a pole a hundred feet away. Once more he left the field, regretting every lost moment. When he reached the base of the pole, he saw that it was small and braced by two guy wires. Twisting the hardware quickly, he loosened the wires, cutting his hands as he did so. He paused a moment, and, pulling a handkerchief from his pocket, he held it between his teeth while he wrapped it around his cut hand. Satisfied that there was nothing more he could do for himself, he set his back to the pole, dug his heels into the ground and shoved as hard as he could. Minutes seemed to pass before the pole gave even slightly. He rocked it back and forth, listening to the wires above as they rubbed together. Then the final effort and the pole toppled. A splutter of sparks as the wires shorted and the field behind him went dark.

Half running, Barney dove into some nearby brush and then made his way back to the field. Twice he stopped as he heard the shouts of passing sentries. Then he moved on only to halt and throw himself into the brush once more as a small truck passed him, lighting the way to the power pole. At the edge of the dark field, Barney could see a detachment of soldiers running along the edge of the field now, taking positions closer together as they prepared to prevent any intrusion.

After a deep breath and a glance at his watch, he dashed onto the field. Soldiers filled in the gap a moment after he had moved through it. Another look at his watch. Twenty-five minutes left. Reaching into the musette bag on his back, Barney pulled out two limpets. On his knees now, he moved toward the first plane. He snapped the glass tip of one limpet timer and stuck the magnetic side to the bottom of the gas tank. A deep breath, and he moved to the next plane. He had to move faster, and as he approached the third plane, he saw a pilot running across the field to check it. Barney hesitated, bypassed the plane and moved to a different one. More pilots on the field now, and he hid beside a stack of oil cans. The pilots scrambled into their planes as if their very presence would protect them. Barney waited until a pilot was in his plane, then moved under the belly of it, set his limpet and moved on. Five planes. Then ten, and he stopped to look at his watch. Three minutes left of forty-five, and he knew he had to get off the field now if he was ever going to. Dropping the musette bag as a present for the Chinese, he scrambled away from the planes. Then he dropped to the ground. The row of sentries he had so narrowly avoided when he entered the field was blocking his escape. He glanced once more at his watch and then rubbed his hand over his face. He was trapped. Trapped. Very slowly, he opened his holster and drew out his revolver. Slipping off the safety, he crawled forward, looking for a gap in the row of sentries. But there was no gap. He looked at his watch and knew he had no time left.

Suddenly, shockingly, there was an explosion on the far side of the field as Hac Quan's first limpet threw the pieces of a bomber into the sky. Another explosion and then a third as a gas tank caught fire. The line of soldiers fell back and then broke toward the exploding planes. In that moment, Barney dove through the line in the darkness. As he did so, the first fighter plane blew on the strip. In the darkness beyond the field now, he trotted back toward the knoll. Behind him he could hear the explosions one following the other. When he reached the knoll, he threw himself on the ground and crawled up beside Hac Quan. In the light of the exploding planes, Barney could see his companion smile.

The field below was in confusion; the sentries could not decide in which direction to run and the officers shouted meaningless orders to them. The gasoline from ruptured tanks spread over the field and caught fire, making one great torch of the planes and the brush which covered the near end of the field.

Touching Hac Quan on the shoulder to gain his attention, Barney waved toward the darkness and moved off the knoll. Hac Quan took one more look at the holocaust behind them and then he joined the Colonel at the place where they had left the bazooka. Barney picked it up and set it on his shoulder as Hac Quan took the two shells. They were pleased with themselves as they moved off toward their final target.

Two hours later and six miles away, Barney and Hac Quan started to climb one of the small mountains that rimmed the valley of the Song Koi. Neither one of them would really have called this worn height a mountain, but they knew that in the cradle between it and the one beside it lay their next target. The sides of the rise were steep, and at times they had to move forward on all fours, reaching above for small trees and bushes to haul themselves up. They tried to remain as quiet as they could, but twice the heavy bazooka Barney was dragging after him struck rocks; though the noise probably did not carry far, they stopped where they were and waited to see if anyone had heard them. There was no activity anywhere as far as they could tell, and they kept moving up.

Once, as they approached the top, Barney touched Hac Quan and pointed back toward the valley behind. Though they had traveled six miles, they could make out the burning airfield. They crested the top behind some brush so that they would not be silhouetted against the skyline and then looked down into the saddle made where the two small mountains folded together. There were lights below. A sentry house, and beyond it, bathed in a spotlight, was the mouth of the tunnel they had come to destroy. A single row of railroad tracks led out of the tunnel and twisted through the fold of mountain toward the valley behind them. They were at least a half kilometer away.

Barney drew the bazooka up before him and, arming it, moved slowly down toward the tunnel. Hac Quan edged after him and then off to one side where he could keep a closer watch on the sentry post. From where he lay, he could barely see three men. There could have been more. Then he saw two men walk out of the tunnel mouth and stand outside the hut.

Barney could see Hac Quan turn to look at him, and with his hand he gestured that he was moving the bazooka up. He moved forward on his knees and down the side of the mountain. His foot loosened a rock, and he froze as he saw the two soldiers outside the hut glance upward. He was too far away to be seen in the darkness and he knew it. Then Hac Quan moved forward. Barney paused to look at his watch. It was almost one now, and he had four hours to make the six miles back up the river and the three miles north to the field. If they were going to get out of here, they had to make it by two hundred hours or two hundred thirty at most. And Fannin was tired. Stretching himself out on a flat space behind a rock, he brought his bazooka to bear on the mouth of the tunnel. Hac Quan had his revolver in hand and was trying to crawl closer to the sentries when the door of the shack opened and the side of the hill was suddenly bathed with light.

Barney's head dropped and he hoped that the engineer had been able to take cover. The door of the shack closed and Barney looked down once more. There were four men standing together now, and he guessed that he was watching a changing of the guard. It was not Buckingham Palace and these men were not toy soldiers. A quick glance to his side and Barney could see Hac Quan lying near some brush. The Oriental was trying to move behind it when he kicked a rock loose. The men below looked up and one of them ran to the searchlight that focused on the tunnel mouth.

Barney reached for his pistol, keeping one hand on the bazooka. Shouts came up from below and the searchlight started to swing over the mountainside. More shouts, and one of the men was pointing upward. Barney's lip went between his teeth as he weighed the risk of shooting out the searchlight. His head went down as the light passed over him and then swung back once more. There were more shouts from below and suddenly Barney saw Hac Quan rise to his feet and move toward the searchlight, firing at the guards as he half ran and half tumbled down the mountainside.

Two sentries dropped to their knees, took aim and fired. Deliberately drawing the searchlight toward himself, Hac Quan continued to move forward. Two rifle shots from below, and the engineer flung out his hands and toppled forward, dropping his revolver with a clatter as he fell.

For an instant, Barney was rigid; then, as Hac Quan rolled over and over down the mountainside, Barney grabbed his bazooka and moved his position, throwing himself behind a large rock looking directly down at the tunnel.

The excited sentries below kept the light on the Annamese engineer, who was twisting from side to side as he screamed in pain. From where he lay, Barney could see that the sentries were trying to decide what they should do about the fallen stranger. The screams came louder through Barney's weary brain, and he rolled over in the darkness and leveled his revolver at Hac Quan, hoping to silence the noise and help his friend. Then he saw that from where he lay, he could not make the shot unless he rose, and he braced himself to spring when suddenly he heard a burst of automatic rifle fire. One of the sentries had silenced the dying man.

Relaxing, Barney took his bazooka in hand once more and kept his head down as he heard one of the sentries climb the hill toward the place from which Hac Quan had first risen. For a few minutes the sentry searched the area, and when he found nothing, he descended once more to the tunnel mouth. From where he lay, Barney could see the searchlight sweep the mountainside a final time before the guards were satisfied and turned the light back onto the tunnel mouth.

Barney looked at his watch. Almost two hundred hours now. He had to wait. There was nothing else he could do. He knew that he dare not even move for fear of loosening a stone; as his legs became numb, he rubbed them one at a time with a restless hand.

Suddenly he heard a distant sound and, nestling his bazooka, he stiffened. A train roared through the tunnel, and Barney half rose in the darkness to fire when he saw the first car. A passenger car. Soldiers inside. The second car, and he knew he was watching a troop train moving through the night. When it was gone, there was silence again. Once more he settled back to wait. It was two hundred hours fifteen minutes now. And there was nothing he could do but wait.

Then the ground beneath him began to tremble, and he pointed the bazooka once more at the tunnel mouth. There was music coming from the sentry shack as the door swung open and two soldiers stepped out to watch the emerging train. The bright light mounted on its engine washed the mountainside and then moved away as the diesel followed the turning track between the mountains.

Barney came to his knees. The first car lighted by the spot on the tunnel mouth told him nothing. Then the second car moved through and he recognized the symbol of the house in six parts. He had found his target. A deep breath as the next car rolled forward. The same sign, and he fired. The small rocket streaked through the night and pierced the ammunition car as it emerged from the tunnel mouth. Barney came to his feet and waited. A moment of silence and then the explosion, followed by a larger one. The entire mountainside rocked; boulders broke loose and tumbled into the fold below. From where he stood, Barney could hear the muffled explosions as car after car blew up inside the tunnel. The countryside shook. The roof blew off the top of the mountain, collapsing the entire length of the tunnel. Barney was satisfied now that nothing less than an ammunition train would have done the job. He could see the falling rocks and the smoke billowing out of the broken mouth of the tunnel. The shack and the searchlight had disappeared in the hell he had created and he was alone in the darkness.

Turning toward the body of Hac Quan, which he knew lay on the mountainside, Barney Fannin came to attention and saluted the man who had given his life as a decoy. As his hand came down and he turned away in the darkness, Barney recalled his friend's words, "You can thank the Chinese for that, Colonel." The engineer had left a mark on the valley of the Song Koi that would not be forgotten as long as an enemy occupied that valley.

Barney made his way back up the mountain; and when he reached the top, he did not look back at the destruction behind him. Ahead lay the valley and the river. If he was going to meet LeGrande and the others, he would have to move quickly, and he was tired. The need to force himself was behind him now. He was numb. He was drained. There was no elation with success. The five targets had been sought out and destroyed. Now the drive was gone, and all that was left in its place was fatigue and a desire to rest for a long time. He did not bother to look at his watch to see how much time he had left. With all emotions spent, he was too tired to care.

General Richard LeGrande looked at the small group he had brought to the airstrip. The girl lay with the crippled Joe Brodsky beside some bushes. LeGrande had checked the wrapping on Brodsky's legs before they had left the house, and from what little he knew about medical matters, he was convinced that the young soldier would probably never walk again. When he considered the tale the youth had told him about his part in the mission, LeGrande believed now that this boy need not even have been dropped in, but the General was the first to admit to himself that his judgment was long after the fact, that none could have foreseen what would happen in the valley. Any criticism of Barney's team was worse than second guessing. It was cruel.

Leon Bryant, who stood at the far end of the small pasture, turned back to look at the General. He had known LeGrande for the six years that the older man had directed the agency, and in all that time he had never known him to make a mistake for which he would not accept full responsibility. But now, as he saw the General staring at the young boy and girl in the bushes, he wondered if LeGrande realized just how great a mistake he had made by bringing a second team into the valley.

Seeing that Bryant was watching him, LeGrande's hand went up in a gesture of recognition, and he looked at the pilot kneeling on the ground nearby. Of all the men who had no business being in the valley, this was the man; yet, since his plane was destroyed by Barney Fannin, the pilot had not complained or even shown any resentment against the trap into which he had been led.

A single thought wove its way through LeGrande's weary brain. These were the ones, the only ones left of the two teams that had entered the valley. Looking at his watch, the General saw that it was already four hundred hours and fifty minutes. Ten to go. Ten, and they would be gone themselves. The radio contact had been made easily and the radio again buried in case something went wrong. Now all they could do was wait. The ground had stopped rocking over two hours ago. When it had rocked earlier, LeGrande had assumed that Barney had struck his last target. Either he had destroyed it, or something else had gone wrong in the valley, but he had faith in Barney. His head went back now and he looked at the night sky. It was as dark as he could ever remember it. Faith in Barney Fannin. He wondered if he would have come to the valley himself if he had had the talk with Barney in Washington that he had had in the small house only that afternoon. He wondered. Of all the evaluations of Barney he had heard and read and feared, the only one that still lingered with him was Barney's own. Was survival part of being a mercenary, which was the way Barney looked upon himself? LeGrande did not know.

There was a sound above, and he was looking up again. Then he saw the pilot come to his feet, and as the sound moved closer, LeGrande looked at his watch again. Three minutes to the end. His hand went up and he could see Bryant light a match and touch it to the paper he had shredded earlier, paper from his pocket—some dollar bills, old orders and a letter from a girl in Istanbul. A moment later the paper caught. It was a small light, but it was all they had. The plane above circled slowly. Finally, LeGrande could see it. Small. Smaller than he had hoped, but then the pilot had told him this field was smaller than he had been led to believe. LeGrande was no expert on this and he could only hope.

The pilot, at his side now, was shaking his head. "It'll be a tight fit, General. Very tight."

LeGrande nodded.

Then the pilot said simply, "It's not one of ours." The General started to reach for his service revolver, when the pilot added, "Navy. C-1-A. Must have catapulted it off a carrier."

A low sweep as the plane's pilot judged his field and circled back once more. As he moved in toward the field, he touched his wheels down, bouncing as he came. Then his flaps were down and he was fighting to keep from reaching the end of the pasture, from ripping into the row of bushes that rimmed the south end of the field. At last the plane stopped.

Bryant ran over to pick up Joe Brodsky, and the grounded pilot ran to open the door of the plane. LeGrande remained where he was, gun in hand, hoping he had time to get his people aboard and time to wait for Barney Fannin and Hac Quan. He stood very still as Bryant carried the youth to the small plane and lifted him up to the two pilots, both inside now. Then Bryant turned back to the General, who still had not moved. The girl drifted over and stood beside LeGrande; without realizing he was doing it, he put out one arm and drew her to his side, a gesture of comfort and protection to someone who had been a friend.

The girl did not object as she felt the tall man's arm about her shoulder, and she half smiled as she watched the stranger the others called Bryant running across the field toward them. "The kid's asking for her, General. He wants to say goodbye or something."

LeGrande merely nodded and looked at his watch once more. Five hundred plus now, and he should be airborne. The small fire lighted to bring in the plane had already burnt itself out and it was dark again. Nothing could be seen or heard but the sound of the plane's idling motor. Bryant looked at the General and drew back the bolt on the automatic rifle he was carrying. If they waited much longer, there was going to be company. Still LeGrande kept his ground. The girl knew it was getting late; she could see the first streaks of dawn in the sky now, and from what the invaders had told her earlier, she knew that the Vietcong and the Chinese had tracked this plane ever since it had entered their country. They knew where it was at this moment and they were on their way. Li felt the tall General's hand on her shoulder stiffen slightly, though he himself was not aware that he was showing any sign that the wait was making him as tense as it was making the others. She saw the man called Bryant drop to his knee and set his rifle against his side. He was ready to fire even though he had no target as yet.

Then there was a yell and the pilot was shouting, "Let's get the hell out of here, General."

LeGrande looked at his watch once more and, with his arm still about the girl's shoulder, he started slowly toward the plane. Bryant rose and moved behind his chief. When they reached the plane, the grounded pilot called to the girl, "He wants to tell you something," and she looked at LeGrande, who seemed to avoid her eyes. His arm remained about her shoulder and so she stood very still.

Then there was a sound behind them and both Bryant and

the General whirled. Someone was emerging from the brush near the end of the field. His hands held high, Barney Fannin was coming toward them.

The others stood where they were and waited for Hac Quan to appear behind him, but the Annamese engineer did not come out of the darkness.

Barney stopped and looked around. "Joe?" was all he asked.

"In there," LeGrande said, pointing to the plane. And then, because he could wait no longer, he asked, "Did you get them?"

"Scratch five," Barney said, and then before he could even take pride in what he had done, he ordered, "Get in there."

Understanding that Hac Quan was not coming, LeGrande waved for Bryant to climb into the plane. He was about to follow, when Barney Fannin touched his arm and motioned for the girl to enter. She looked from one officer to the other and saw that LeGrande was smiling as if what was happening was very important. She took the hand held out to her by Bryant and was drawn into the plane. Then Barney waved for LeGrande, who smiled even more broadly now, but as he started to climb in, the grounded pilot emerged from the plane, saying,

"We've got problems, General. Coming off a carrier, the plane was catapulted, but this field is small for the weight she'll be carrying."

LeGrande considered this and shook his head. "We told them six men."

"They sent what they had, General. This one's jammed with permanent equipment."

Both men turned toward Fannin, who waved them aboard as he asked, "What are our chances of all making it?"

The pilot shrugged. "Just possible if we drop some gas and try for the carrier instead of going south."

"Drop it," Barney snapped. The pilot climbed back into the plane, followed by LeGrande and then Fannin, who found himself squeezed between the door he was closing behind him and the seat where the General had settled himself next to Bryant. Remaining on his knees, Barney shouted, "Get her off."

The pilot at the controls nodded and jerked a switch. There was a sound beneath them as a gas tank fell away and the plane slowly swept around to face the length of the field. There was little wind and only the breaking light of day. The motors raced and the small plane started down the small field. Faster and faster. Then suddenly it swerved as the pilot gave up the attempt to take it off. Once more he taxied down to the end from which he wanted to start and once more he started to race his motors. His passengers closed their eyes and waited. They rolled forward but again the plane swerved, unable to leave the ground. LeGrande knew what had to be done, but he had promised that he would go with Barney to the end and he would keep that promise.

The pilot was taxiing toward the far end of the field once more when the first shots came. Two bullets ripped through the plane; without hesitating, Barney reached across LeGrande's lap and grabbed the automatic rifle from Bryant. Barney smiled at the others, waved goodbye, opened the door behind him and tumbled out of the moving plane.

LeGrande rose from his seat and leaned out of the door. Barney was lying flat now, and as the firing from the far end of the field began to strike the plane's wings, Barney returned it. The wing passed over Fannin, and LeGrande stood by the door of the plane until the pilot was ready to make his third try. Three bullets tore through the tiny cabin and Bryant grabbed his shoulder. Still on his belly, Barney continued to lay down a field of fire, disrupting the enemy attack. The motors raced and the plane jerked forward, faster and faster until its wheels left the ground and it skimmed over the bushes at the field's end.

From where he lay on the ground, Barney Fannin did not even bother to look at the plane. The enemy was moving across the field toward him and he could see a grenade thrown and the fire from a dozen rifles. Then he was rising from the ground and hurled back; as he saw the sky bright above him, his eyes closed and it was dark again, and he was wondering if the stars he saw behind his closed lids would always be there.

The small plane rose higher and higher over the valley of the

Song Koi, and at the direction of General LeGrande, the pilot made a single broad sweep of the countryside. It was already dawn. Below lay the ruins of a once beautiful bridge. Not far away water spilled through a great crack in what must have once been a dam. Flying low, the pilot pointed toward a large black blotch of burnt and torn tanks. LeGrande nodded. They were over an airfield now, but none of the twisted planes was coming up to greet them. On toward the coast and rising over the small mountain at the end of the valley, where a cloud of dust hovered over a smashed railroad tunnel.

The General's hand went out to wave the pilot on and he turned to look at the girl behind him, cradling the head of the young soldier. Here were two who would never think ill of Barney Fannin. And Richard LeGrande did not care what anyone else might think, because only those seated with him in this small plane really knew what Barney Fannin had actually been.

Without embarrassment at the open sentiment of his gesture, his hand came up in a salute as he paid his final tribute to his old classmate and friend—Barney Fannin, Colonel, U.S. Army, The Man Most Likely to . . .

ABOUT THE AUTHOR

IRWIN R. BLACKER is a professor at the University of Southern California at Los Angeles. Born in Cleveland, he taught English at Western Reserve, Purdue and New York Universities. He served during the Second World War with the engineers in North Africa and Italy and was subsequently a public relations man with a utilities company, the co-director of the national staff of a theological seminary and its congregations, a motion picture writer and producer as well as the writer of numerous television programs. He is the author and editor of sixteen books.